THE FIRST TEARING

CHRISTOPHER J STEELY

First Printing, 2026

For my Ashe. Your journey is the heart of this story, and watching you become who you were always meant to be has made me stronger, braver, and more proud than I ever thought possible. Thank you for trusting me with your story.

"We are not born all at once, but by bits. The body first, and the spirit later."

Mary Antin

Prologue

Pines hated coming to Nashville.

It was loud and crowded, and he'd never cared for country music. During the last visit, buskers had claimed every block, each howling about a broken-down pickup or glorifying bar fights with drunk friends.

He'd been told the scene was changing, that Nashville had drawn new crowds beyond country. It was difficult not to remain skeptical as he passed the "Honky Tonk Highway" and turned onto 7th Avenue. Nearby steel strings twanged sharp against his Lycan hearing, setting his teeth on edge.

Pushing the annoyance aside, he continued on. This wasn't a pleasure trip anyway; it was a mission.

Pines had long ago stepped down as an elder of the Southeastern Moote. He was tired of politics, tired of the posturing. All he wanted was to serve Gaia directly, the way Lycans were meant to.

Gaia herself cared nothing for meetings or manifestos. She cared for rivers running clear, not black. For deer birthing in peace. For mountains standing whole, ungutted by machines.

So he'd joined a small group that had settled in Huntsville, Alabama. Their focus was protecting Monte Sano Mountain and the greater Madison County. Simple work. He'd imagined spending his remaining years watching for genuine threats to the earth and its spirits.

So why had he been summoned here?

The message hadn't come from the elders. At least not officially. The runes etched into the missive bore no signature, only urgency and a warning that time was running out.

Maybe it wasn't the Moote that had called on him. Maybe it was the Seer itself.

He frowned. It wouldn't be the first time the spirit acted without the Elders' knowledge.

His thoughts drifted as he cut through the Bicentennial Capitol Mall State Park. The eleven-acre park was a small oasis of green in the asphalt jungle. At least Nashville, under the local packs' influence, had worked hard to conserve green spaces around it. He paused near a magnolia tree, catching his reflection in the lit pond.

He was probably getting too old for this. Nearly eighty years old now, though he'd stopped announcing that particular milestone. The wrinkled skin around his eyes had deepened into permanent creases, and his hands bore the liver spots that no amount of Lycan resilience could prevent. Sure, his kind aged slower than humans, but time still caught up, eventually. It always did.

"For everyone except the damn bloodsuckers. They stay pretty for centuries, and all it costs them is their soul." His words carried a bit too far, and he saw a couple look over and hurry away. He moved on from the pond, enjoying the rest of the park. He'd take his wrinkles and his mortality over that hollow existence any day.

Pines worked to pull his mind back to the matter at hand as he stepped out of the park. This was of vital importance, or at least, that was what the message had promised.

"Damn thing can't just text what it knows," Pines mumbled as he dropped some cash into the cup of a sleeping man nestled in the shadows of Madison Street. "Has to make it a pilgrimage so it can have its audience in person."

That probably wasn't fair, he admitted to himself.

Not many five-hundred-year-old spirits could grasp concepts like text or email. The Seer still preferred crows as couriers, though lately it had experimented with fax machines. He smiled at the thought of The Seer buying a scrying app on an iPhone or hosting a séance over Microsoft Teams.

Hell, even many Lycan elders still preferred the old ways. And of those he could name, most were barely half a century old, much less half a millennium.

He felt his phone vibrate once in his pocket, but he ignored it. He was already running late, a big faux pas when visiting the spirit of time.

The brownstone loomed in quiet defiance of the modern skyline, its ivy-choked portico and soot-stained brickwork standing out.

"How does a spirit of time own a house in the city? The taxes alone must be hell," he muttered.

Maybe I'll ask it this time, he mused. He knew he wouldn't though. He'd get the information as quickly as possible and get out with the minimum required social niceties.

Not many cared much for conversations with The Seer. It struggled with the idea that people liked pretending they had free will. Sure, the spirit claimed everyone had control over their destiny. It just also happened to know exactly how things would play out.

Most of the time.

As Pines reached for the doorbell, the buzzer clicked. He switched to the handle instead.

"I'll never get used to that," he muttered, running a hand through his silver-streaked brown beard as he stepped inside.

The air hit like a time capsule, thick with patchouli, incense, and melting vinyl. Shag carpet in a violent shade of burnt orange clawed at his boots, while the walls wore cheap wood paneling. A lava lamp pulsed on a kidney-shaped side table, blobs of color drifting in slow rhythm.

A poster of *Jimi Hendrix at Woodstock* stared from across the living room, the psychedelic swirls behind the guitarist nearly hypnotic. Beside it hung a faded print of *Farrah Fawcett*, her grin untouched by time. A sun-yellow rotary phone dangled over the edge of a sideboard, resting beside a stack of vinyl records.

The furniture looked scavenged straight from a thrift store curated by someone on a manic decorating spree: avocado-green cushions, low-slung suede couches, and a coffee table with a built-in ashtray and a copy of *Popular Mechanics* from 1974.

The Seer enjoyed decorating in the styles of different eras. Pines' favorite had been twenty years ago, when he'd stepped into what The Seer claimed was Rome, circa 100 BC. Murals covered the walls in crude pigments but exquisite detail. Mosaics tiled every floor. Instead of appliances, there had been a clay wash pot and a stone hearth blackened with charcoal.

Pines was pretty sure the spirit handled the remodels himself on a whim. Still, he liked to imagine hunting for a contractor who specialized in 15th-century Dogon work.

Now, the 1970s struck hard. Pines blinked and tried not to breathe too deeply. Meticulous. Absurd. Of course it was. The Seer always had a flair for excess.

A small part of him still hoped to see the Spirit of Time and Space in a paisley shirt and bell bottoms. Maybe even goldfish heels.

But the host descended the stairs, dressed as always: draped in a dark robe, hood drawn low. Tiny stars and planets drifted across the fabric in no pattern Pines could follow.

Still impressive, he supposed. But damn, the disco look would've been something.

"Greetings, friend and protector of Gaia," the apparition of time spoke.

It walked past Pines and into the living room, sitting on a light tan beanbag chair. The spirit gestured toward another beanbag across the coffee table. Pines nodded and sank into the padding. On the table sat his favorite beer.

"I have to admit that this is my favorite renovation so far."

"Your favorite renovation," the spirit replied.

"Goddamn, you don't gotta be so weird," Pines huffed.

The Seer lowered its hood, revealing its current host: a Hispanic man in his late thirties. Tired eyes, greying temples, a pleasant enough face if you ignored the sense of vast cosmic weight behind it. The man's skin looked worn, not from life, but from use.

When the spirit had introduced itself to Gaia's protectors, it had promised that any person The Seer "borrowed" was a willing participant. It also reassured them that each human was compensated for their time.

Not that it really mattered in the end.

The ethereal being had been right far more often than wrong in the visions it passed to those it judged worthy.

There was one tip Pines had heard about. A situation outside Jacksonville. Something about a pack stronghold nearly sinking into a river. Or maybe it was a swamp. The elders hadn't exactly clarified.

It didn't matter. They trusted the Seer. And when it spoke, everyone acted as if the world was on fire.

Pines took the ice-cold beer in his hands and got to the point.

"Okay, tell me why I'm here."

Across from him, The Seer mouthed the words in perfect sync. That was the thing. The spirit always knew what you were going to say. It wasn't cruel about it, but it didn't try to hide it, either. Like a child reciting the lines of a show they'd already watched a hundred times.

"This is of great importance. You must be prepared for what is to come." The spirit leaned forward. "It may also be the last vision I'm able to give to you and yours."

"Ominous," Pines replied.

But internally, he understood the weight of what had just been said. If this really was its final message, it demanded his full attention. What clenched his gut, though, was the uncertainty in the spirit's voice.

"You finally going back to the Realm of Renewal?" Pines asked.

The Hispanic man only looked at Pines, then down at the notepad and pen, waiting for him to take the hint.

Picking them up, he flipped open the notepad. The paper felt older than it should, yellowed at the edges, words already faintly pressed into the fibers as if someone else had written them first.

He looked the possessed human in the eyes. "Okay, let's go."

Two hours later, Pines stepped back into the night air, heart pounding like a war drum. He stood there a moment, letting his pulse settle before remembering the missed text. The city hummed around him, but it felt a world away.

This was more than a simple pack stronghold possibly disappearing. If Pines didn't succeed, the Dust Bowl of the 1930s would be a fond memory compared to what was coming for the Southeastern United States.

He didn't have much time. And he didn't like the way he'd have to tackle the tasks ahead.

Flipping to the first page of the notepad, he keyed the address into his phone's GPS.

Remembering the missed text, he opened his messages. Under an unknown number was a reply to a question he hadn't yet asked.

It's easy to own property when you've already seen the foreclosure notices.

Pines stared at the message until the words blurred, a cold reminder that time wasn't just watching, it was already moving the pieces.

Chapter 1

The second time Ashe left their parents' house that night hurt worse than the first.

They stood in the driveway, chest tight and fists clenched, blinking back burning tears. The night pressed in around them, thick with Alabama summer. Humid. Stifling. Too close.

Ever since coming out as nonbinary, the twenty-three-year-old had faced persecution and bullying at every turn.

They'd lost their job at a government contractor the week after coming out. The excuse was "lack of work," but Ashe had seen the next quarter's customer sheet.

Their partner had said that being with Ashe was too confusing for her sexual orientation. Ashe still heard the words in her voice, detached but certain, as though loving them had been an experiment that failed.

Family had been the one thing Ashe thought they could still count on.

After the usual hugs and promises to visit soon, Ashe stepped into the night on a high note. They looked up into the sky. The graphic designer loved tracing new patterns in the stars, creating their own personal constellations. One cluster looked like a dahlia from their garden. That's when they remembered they'd left the present for their mom in the car.

Not wanting to wait, Ashe grabbed the gift and ran back up the steps toward the kitchen. They knew their mom would love the fresh-cut flowers and the handcrafted vase, all made from Ashe's small garden. It was a thank-you for being a rare light during the darkest stretch of their life.

They stepped into the house and headed toward the kitchen, where a wall separated it from the living room. Just as they rounded the corner, vase in hand, they heard their father's exasperated voice.

"I just don't understand," he said, his voice thick with frustration. "She... well, I guess *they*... are hurting their career potential by jumping onto this silly bandwagon. I mean, I supported gay marriage, but there's got to be an end to the extremes."

Grandma Perkins chimed in, as reliably ignorant as ever. "I still think you've gotta be one or the other. She was born a girl. Maybe she just wants attention."

Ashe's mom placed a soothing hand on Grandma Perkins and said gently, "Give her time. She's young and just went through a stressful breakup. This will pass. Until it does, we are going to go along with it and give her whatever she needs."

Go along with it.

"I can't do this," they whispered, breath shallow, already turning to escape. And ran straight into their big little brother.

He didn't budge as Ashe bumped into him. He peeked around the corner to make sure the elders were still ranting and whining. Then he turned back to Ashe, gently took their arm, and led them into the dining room. The two siblings had not always been close; a six-year age gap will do that. But over the past few years, they had developed a much closer bond.

"I'm sorry," Kyle whispered, his face a mixture of empathy and guilt. "They've had this talk more than once. Every time I try to defend you, they pat me on the head and say, 'That's a good point.' Then they go back to being ignorant."

"Maybe I shouldn't be mad," Ashe whispered, wiping a stray tear from their cheek. "At least they love me."

Kyle frowned. "If they love you, they need to love *all* of you. Maybe it'll come in time. I mean, they're old and think they know everything." Kyle worked up a small smile and looked into his sibling's eyes. "I'm here for you, and next May you're gonna have a new roommate whether you like it or not."

Despite everything, Ashe smiled. For the first time all night, they felt anchored, just a little, by his stubborn certainty.

Kyle was seventeen, all shaggy hair and bright green eyes wet with unshed tears. They hugged, and as a jab of levity, he made sure to put his chin on top of their head.

"Shortstuff."

As Ashe pulled back, they noticed they'd soaked his shirt.

It was another one of his band-tees, the name so obscure it might as well have been written in Latin.

"King Gizzard and the Lizard Wizard?" Ashe frowned, glancing from the shirt up to his face.

"Hey, you should hear them," Kyle said, perking up. "They're actually touring and going to be in Atlanta soon. We could probably still get tickets."

Ashe opened their mouth to decline politely, then froze. Their mom had entered the room, wearing a startled expression. Kyle reflexively stepped in front of Ashe in a subtle attempt to protect them.

"Oh Ashe! I thought you had left. Have... have you been here the whole time?" Her voice pitched high, almost guilty, like she'd been caught stealing.

The air cracked like a dropped plate. All the weight Kyle had lifted came crashing back down. Ashe couldn't even look at her.

It took everything in Ashe not to challenge Mom then and there. But they didn't handle conflict well, and storming out shouting would only reinforce her beliefs that Ashe was just "a young person going through a phase."

"I made you something," they said quickly, holding out the vase.

"It was in the car. I... wanted to make sure you got it. I might not be around for a while."

That hadn't been true, not at first. Ashe had planned to come back later in the week to help with meal prep and maybe do some laundry. The house they were renting still didn't have a washing machine.

But now? They no longer felt safe in their parents' house.

Their mother gave them a skeptical look. She waved off the tears and the shake in Ashe's voice, choosing willful ignorance to keep the peace. Ashe gave their Mom a quick hug and squeezed Kyle tightly before bolting down the steps and through the garage. They knew the exit was abrupt, but they couldn't maintain the suffocating facade any longer.

Now on their knees, they felt heavier and more alone than ever. What Ashe and Kyle called the Pringle Moon shone through the clouds, providing just enough light to see.

The street was empty. Still.

Quiet.

"This can't be fucking happening!" Ashe roared at the sky.

Depression and sadness turned to rage. Another connection, another part of their life, burn away. The rage felt different this time. It burned through their chest like acid. Their breathing turned rapid and shallow, coming faster and faster. Their heart raced desperately. Panic curled in, smoke under a locked door.

Breathe. Just breathe.

They tried to remember the breathing exercises the therapist had covered last session. Taking a deep breath was impossible as summer had come on strong in Huntsville.

The thick, wet air was like breathing in a steam room. Ashe started hyperventilating. The weather and emotions made it impossible to maintain control.

All Ashe knew was they couldn't go back inside. They needed to get to their car and get the A/C going. The artificial air would help push out the humid muck, and maybe then they could regain control.

Ashe staggered and leaned against the driver's side door of their very used RAV4. As they were reaching for their keys, the pain struck.

Ten thousand needles stabbed and wriggled into Ashe's back. They dropped their keys and wrenched backward in an unnatural bend. The agony spread from their back and twisted through their body. Fire burned in their chest from the lack of oxygen. Ashe collapsed to their knees, too paralyzed to do anything more than suffer.

From the shadows of nearby pecan trees, a short, muscular man ran toward them.

Ashe managed a glance at the approaching stranger, older than their grandparents, wearing an oversized black shirt and gym shorts. When he reached out to touch them, Ashe rasped, "Don't," fumbling for the knife in their pocket.

They tried to recoil from the extended hand. The panic and pain spiked, doubling them over.

His hand landed firmly on their shoulder.

The agony *vanished*. Not completely. But enough to draw in air again. Enough to think.

Something else threaded between them now. A calming bond. Grateful but still panicked, they reached shakily for the fallen keys, never taking their eyes off him.

"I'll get them," he said, voice tight and strained.

He looked worse than Ashe. Pale. Trembling. Sweat poured from his beard. Something about him felt... off. Wrong. Not dangerous, but definitely not normal.

Maybe he was a local jogger? Someone out late who saw Ashe collapse. It would explain the clothes and sweat.

The man bent down awkwardly, still gripping Ashe's shoulder. Sweat dripped from his beard, dark brown streaked with silver, as he hooked a finger through the key ring and stood up.

"You need to get in; I'll drive," the man said, locking eyes with Ashe.

Ashe tried to speak. To protest. But the man cut them off.

"We don't have time. We need to get away from people. *Now.*"

Ashe went cold in the hot July air and tried to pull away. Sliding from the stranger's grip, they could feel the pain pour back in. It was worse than before.

The older man grabbed Ashe, and the bond snapped back into place. The pain reluctantly subsided again.

Ashe wasn't weak. They worked out three days a week at the local CrossFit gym. But that didn't matter as he yanked Ashe's face to his.

"We need to go now. Before you hurt someone, someone you love." His hot breath washed over their face.

The stranger opened the back door and kept hold of them, guiding Ashe into the seat. They were still struggling to stay in control, each inhale ragged, their lungs burning, and the pain hovered on the edge. It squirmed like something alive, eager to claw its way back in.

Ashe stretched out across the back seat, hoping, praying, they'd misunderstood him. Maybe he was going to take them to the hospital?

Not like I got the insurance for it, Ashe thought. *Maybe I can still use Mom and Dad's?*

Thinking of their parents only stoked the rage simmering beneath the surface.

The old man gasped, almost losing his grip. His hand slid down to Ashe's arm but never lost contact. He was looking worse, spiking concern in Ashe.

What if running or whatever he had been doing in the trees had been too much for him? The heat couldn't be helping, and Ashe didn't want him to have a heart attack on the way to the hospital.

The stranger gasped, "I'm going to let go. It's going to hurt. Bad. I need you to fight it. You have to stay in control while I drive us to safety."

Ashe could only nod and brace themself as the stranger let go. The torment rushed back in. But instead of needles, wild animals were let loose inside.

The SUV tore out of the neighborhood, clipping a stop sign on the way out.

Any protest died on Ashe's lips. More beasts joined the frenzy, rending Ashe's insides apart. They tried to focus on something, anything, other than the pain. Ashe stared at their arm, forcing steady breaths. Goosebumps rippled over their skin as thick, dark-blonde hairs pushed through, swelling and lengthening. Each strand forced its way out with a wet, prickling sound, stretching pores wider than skin should allow. Within seconds, the hairs reached six inches, with more erupting across their hands.

The crawling shiver spread down their chest and stomach. Panicking, they yanked their shirt, the fabric tearing under their grip. Tiny bumps raced around their torso. Their chest binder vanished beneath a surge of fur, dark brown streaked with blonde, and then a sharp snap split the air as the binder gave way.

Guess I'm getting chest hair after all, Ashe thought wryly.

Delirium blurred into a laugh, then a sob. This had to be what madness felt like when it hit all at once. People just don't turn into monsters.

Then, Ashe remembered they were not alone. Through the red haze clouding their vision, they could see the old man laser-focused on the road. Gone was the pale, trembling figure who'd been drenched in sweat moments before. Now he looked steady, composed, as if whatever had been draining him had lifted the moment he let go.

Even with Ashe's mind slipping, they could tell the SUV was heading in the opposite direction of the hospital. They were rocketing north on Wall Triana Highway, pushing 100 MPH.

The stranger weaved past anyone still out on the small two-lane highway. He pulled out to pass a small silver sedan, but an oncoming truck forced him to cut back too quickly, sideswiping the sedan as he yanked the wheel.

"Too many damn houses," the old man barked. He was looking for something Ashe couldn't see. He floored it, the engine groaning as they pushed past 115 MPH. Streetlights gave way to scattered porch lights, then darkness.

He looked back again, voice sharp.

"You *cannot* let the wolf out; you *need* to stay in control."

What was he talking about?

Ashe opened their mouth to yell.

And barked.

Turning back to the road, he let out a long, connected string of curses. Then he jerked the wheel hard. The bright blue RAV4 went onto two wheels, teetering, but landed in a fishtail heading directly into the trees. The bumps were violent, but Ashe didn't move like they should have. Their body felt... denser. Bigger. Wrong.

A sharp screech tore through the night as metal scraped against oak. The old man jerked the wheel, forcing the SUV deeper into the woods, still barreling along at a reckless sixty. The tires skidded on loose earth, offering little traction, and every swerve dragged the vehicle through brush and branches. He clipped a young cedar head-on. The impact shuddered through the frame as the tree splintered and toppled behind them.

In the chaos of their wild ride, Ashe suddenly noticed something had changed.

The pain was gone.

Relieved, Ashe tried to sit up but couldn't move. They were pinned in the back seat. Looking down, there was a hulking mass of wet, matted fur and muscle where their body had been. Brown streaked with blonde, it was easily four times the size they'd once been.

Not human.

Inside, Ashe felt different. The concerns from minutes ago had dissolved. They'd been replaced by a primal lust.

Hunger. Power.

A voice echoed in their mind, whispering to embrace these feelings. Ashe tried to hold onto their humanity. They reached out for familiar images. Kyle's face, the vase of dahlias, their own name. But each thought slipped away like water through fur.

Hunt. Chase. Kill. The voice sang to the newly turned werewolf.

Chapter 2

Pines knew he had to stop. *Now.*

Ashe was nearly through their First Tearing.

He slammed on the brakes. The car fishtailed before jerking to a stop. A mass of fur collided with the back of his seat. The impact drove his face into the steering wheel with a crack. Blood spattered the dash as his vision went white-hot for a second.

He wiped his face and shoved at the driver's side door. Nothing. It wouldn't budge.

The last tree he clipped must have bent the frame. He rammed it hard. Once. Twice. It burst open on the third shove with a wrenching screech.

Wrecking the kid's car was not going to build the trust he needed. He grabbed the door and wrenched it shut, hearing a loud pop.

"I can fix that," Pines muttered.

Glass shattered in the back of the SUV. He could feel the car vibrate under a low, rumbling growl.

The forest pressed in close; typical Appalachian second-growth with a tangled mix of oaks, pines, and spindly maples. Shrubs and saplings clustered wherever moonlight slipped through the canopy. The air was thick with humidity. Even after midnight, the temperature clung to the high eighties, the heat of the day refusing to let go.

Pines tasted copper in his mouth, wiping more blood away from his nose. The bleeding had slowed, but the blood would make it easy for the werewolf to track him. He needed to mask his scent.

He reached down, tore off a strip of his shirt already soaked in blood and sweat, and flung it left. Another scrap to the right. Another behind him. Scents meant to confuse the young Lycan, if Pines was lucky.

Hopefully, I've gotten us far enough from civilization.

Behind him, the SUV groaned. Metal popped and tore as Pines turned to see the back door fly off and land thirty yards into a thicket. Then, silence.

Nothing surrounding the SUV dared move. The leaves refused to be swayed by wind. Wildlife froze like statues. Nature held its breath in horrid anticipation.

A howl ripped through the silence. Long, ragged, not quite human. The sound rattled his ribs, made the fillings in his teeth buzz.

I'm not going to make it to cover.

Back in his thirties, he could've run a mile in under five minutes, even on terrain like this. Now, he wasn't sure if he would make it a thousand yards before Ashe caught up to him.

"Shit," Pines muttered.

The small, five-foot-seven frame was gone. In its place stood a towering mass of fur and muscle. Seven feet tall, four hundred and fifty pounds of raw instinct and violence emerged from the wrecked back seat with an eerie fluidity. It rose on its hind legs and sniffed the air. Its snout twitched. Then its eyes locked onto Pines.

A thick rope of drool slid from its muzzle. A low, guttural snarl pulsed from deep in its throat. Lips peeled back slowly as if savoring the thought of pursuit.

"Shit, shit, *shit,*"

Pines skidded to a stop and turned to face it. This wasn't just a werewolf. It was something built for carnage. Even raw and untrained, it had enough strength to tear him apart without breaking stride.

Hell, he had hoped for a spiritual change. Rare, but he had seen it. Even with a body shift, he had expected a Veilshaper or a Singer, something he could reason with. What he saw instead was a Warhide, one of the most dangerous forms a Lycan could take.

This isn't how it was supposed to go.

If he'd gotten farther. If he'd put another mile between them. Maybe the scent of a deer or a wild turkey would've pulled Ashe's instincts away. But now? Now, he was the only thing moving. The only thing bleeding. The only prey in reach.

Well, if this is how it's gotta be, then let's get this over with.

He let the change begin. He didn't want a Full Tearing, but just enough. He wasn't letting the wolf all the way in. That kind of surrender could cost Ashe—or both of them—their lives.

But he needed help. Strength. Speed.

The Grayskin transformation hit slowly, like a fuse burning toward something dangerous. Bones lengthened. Muscle packed on. His skin itched as hair thickened along his arms. He grew six inches and gained a hundred pounds in seconds. Not monstrous but not completely human.

He was still outmatched. A foot shorter and nowhere near as strong. But it might be enough.

The beast howled again, scattering birds in all directions. Then it dropped to all fours and sprinted towards him.

***

Prey, the Wolf Spirit whispered.

The voice was seductive, as were the feelings of bloodlust and superiority. Ashe was an apex predator. No one could bully them, and no one could escape them. Part of that didn't feel right, but Ashe shoved the doubt aside.

The beast stared at the figure ahead. It wasn't a person. Just movement. Heat. Blood beneath skin. The scent was strong, rich with fear and pain. This was the one who'd dragged them from the street. Maybe even the one who made them like this.

A reason for vengeance, but it didn't matter. What did was this thing was *alive*. It could be torn. It could scream.

Muscles coiled. Jaws parted. A string of drool stretched from tooth to earth.

They continued to sprint toward the old man, unrelenting, even as his body began to twist and swell. Muscles packed on with unnatural speed. It didn't matter how much stronger the stranger got. This wasn't going to be a fight. This was a hunt.

Claw. Bite. Feast. The voice cooed.

They covered one hundred yards in seconds and swiped at the old man's head.

He was surprisingly quick for his age. He ducked the blow, catching a small scratch on his back. The stranger then turned the duck into a dive between Ashe's legs.

The fresh smell of blood welling up on the man's back only excited Ashe more. It was a perfume sweeter than honeysuckle, drowning out every other thought. They turned, arm extended to take another swipe. This time they would aim for the chest. It would make it more difficult for the quick little prey to dodge.

They searched for the prey when their snout met wood. The large branch shattered on the Lycan's nose with a crack. A short yelp escaped their mouth before they could control it, angry at themself for showing weakness.

The pain faded quickly. They could already feel the torn skin and broken cartilage repairing. The bright white and yellow spots dimmed. Something that would have put them in the hospital in the past was now only a minor inconvenience.

This is great! Nothing can stop me! Ashe thought, reveling in their power.

The voice of reason cried from somewhere deep in their mind.

What are you doing?

Ashe tried to shake the voice off. They didn't want to think; they wanted to act. Thankfully, the small voice was easy to ignore, but it didn't go away.

Hunt, the beast commanded.

Ashe dropped to all fours and began sniffing the ground. The old man had used the moment of confusion to escape. Ashe could detect multiple scent tracks, but one was larger, leading deeper into the woods.

A savage grin tore across their face. Lips pulled tight over glinting, razor-sharp canines. Without a second's hesitation, Ashe sprang forward. Claws dug into the earth as they tore through the shadows, closing in fast on their prey.

Hunt. Fight. Kill.

***

Pines figured the scent distraction wouldn't work.

But he had hoped that it would at least slow the beast down. He was nearly out of shirt as he had ripped off another piece, wiped blood and sweat onto it, and tossed it away. His heart thundered in his ears as he ran.

It wasn't only his heart thundering.

Ashe was not trying to hide their pursuit. Footfalls thudded. Limbs snapped. Pines could hear the quick, sharp breaths of the predator. The Warhide was gaining. He was losing ground, tripping over brush and loose rock.

Still running, Pines closed his eyes, focusing his other senses on the surrounding terrain.

He pivoted hard. The shift in the air was his only warning.

Something moved behind him. Fangs snapped shut where his neck had just been. A sharp click of teeth closing on empty air sent a cold shiver up his spine. He'd dodged the lunge, but his quick turn became a stumble. Then he rolled down a short hill into thorny brush.

Not the night I'd imagined, he thought, brushing grass and dirt from his face.

He needed to refocus. Keep moving. If the Warhide made a mistake, it would only slow them, but if he made a mistake...

Standing, Pines did a quick check. Nothing broken, and the scratches, like his face from earlier, would heal quickly. His clothing was shredded. He considered stripping the rest off and going full birthday suit. But he couldn't bring himself to get caught running nude through the woods. Again.

Last time, there were pictures. He didn't need a repeat of other packs commenting on how cold it must be in Alabama summers.

A howl at the top of the hill could be heard for miles. The Warhide stood above him. Eager. Hungry.

"Welp, hopefully no one calls 911 to report coyotes," Pines muttered. If the cops came, bullets would only make things worse.

"Let's see if I can beat you to the creek," he yelled. To keep it focused on him, he flipped the beast off.

"Here's two fingers for ya."

Then he ran off in the direction of running water, with the beast in quick pursuit.

***

Break him, the seductive voice murmured.

Ashe had to admit it. The old man had caught them off guard. Twice. And now, somehow they had lost him. They'd been distracted by several rabbits scattering into the underbrush, each thinking itself the target. The small prey had tempted them for far too long. They had finally decided to ignore them. The wolf wanted a bigger prize.

The moon had dropped; the light of the sun was only hours away. Ashe finally picked up a lingering scent again. This was their prey. The wolf agreed.

Ashe took off through the creek and up a nearby hill into denser woodland. This time, they moved a little slower. Focused. The old man wouldn't trick the hunter again.

He's human. This isn't right.

The voice of reason had grown during the pursuit. Ashe hated how convincing it had become. The longer the hunt dragged on, the more it crept in. They needed to end this.

But they also didn't want it to end. The stalking. The challenge. The fear in the prey. It was exhilarating to be in the woods, chasing something cunning, fast, and scared of Ashe. The soothing voice promised the hunt could last forever if they wished.

Part of them wondered if this was even real.

A fever dream. A nightmare.

But Ashe didn't care. Not now. They wanted to give in to the voice. Let it pull them deeper.

To hunt. To survive.

***

It had been hours. Ashe constantly on his trail.

Pines couldn't go on any further. Alabama summers could kill a man, even at night. His old wounds ached, and his vision was blurring. He was exhausted. Thirty years in this state, and the heat still stole his breath like it had something to prove.

He had hoped that the rabbits he startled would be enough. A quick distraction. A better target. But Ashe's Wolf Spirit was a greedy little bastard.

Not running meant Pines needed to hurt the Lycan badly enough that it shifted back. Then he could deal with the human. Apologies could come later, when they both made it out of the woods.

"If I get out of here tonight," the old man spoke into the wind.

Wiping sweat from his eyes, he mentally went over the impromptu plan he had laid out. This was all he had. No shadows to hide behind. Just the monster's blind hunger for its prey.

He knew from experience that Ashe's beast was running on instinct. However, if it suspected a trap, everything would come crashing down.

There was no room for error.

A movement of shadow in the distance cut off his thoughts. Ashe appeared over the hill on their back legs. Their eyes were a soft white-yellow glow, reflecting the last light of the sinking moon.

They howled a challenge toward him.

Pines had purposely cornered himself in the dry creek bed. The slope was too steep with no quick way out. He had crossed the active creek upstream, hoping it would funnel Ashe right into the trap. The beast came exactly where he had planned.

Lucky me.

Pines looked around and confirmed he was cornered. He knew it. The beast knew it. But what Ashe would see was a small natural dirt ramp behind him. It should stay hidden from their view until Pines was able to use it.

Okay, let's get this started.

Pines picked up a large stone half-buried in earth. With a grunt, he chucked the stone at the Warhide. It was over fifty yards and uphill, but he managed to hit them.

There was a sharp, confused yelp. He doubted Ashe was really hurt. More likely just surprised to be attacked again. The Warhide quickly shook off their lethargy and charged straight for him.

***

Soon.

Ashe felt the warmth of the night filling their soul. Their prey was tiring and trapped. It would not be long now.

Please!

Ashe faltered just a step as the voice of reason pleaded. Its voice was louder. The guilt of the hunt crept to the forefront of their thoughts.

No. So close. It urged and Ashe continued on. The old man had run up a hidden shallow embankment.

Ashe sprinted on all fours, legs and arms pumping in steady rhythm. Their eyes stayed locked on the prey. Instinct would guide the path, but they weren't letting him out of sight again. Ahead, the old man turned sharply down an animal trail, stumbling through the dark like his legs were barely listening anymore.

But Ashe didn't need trails or footing. They pushed off the slick soil of the creek bed and launched upward, landing in a crouch just thirty yards from their prey.

The look of surprise pleased Ashe and the Wolf Spirit. The final strike would come soon.

The old man was up to something. His shambling movements looked choreographed. His pace slowed, allowing Ashe to get far too close.

Then, he pretended to trip over his feet., shoving a thick limb aside with a practiced, panicked motion. The branch was young and still springy. The base bent low, then snapped forward.

Right toward Ashe's face.

A human memory surfaced through the haze of hunter's instinct. When they were younger, Ashe's family would go hiking during the first of spring. A preteen Kyle would always run ahead, bend a branch back, and let it snap straight into Ashe's face. Then he would laugh at his trick. At their pain. It never failed to piss them off. Kyle would run off laughing, and they'd chase after him, swearing.

Clever prey, the beast warned.

Yeah, but I know this trick, Ashe thought.

They hopped over the branch, dodging the swinging club, and landed on all fours, maintaining their momentum. Up ahead, the old man dove off the trail and rolled away. The same trick as before, but this time Ashe was ready.

They turned their focus forward and saw a tree in the middle of the animal path. Two large limbs had been purposely broken into jagged edges. One was at neck height and the other near their chest. If the swinging branch had hit, it wouldn't have just blinded them. It would've driven them straight into the spikes.

He wanted to spear me!

Outrage surged. The nerve of this weak human! Trying to fight instead of run. He actually thought he could outwit a predator. They would prove him wrong.

Still running, Ashe adjusted slightly to the right and jumped onto the tree, just above the broken limbs. The old oak shuddered under their weight, but its roots held. They pushed off and launched toward the prey.

He saw his plan had failed and was on the move. But Ashe had planned their jump well. They knocked him to the ground, his face and chest slamming into the hard clay soil.

Ashe's mouth watered in victory. The beast was done with the hunt; now for the spoils. The prey struggled uselessly. The Warhide sank their teeth into the old man's shoulder. His scream of pain matched the height of Ashe's delight.

Bite. Rend. Devour.

Ashe could already taste the salty blood welling out of his body. They had never felt so powerful. This man had kidnapped them, hurt them, and turned them into a monster.

This is what he deserved!

It wasn't just revenge that drove Ashe now. It was the feeling of something primal and consuming.

Power.

It filled the hollow places inside them, like vines forcing their way through cracked stone. The wolf had whispered of eternity. Of never being alone, never being judged again. Ashe wanted it. Craved it. To hunt with the beast. To become it forever.

The old man tried once more to shove the monster off him. But the effort only tore his wounds wider. Weakened from the night's brutality, his body gave in, shrinking to its previous size.

Ashe's jaws released. They used their claws to keep their prize pinned. They prepared to give this honorable prey a quick death. Then they would feast. Ashe's canines touched the back of his neck, puncturing the skin.

Then the voice came.

It didn't whisper this time. It roared.

Human, like you, like Kyle.

The voice hit harder than any branch or stone. Ashe jerked back, releasing the man. He quickly twisted and crawled away. The Wolf Spirit wrested control back, driving Ashe's body forward instinctively, not wanting to lose their prize.

The old man's face was a blend of blood, leaves, and bits of dirt. His eyes still held defiance, but Ashe could see the fear.

For a brief second, Ashe saw Kyle's face in place of his. The image was so sharp it stole their breath. The same green eyes, the same crooked grin from years of teasing. Surprised, they regained control and staggered back. They shook their head and looked back to see Kyle was gone.

The Beast tried to soothe and encourage Ashe back into attack, but they stayed frozen in shock. Seeing Kyle's face forced lucidity to seep into Ashe's conscious mind.

Ashe dropped to the ground, hairy elbows digging into the earth, and pressed their forehead into the soil.

What if this had happened at their parents' house?

The thought of hurting anyone now turned Ashe's stomach. The image of Kyle's screaming face as they rent him apart was all they could focus on.

Bones cracked, muscles unknotted. Their body shrank, skin pulling tight as the fur began to vanish. Ashe was becoming human again.

A blessing and a punishment.

The old man rose, blood dribbling from his shoulder and down his back. He stepped over to Ashe, offering his hand. A slender hand gripped his in return. With a grunt, he pulled them to their feet. They stood together, unsteady. The trees rustled gently around them as the worst of the night began to settle.

"Well, that's new," the old man said. "Never seen someone stop mid-hunt during their First Tearing. Not without killing first."

Ashe could only nod, a gesture of acknowledgement rather than understanding.

The old man smiled, with a small wince of pain. "My name is Pines."

"Ashe," they said softly.

"You were pretty smart during your first change. Were you in control?"

"I dunno, I'm not even sure this is real," they admitted.

"Fair enough." The old man glanced around.

Ashe looked too. A fragile peace settled over the landscape. The tension had bled away, replaced by the soft chirring of insects and distant birdsong. Too normal to feel real.

"Let's get out of these woods and get some clothes on for both our sakes."

As they both began heading back toward the road, Ashe's memory finally snapped into place, filling in the last missing pieces. Stopping abruptly, Ashe glanced at the stranger.

"How messed up is my car?" Pines kept walking but hesitated just long enough before answering.

"Got a small shop behind my place. Give me a week, and I'll have it good-as-new."

Ashe caught up to him, staring forward, doubtful their car would truly ever be the same again.

Chapter 3

Cole wondered, not for the first time, how the hell he'd ended up on this drive.

July's heat bled through the van's cracked windows. The vinyl seats stuck to his legs, peeling with every shift, the fan squealing with every turn of the road.

The winding road up Monte Sano did nothing for his stomach. Pines hadn't said a word since they left. The old man might have been worse company than the heat.

If Rebecca hadn't taken their only car, Cole would've driven himself. Alone. Windows up, A/C on, and the option to turn back.

Instead, he was stuck here, wondering if a tuck-and-roll would kill him. Probably not. Not with what he was now. That was one of the few things Pines had shared since their first meeting. Whatever was happening to Cole, he wasn't human anymore.

He'd probably track me down and drag me back if I did try to run.

Besides, Cole wanted to know what was happening to him. He needed to know.

He closed his eyes, drawing his memory to the previous night. The night of the half-moon.

He and Rebecca had the worst fight of their relationship. She was frustrated with how little time they spent together. Cole had tried to explain. Sixty hours a week split between the post office and teaching music. Rent wasn't going to pay itself. And he was pursuing his music career. He'd just started to gain traction with several gigs at local venues.

Cole hoped she'd eventually see the short-term struggle was for the long-term reward.

But last night, he'd forgotten their anniversary.

Three years. Rebecca had lost it, and he didn't blame her. Cole tried to explain that work had called him in. They needed the extra money, especially now. He was leaving later in the month to tour with some local bands. Even with the low pay, he would get his music beyond Huntsville, and record labels would be scouting the events.

The fight had dragged on until early morning. Rebecca left, taking the car, and said she was staying with her parents for a while. The front door slammed. He was left with two candles flickering out beside untouched dinner plates. Their last gasps of flame died in waxy puddles.

Cole ate in silence. The fridge's hum seemed to judge him.

His body ached from the day's grind, but his mind wouldn't shut up.

He retreated to the garage studio. The secondhand office chair groaned under him. The glass on the desktop had been scratched and nicked long before they had found it. Across the cracked concrete, the mystery-stained couch sagged in defeat.

He picked up his acoustic guitar and let muscle memory take over.

Music had always been his pressure valve. Lyrics flowed more easily when he was emotional. Tonight was especially inspired.

Cole typed lines on his laptop between chords, trying not to think of her.

But his eyes drifted.

His attention rose to the poster hanging above the desk. His first album cover. Rebecca had commissioned it and paid for it with the part-time job she was working. The entire amount she had from that job paid for the album release.

A bittersweet mix of memory and regret.

Refocusing, he went back to strumming the guitar. After another hour, his fingers slowed. The chords faded. Then stopped.

He drifted to sleep at the desk. The last note still hummed in his ears, echoing in the studio. When the silence broke, he was standing in a vibrant grotto, untouched by human hands.

Wildflowers blazed, wheat swayed in the breeze, and a far-off field of lilacs sweetened the air. The grass was impossibly soft beneath his bare feet, yet somehow it felt like home.

A waterfall roared in the distance with the sound of an eager crowd. Cole stepped toward the rushing water. Sunlit mist broke into impossible colors as the falls struck a silver field, birthing animals that scattered into the trees.

Birdsong and harmony filled the air. Familiar. A melody he only half-remembered. Lines of verse stirred at the edges of thought, half-formed but insistent, carried on the music.

The musician hoped the dream would last. He felt safe. He knew he would be cared for in this strange nirvana.

Then he heard the growl.

Low. Deep. Very Close.

He turned slowly. And froze.

The wolf towered above him. Three times larger than any he'd seen in zoos or on documentaries. Its fur was shades of ash and soil, with white streaks at the neck and a white spot over the right eye with red-tipped ears. A scar ran from its muzzle to a jagged mouth lined with yellowed fangs.

Its glowing amber eyes locked onto Cole's light brown.

Cole's heart thundered as the wolf stepped forward. Fight or flight pushed him back, fists clenching, chest puffing in a pose that felt absurd even as he struck it. His heel slipped at the edge of the ledge, arms flailing for balance.

The wolf barked once, a sharp warning, then lowered its shoulders. Muscles bunched, fur bristled. It was ready to strike, and Cole had nowhere to go.

He closed his eyes, hoping it was only a dream. If not, he begged whatever was listening to watch over the ones he loved.

To watch over Rebecca.

As the plea left his lips, warmth touched his cheek. The same peace as before washed over him. The predator stopped. Waiting. Watching.

Cole opened his eyes and dropped to one knee. He slowly extended one trembling hand forward.

The beast flinched, then sniffed.

Cole's heart hammered as he hummed quietly, searching for the calming birdsong melody. Anything to still his fear.

The wolf blinked. Its snarl softened. It tilted its head, working through something Cole could not comprehend. Then, decision made, it approached and greeted the musician with a lick.

The warm, slobbery tongue should have disgusted him. It didn't.

Nuzzling beneath his arm, Cole continued to hum. He stroked the beast, fingers brushing through thick fur. The animal's final tension melted away beneath his hand.

Then something changed.

Relief and melody vanished as the wolf's body stuck to him. Fear cut through the melody, sharp and sudden. Cole tried to pull away, fur yanking with him. The wolf also panicked, its head jammed beneath his arm, and thrashed hard enough to drag him across the ground.

"No, no, no..."

Cole's hand sank into its shoulder like hot wax, heat pulsing around his fingers. The wolf's muzzle pressed into his chest, its eye and half its jaw disappearing inside him. Panic fed panic as the beast clawed at him, raking bloody ribbons from his thigh before its legs fused into his skin.

Cole screamed as blood and sinew writhed beneath the surface. He could feel its limbs stretching inside him, bones breaking and knitting around the intrusion. The wolf's chest heaved against his ribs, gasping for air it could no longer reach, until its whole body dissolved into him.

Please wake up, he begged.

His frame warped with it. Shoulders bulged, spine twisted, tufts of fur erupted in wet clusters. Pain lanced through him as his own bones reformed, merging and growing with the wolf's. His body swelled, skin stretching, until he was something monstrous.

Then the pain receded. Relief and awe flooded him, along with something else. The wolf's spirit had merged with his own, its desires raw and overwhelming.

Run. Be free.

He staggered upright, disoriented, two minds bleeding together. At the riverbank, he leaned down and stared into the water.

A beast stared back: furred, fanged, and wide-eyed, yet still Cole. Mottled gray and brown fur cloaked his frame, marked by a white blaze over his right eye. Claws twitched, legs bent too sharply, a body built for pursuit.

Instinct surged. He threw back his head and howled. Birds scattered like ash, the woods emptying in his wake.

Cole jolted in his studio, vision swimming.

He looked down. Tufts of gray and brown hair lay scattered around him. The guitar strings had been cut cleanly, sliced through by something sharp.

Cole's senses prickled. Something in the room didn't belong.

A stranger stood five feet away. An old man in a black T-shirt and sagging gym shorts. Gaunt eyes too still, his limbs hanging just a little too loose. His skin was pale, almost waxy, as if he had frozen in place for years.

Cole's breath caught. There was something wrong in the man's stillness. A new kind of tension crept under his skin. Numb. Confused. Instinctive. The man looked just as bewildered as he felt.

They stared at each other, both waiting for someone to move first.

Pines looked him up and down and asked, "Country singer?"

Cole stared back. "Indie pop," he replied, because what else could you say to that?

Pines gave a disapproving "Hrmph." Without invitation, he sat down and explained what had just happened. Cole wasn't sure how Pines had managed to calm him down. Most of the experience had blurred together, a dream that trailed into another dream.

The old man gave only the briefest summary. Cole had just had his "First Tearing, and it had happened in the Wildlands, Gaia's home plane. Pines claimed he'd been standing outside the house when he heard the howl. He'd rushed in, breaking down the side door to the studio garage.

"I rent this place. That door's going to cost me a fortune."

Pines mumbled a halfhearted promise to replace it later. When he'd forced the door open, he explained, he found a six-and-a-half-foot werewolf typing on the laptop. Before Pines could react, Cole had "Veiled" back to human form.

Cole looked at his laptop screen. A four-line stanza glowed there, and a chill tightened in his chest. He was certain it hadn't been there when he fell asleep.

My claws dig deep into the ground
And rip apart the verdant mound
The green spreads and the light shines
Like a cancerous growth expanding with time

The words still pulsed on the screen as if freshly typed, the same ones that had risen in his mind, half-sung in the dream's melody.

Pines had answered only a handful of Cole's dozens of questions, promising to share more the next night. Once he'd been introduced to the rest of the pack.

Now, he was being driven up to the top of Monte Sano in a white, unmarked van with no AC. Before the ride, Cole had made one last attempt to pry more information out of Pines. The old man just opened the door for Cole and muttered that he'd explain once everyone was together.

"Some things gotta be experienced to be understood."

Now, as they pulled into the parking lot, Cole hoped the answers would be worth the damage already done.

Chapter 4

"Is that going to be a problem?" Cole nodded toward the sign warning trails closed at sundown.

"I know a few rangers," Pines said.

The sun hovered low, casting long shadows across Monte Sano's canopy. At the entrance to the lot, a few cars were already pulling out.

The van slowed with a loud pop as its tires crunched over loose gravel. Cole leaned forward, peering out through the cracked windshield. Three vehicles were parked up ahead, and three people stood waiting, their outlines sharp against the dying light.

Pines came to a stop beside a beat-up blue SUV. Scratches marred the paint, a mismatched white back door stood out, and the passenger quarter panel was missing entirely, exposing mechanical guts like torn muscle and bone.

The old man climbed out without a word. Cole followed, eyes lingering on the battered vehicle. Pines walked past one of the figures who glanced at the SUV, then at him.

He shrugged. "Working on it."

That was all he said before striding toward the trailhead. The others exchanged glances, then fell in behind him.

Cole surveyed the odd group.

The first to catch his eye was a woman in her late fifties. She had a strong jaw and bob-cut brown hair streaked with silver. Her eyebrows were sharply manicured, and her dark eyeliner suggested someone who still cared about appearances. A silver nose ring glinted in the last rays of sunlight. Her gaze swept over Cole once, as if a single glance told her everything she needed.

Celtic tattoos curled around her forearms, disappearing beneath the sleeves of a nylon shirt. Nothing matched. Olive shirt, faded cargo pants, scuffed brown boots, but she looked ready to climb a mountain without breaking stride.

Not that Cole was in any position to judge. He wore a Chargers T-shirt, which he was pretty sure was Rebecca's, and jeans with more holes than denim.

The second person was the one Pines shrugged at. Tall, maybe early twenties, with a pixie cut dyed a fading purple. Roots showed through, a soft brown that clashed in a strangely pleasant way. The outfit was loud: K-pop crop top, bright red Dockers, and rainbow-striped socks. A tattoo of a six-sided die inked the back of their hand.

The last member of the group was a tall man in his early to mid-twenties, easily clearing six feet. His copper-brown skin and lean, muscular frame made him look like he'd stepped out of a casting call. Warm brown eyes and a porcelain-white smile radiated effortless confidence.

Cole guessed he was a former high school quarterback, or something equally popular. His long black hair was tied back in a sleek ponytail. The only flaw Cole could spot was a patchy beard that didn't quite fit the clean angles of his jaw.

Pines stopped beside the trail sign. The map showed a two-mile route up to the fire tower. He turned, gave the group a stern look, and said, "Alright. Let's go."

They started up the trail. Gravel shifted underfoot, quickly giving way to packed earth and soft pine needles. The air thrummed with cicada song. Light filtered through oak, maple, and hickory, dappling the path in honey-gold and deep green. On one side, the slope fell away into thorn-choked underbrush mixed with tall ferns. To the other, moss-covered boulders dotted the incline like a giant's knuckles, slowly worn by time.

Before they'd gone far, the older woman stepped in front of Pines.

"I thought there was one more," she said. Her posture was sharp, but her eyes were weary. He wasn't alone in being kept in the dark.

"She's meetin' us there." His tone was flat. Not hostile, but final.

No one pushed further. The woods around them swallowed the moment, filling it with nightlife and a warm breeze.

Cole breathed it in. Monte Sano had a quiet beauty. He regretted never visiting before. For a moment, the memory of his dream returned. That impossible wilderness. The waterfall. The glow. This wasn't that exactly, but it was close, and sometimes, close was enough.

He watched Pines, noting how the old man relaxed the moment they hit the dirt. His stride was easy, his pace brisk. For someone half a foot shorter and old enough to be their collective grandfather, he set a pace that kept the rest sweating.

Cole shifted his attention to the tall, lean Latino walking just ahead of him. The guy hadn't said much yet, but Cole quickly noticed how often he glanced at the purple-haired figure. His eyes lingered a little too long, and he seemed just a bit too eager to stay close.

The silence broke when the guy cleared his throat, trying a little too hard to sound casual.

"Hey, I'm Ryan," he said, aiming it toward the purple-haired stranger.

A pause followed. Not hostile, just awkward and long.

"I'm Cole," the musician offered quickly, trying to smooth things over.

"Ashe," came the curt reply.

"Renae," added the woman in green and brown.

They moved deeper into the woods. Pines led without slowing, the trail narrowing beneath thickening trees as the sky dimmed toward twilight.

Ryan tried again. "So how did you, y'know... handle 'The Change?'" His fingers made quotes as he drew out the last two words.

Ashe seemed put off by being the focus of attention. Ryan only stared back with a goofy grin and too many teeth to seem sincere. That smile had probably won him plenty of admirers.

Eventually, Ashe gave a lopsided grin. "I almost ate the old man."

A snort came from up ahead.

Cole's laugh caught in his throat. The others chuckled, but the sharp edge in Ashe's eyes told him it wasn't just a joke.

"He found me right as I was 'Changing," they said, mimicking Ryan's finger quotes. "Had to drive me out somewhere safe. By the time we got there, I was a full werewolf. Then I hunted him for a while."

"I led you by the nose," Pines muttered. "Was never in any danger."

"Riiiiight," Ashe drawled, shaking their head for the others to see.

The others smiled at that. Even Renae, who had been working hard to appear unapproachable, let out a quiet chuckle.

Cole tried to laugh again, but a knot tightened in his gut. His First Tearing hadn't been violent. The dream had been intense, but no one had gotten hurt. The thought gnawed at him: why had his wolf welcomed him when theirs had tried to kill?

As the others laughed at what could've been a nightmare, Cole wondered if he was truly safe with them. Pines had called them a pack. But were they really? Or just a handful of strangers tied together by something none of them understood?

Cole needed to learn more. About the dream. What he had become. All of it.

The group opened up after Ashe's tale. They continued in good spirits, with Cole shaking off his worry until Pines came to an unannounced stop.

They were still not at the Fire Tower. Only trees and underbrush littered the terrain around them. Pines touched a few trunks, silent, then nodded and stepped off trail.

The group hesitated but followed.

"Seriously?" Ryan asked.

No one answered.

The banter died as the dirt path disappeared behind them. Roots and shadows took its place. Darkness settled in where the sun had been, but Pines didn't slow.

The air thickened with the smell of pine sap and rotting leaves. Somewhere ahead, a creek burbled over stone. The heat clung even here, pressing against Cole's skin like wet cloth. Wiping his eyes, he stumbled on a half-buried stone, catching himself just in time.

Renae was the only one truly prepared for this part of the hike. From one of her many cargo pockets, she pulled out a small LED flashlight. She'd already deployed mosquito spray and a canteen without comment. Now she flicked on the beam, casting a path of light that cut through the creeping dark.

Ryan pressed on, spinning stories about college hijinks, old flings, and a summer playing semi-pro ball in New York. Each tale aimed at Ashe like a spotlight. Each tall tale made Ashe's jaw tighten just a little more. His voice bounced against the trees, too loud, a jarring note against the forest's stillness.

Cole offered polite laughs and comments where needed. But Ryan's attention never strayed from Ashe. It wasn't charming. It had become needy. Desperate. The others distanced themselves from the braggart, creating small gaps in their line while still staying within range of the flashlight beam.

Eventually, even Ryan noticed. He went quiet.

Cole, sensing the awkwardness, hummed. The melody floated softly between trees. Familiar. Peaceful. He shifted into one of his own songs from his first album. It hadn't done well on streaming services, but it was Rebecca's favorite. He always played it when she came to shows.

Ahead of him, Ashe's head lifted. They turned, eyes wide.

"You're Cole Stone?" they asked.

He lit up like a spotlight. "Yeah!"

Ashe grinned. Their entire posture opened up. "You're The Indigo Jay. My brother has your songs on Spotify. I think he even bought one of your shirts."

Cole couldn't help the dumb grin. "Want me to sign something for him?"

Ashe laughed, full and genuine. "Maybe when we get back to the parking lot. It's not really my thing, but he's gonna flip."

"Sounds like she's not a fan, bro," Ryan cut in. His voice landed with a thud. "Maybe don't interrupt when we're having a conversation."

The woods seemed to freeze in the summer heat.

Even Renae blinked at him and shook her head, a quiet warning written all over her.

Another quiet snort came from Pines' direction.

Ryan's smile faltered. He flushed, sped up, and positioned himself closer to Pines, putting distance between himself and the others. An island of awkwardness. Alone.

No one spoke for a long stretch. Leaves crunched. Flashlight beams danced across the landscape. Cole's attention drifted, pulling away from the group.

Ashe slowed. After a few dragging steps, they stopped.

The others followed suit, pausing with a cautious distance between them. Pines didn't notice until the silence held too long. Then, even he stopped and turned.

Ashe exhaled sharply. Their gaze stayed down, breathing controlled.

"I don't know how to say this without sounding like a bitch," Ashe began. Their voice quivered, cheeks red. "So if that's how you take it, fine."

Cole held his breath.

"First. I'm not a 'she.' I'm nonbinary. I go by they or them. You didn't know. That's fine. Now you do. It's only a problem if you make it one."

"Second. I do like The Indigo Jay's music. I'm just not into collecting autographs. My brother is. That's why I said it wasn't my thing. He's gonna freak."

Their words came fast, with no room to interrupt. Most of it sounded rehearsed. Ashe had probably been going over what to say in their head while they walked.

"Third. Don't be a dick unless you want to lose it."

Their eyes flared, caught in the beam of Renae's flashlight.

The night had gone unnaturally still. No one spoke. Even the wildlife seemed more interested in the confrontation than in their usual nighttime songs.

As the group's attention shifted from one face to the other, Ryan's breathing came heavy and uneven. Ashe, too, was struggling. Each inhale sharp and shallow, barely under control.

When Ashe finally steadied their breath, the focus turned fully to Ryan. Everyone waited to see how he'd respond.

Ryan's breathing quickened, uneven and shallow. He looked as if he might speak. His face tense; ready to say something defensive, or worse, something cruel to deflect the blame.

Pines moved first, stepping toward Ryan and placing a steady hand on his shoulder. He leaned in, whispering something the others couldn't hear.

Ryan, seemingly emboldened, lifted his hands.

"I was rude," he said. The words scraped out like they hurt.

"I'm sorry. I don't have a problem with your choice to be a non-bina—"

Ashe's entire demeanor shifted. A wave of wrongness radiated from them. Sharp and immediate.

"My choice!" Ashe snarled. Their body grew. In the low light, hair spread across their arms and stomach. Something stirred in Cole's chest, an echo of fur and instinct. His wolf recognized the threat before he did.

"Shiiit," Pines blurted, inching towards Ashe.

Ryan backed up, wide-eyed. "I don't got a problem! I just, I dunno. Bad word choice. Probably why I got mostly Ds at community college, y'know?"

Pines reached Ashe and laid a hand gently on their arm. At the touch, Ashe's eyes shifted from Ryan to him. No words were exchanged, just Pines' steady, stern look and Ashe's face, still lit with anger.

Sweat traced new lines into the old scars at Pines' temple, his body holding an invisible weight.

Pines edged back, stepping between Ryan and Ashe.

Ashe exhaled, their stance loosening just a little.

Comforted that he wasn't about to be lunch, Ryan continued, "Look, I'm nervous as hell about all this, and when that happens, I can be a dick. But don't rip it off... please?"

Renae snickered at the self-deprecating remark, and that seemed to further calm Ashe.

Then Ryan's goofy smile returned. "I was actually trying to mack with Renae, anyway."

Renae winked in reply, drawing a round of chuckles. Just like that, the standoff softened into an awkward gathering.

Pines took the lead again. "We're close," he said. "Might be good to get there before someone else tries to throw hands."

When it seemed safe enough not to be overheard, Cole drifted closer to Ashe and whispered, "Did you know your shirt is signed by every member of that band?"

Ashe glanced down at their favorite K-Pop shirt and briefly blushed. "I think I bought it that way." Before Cole could respond, they quickened their pace to walk beside Renae.

Cole smiled. It was enough just to have found another fan.

***

Another twenty minutes passed before Pines brought the group to a stop.

They'd reached a clearing near the mountain's peak. The moment they crossed the tree line, the air changed. Cooler. Cleaner. The humid weight of the Alabama summer fell away as if the grove refused to carry it.

The tallest tree stood maybe twenty yards off, an ancient oak with roots that clawed deep into the earth and branches that reached toward the stars like open arms. Its silhouette was jagged against the night sky, but something about it felt less like wood and more like a door left ajar.

Moonlight washed the grove in pale silver. The grass rippled in the soft night breeze, each blade bending in unison as though moved by a single breath. No trash. No beer cans. No carved initials or tram

It hadn't changed much since spring. The trees had filled out. More green clung to the edges. But the feeling of the grove, the connection to the Wildlands, remained untouched.

Pines took a breath and looked over the group.

They'd been loud. Clumsy. At each other's throats already. He'd seen hyenas with more composure. Still, he wasn't angry. They were raw, yes, but they were his pack now.

And truth be told, the old man was a little excited.

He studied each of them in turn.

Cole and Ashe still hummed with energy. Ryan lagged behind, sullen and still licking his wounds from earlier. Renae... was harder to read. Guarded as ever. He'd been called tight-lipped plenty of times, but Renae might just beat him at his own game.

He looked past them, scanning the trees.

Where was the last one?

If she was out there now, he couldn't sense her. Not clearly. Still, she was smart. Careful. That much he remembered from the first time they met.

Another ten minutes passed. Even Ashe and Cole faded, their energy dimming into quiet shuffles. Before the complaints could start, Pines lifted two fingers to his lips and let out a sharp whistle. High and shrill, it cut through the night and echoed into the trees.

Nothing.

She'd promised to meet him here.

Although English wasn't her first language, Grace understood the plan. He hoped.

Worry prickled at the back of Pines' neck. He'd been told he needed all five of them.

Movement pulled at the corner of his vision, back along the path they'd taken. The others still hadn't noticed. Too focused on the clearing.

Pines stepped forward and raised his voice, just enough to carry. "Grace?"

A shape emerged from the trees. Red-furred. Lean and low to the ground. A wolf.

She padded into the moonlight without a sound, her gold eyes catching the silver wash of the sky.

She sniffed the air, slow and deliberate, then crossed the clearing with careful steps. Her tongue lolled slightly from the heat, but there was nothing frantic in her movement. She was calm. Controlled.

The others stepped back as she passed. Pines chuckled.

The wolf came to a stop beside him and sat, tail flicking once across the grass.

"This is Grace," Pines said, turning to face the group. "The sixth member of our pack." This was always the part where most newcomers would freak out. He waited.

"Uh... welcome?" Cole offered, clearly unsure how to address a wolf. Grace gave a small nod. Or maybe just shook off a fly.

"Oh, I get it!" Ryan said, his face brightening with sudden realization. "She's showing us what we're gonna look like when we turn into wolves, right?"

Pines tilted his hand from side to side. "Yes, and no. You'll be able to take a wolf form. But like you, Grace hasn't gone through any other changes yet. Just her First Tearing and back again."

A flicker crossed Renae's eyes, some unseen emotion, but she was too far off to read it clearly.

Ryan, on the other hand, wore his feelings plain as day. Pines watched the younger packmate piece things together quicker than expected. He hadn't expected the comment that followed.

"So it's just a wolf?" Ryan asked, squinting at Grace like he couldn't quite believe it. "Like... a regular dumb animal?"

The growl was low and immediate. Ryan flinched as Grace rose to her feet, bristling. Her ears pinned back, lips curling to bare sharp teeth. She stalked forward. Deliberate. Quiet. Eyes locked.

Ryan raised his hands. "Hey, down girl."

Pines grunted, "Yeah, she was born a wolf, but she's still got feelings." She kept coming, slow and hungry-eyed, panting slightly in the heat.

"Anyone want to help out here?" Ryan called, backing away a step.

"Popular guy," Ashe muttered, stepping around him to approach the red wolf. About five feet out, Ashe dropped to one knee and lowered themself to eye level. Calm. Steady. Then tilted their head, baring their neck.

"I read somewhere this works with pack animals," they said.

Pines blinked, quietly impressed. There was no fear in Ashe.

Grace stepped closer to Ashe, sniffing their neck and chest. Her posture softened. The bristling fur along her spine smoothed. Whatever she'd been looking for, she'd found it. Then, without hesitation, she began licking their face.

Ashe froze. Joy in their eyes. Face smeared with slobber. They turned to the others with a crooked grin. "See? Told you."

"Yeah, that's one way to earn trust," Pines said dryly. "Though technically, you just presented yourself as the submissive."

Ashe blinked. Concern flickered across their face but then they shrugged. They gave Grace a scratch behind the ears and stood up, unbothered.

Pines looked over the group. All of them were here. There was a chance. He clapped his hands, gruff and sharp, the sound not quite hiding his anticipation.

"All right," he said. "Let's get started."

The group assembled in a loose semicircle. Ashe and Renae flanked the edges; Ryan stood awkwardly in the middle. Enough moonlight bled through the clearing that Renae clicked off her flashlight.

Pines moved around them deliberately, dragging a crescent moon into the dirt around their feet and connecting each person with a single line, then placing himself opposite the arc.

The ritual wasn't necessary. But it helped.

"Okay," Pines said, already peeling off his tattered black shirt. "Everybody strip."

That got some looks.

The three younger ones shifted in place, visibly unsure. Renae, unfazed, had already kicked off her boots and was tugging at her cargo pants.

"You're going to have to get used to this," Pines said, settling into the tone of a well-worn lecture. "As a pack, you'll see a lot worse from each other than just your dangly bits."

Ashe glanced down at his waist, then immediately looked away with obvious regret. The kid's face went a little green. Pines gave them a look. Stern. Unapologetic.

They sighed, peeled off their crop top and chest binder, and stepped forward. Cole and Ryan exchanged a glance, then followed suit.

Pines waited until all eyes were back on him. "First thing we're doing is called Veiling. You're going to become a wolf. Then come back." He paused, letting the words settle. The confusion didn't surprise him.

"These are the most common forms you'll take," he continued. "We'll practice veiling into the wolf and back to human before we touch the other two."

He pointed at the humans. "You four first. Focus on the spirit of the wolf. Breathe deep."

Their shoulders relaxed. The clearing grew still.

"Now," Pines said, voice gentler, "release your joy. Your love. Every good thing this world has given you, offer it to Gaia. When you're empty and still, the wolf spirit will come."

No sooner had he finished speaking than Renae shifted.

Her body folded in on itself with practiced ease, limbs compressing, muzzle lengthened. Bones clicked in a quiet rhythm, her body reshaping with none of the screaming agony Pines usually saw the first time. A Mexican gray wolf stood in her place. Rust-colored fur tangled through the gray like a Rorschach pattern. Her eyes stayed dark. Watchful.

The wolf gave a sharp yip, padded in a loose circle, and laid down.

The other three turned back to Pines, breath deepening again. This time, they were serious.

That was fast for a first-timer, Pines thought.

He studied Renae, looking for some hint of explanation. But she was harder to read as a wolf. Still, it wasn't unheard of. Some caught on quickly. Maybe she did yoga. Or maybe she was one of those older hippie types who'd made peace with herself decades ago.

Whatever the reason, it helped. The others would see it was possible.

Not long after, Ryan and Cole shifted. Both took the form of Eastern Timber Wolves, with Ryan a little larger and more gray along his flank. Cole bore a white blaze over his right eye, just like the night before.

Ryan gave a delighted yip and darted around the grove, leaping over Renae and testing out his four new legs. He bounded in sloppy circles, more Labrador than predator, his tail whipping like he expected applause.

"Before you get too carried away," Pines said, "let's get Ashe shifted. Then we'll run. Get a feel for it."

Four snouts turned toward Ashe.

They stood still in the center of the circle, eyes tight, frustration bleeding from their face.

Thoughts raced behind Ashe's expression. The breathing was right. The wolf was there. He'd seen this before. Someone ready, but not yet able. He opened his mouth to explain. Then paused. Something in the air, just out of reach. A wrongness, faint but growing. Like the air before a storm, but sour. Pines' nose twitched. He couldn't place it.

Grace moved first. The red-furred wolf turned toward the forest, posture snapping from relaxed to alert. Her head lowered. Her eyes scanned the tree line.

Then came the gunshot.

The clearing rang with it, a flat echo bouncing off stone and oak.

Pines' head whipped toward the sound. Then back to the pack. Ryan had fallen. The big wolf scrambled in the dirt, hind leg collapsing beneath him. Blood spread quickly across the gray fur of his hip.

And then Pines smelled it.

It reeked of something wrong: burned hair, rotting marrow, metal gone sour. Wet soil steeped in decay. Not just death, but desecration. The scent of a world that had rotted away long before theirs.

Tzelut, The Cursed Root, knew they were here.

Chapter 5

Ryan's wolf form lay crumpled in the center of the clearing, blood matting his flank, tongue lolling, leg twitching like a fish gasping on land. The sight hit him like a fist to the chest. It wasn't just the injury, but the timing.

This was supposed to be a night of learning and celebration. Gaia should have been honored. The young pack was meant to pledge themselves to her.

Instead, some goddamn Tzelut fanatic had desecrated the Grove and was trying to kill the pack.

His pack!

Another shot cracked through the trees. The echo chased itself through the trunks. A death sentence whispered by the forest itself.

Pines shook off his lethargy and forced himself into motion. He was a guardian of the land, and this grove was one of the oldest the Lycan had ever known. One of the strongest ties to Gaia. He would not fail her or those placed in his care.

He caught Ashe's silhouette just as it started to stretch upward, bones creaking under flesh, skin rippling in unnatural rhythms.

Before the transformation overtook them, Pines launched forward and tackled them, crashing into the mossy earth. Dirt and dead leaves flew as he dragged Ashe behind a rotted log, the ancient trunk barely big enough to hide them both.

He loomed over the human and cupped their face in both hands, forcing their glowing eyes to meet his.

"*DO NOT TURN*," he hissed, breath hot and sour. "*Look at me. Focus. Stay human.*"

Ashe froze, chest heaving. Their eyes stared into his. The shift halted. Muscles deflated with an audible pop of joint and sinew, the change receding beneath skin.

The rifle barked again.

The bullet smacked into a stone a few feet in front of Grace, exploding into sparks. She snarled and sprang northeast into the trees, weaving between saplings and tangles of underbrush. A blur of russet fur vanished among the trunks.

"Scatter and hide!" Pines bellowed, the command rippling through the clearing like a whip crack.

The other wolves, newcomers still learning the shape of their own limbs, shook themselves from shock and darted off. Renae veered west, crashing through ferns and vanishing into the gloom. Cole bolted south toward a nearby mountain stream, paws kicking up needles.

Pines knew they'd eventually figure out how to Veil back to human, but panic and pursuit would make that nearly impossible. The best thing for them was to escape the danger.

He glanced toward the treeline where the last muzzle flash had come from, then back at Ashe.

"I need to give him a single target to focus on," he muttered. "Get Ryan out of here if you can."

With a growl, he leapt over the log and shifted midair. Fur sprouted from skin, bones compressed, and he landed as a red-speckled Great Plains wolf, lean and fast.

He bolted east, zigzagging between young maples and oaks, breath steady, body low. Each stride churned up clumps of damp soil. The shooter would follow the motion. He'd make sure of it.

***

The pressure of the change and the chaos around them pushed Ashe to the edge of losing control.

Not now.

The sensation clawed at them, but they forced it back, keeping low and hunched to make themselves less of a target.

Ryan. They had to get to Ryan.

He lay completely exposed. Breathing shallow. Blood glistened along his flank, fur torn and singed. Ashe bolted out from cover, staying crouched, bare feet digging into rocks and snapping unseen twigs. They were close to him when another shot howled overhead, slicing the air beside their ear.

They dove, curling into a ball around Ryan's body. He'd been near Pines, at the very center of the clearing, when the shot took him. His breath came in ragged bursts, eyes glassy.

"I'm sorry, please don't hate me later for this," Ashe whispered.

With effort, they wrapped their arms under the wolf's belly, lifting. Ryan was heavy, a hundred and fifty pounds of dead weight, but Ashe pushed off and staggered toward a cedar thicket fifteen yards away. The brush was dense. It would have to be enough.

The wolf was heavier than Ashe expected, but somehow they lifted him. Every muscle screamed, biceps and shoulders straining as though they might tear under the weight. Heat rolled off their body, sweat running into the blood that poured from Ryan, streaking their bare chest in red and salt. The air stank of sweet metal and damp fur.

Crack.

Agony bloomed in Ashe's shoulder. A bullet grazed them, spinning their body halfway around. They gritted their teeth, stumbled forward, and with a cry, hurled Ryan into the shadows. A loud yelp came out of the wolf as he tumbled through pine needles and vanished into the brush.

Ashe dropped to their knees five yards short. Every nerve shrieked. They dragged themself forward through bramble and bark. Their hands felt the touch of fabric and realized it was a bundle of discarded clothes.

Bunching the fabric in their hands, they pressed deeper into the brush until they reached Ryan. His breath was thin, nearly drowned out by the wind. Blood slicked his side, and the fur around the wound was burned, bubbling like tar.

Ashe pushed the sounds of the outside world away. They pressed the shirt against the wound, blotting away fresh blood. Gently, they touched Ryan's hip to assess the damage. Fingers brushed something hard in the wound. Pain raced through their skin. It felt like touching dry ice wrapped in fire. They looked to see blisters rising instantly on their fingertips.

"Shit that burns," they whispered. "Are you feeling that?"

The wolf's eye flickered open. Then shut. Ashe gasped as their pain doubled, their body screaming. But underneath it came another rhythm of suffering, pressing inside like a second heartbeat. It was softer, weaker, but carried a weight that dragged them under. Dying. The terrible knowledge of it lodged inside. Ryan's fear, Ryan's end, bleeding into them.

The bullet was poisoning him. Ashe could feel it, burning from the inside out. They needed it gone. Fast.

But first, they needed a clearer look at the wound. Hoping to find Renae's flashlight, their hand brushed against their own pants. Searching pockets, they found their phone. With shaking fingers, Ashe pulled it out and clicked the flashlight app.

The white beam cut through the dark, revealing the wound in grisly detail. Flesh had split raggedly, and a black rot spidered outward from the impact site. The misshapen slug gleamed dully where it sat embedded in cracked bone. Ashe saw fragments of hipbone shattered and curling inward like splinters from a rotten tree.

They forced back bile.

A stray thought whispered: *There should be more blood.* Instead, the tissue around the metal pulsed faintly. The body itself rejecting what had been placed inside.

Gathering their nerve, Ashe poked two fingers into the bullet hole. Ryan howled, and Ashe tried to quiet him. The bullet was slick, impossible to grip as their skin hissed on contact. Ashe withdrew, hand shaking.

"I'm not gonna get this out unless I widen the entry point." They spoke softly, hoping Ryan could understand.

Ashe fished their pocketknife from another pocket. Their dad had given it to them on their sixteenth birthday, with the name *Calder* engraved along the handle. It was meant for protection, though until now its only battles had been with cardboard boxes.

The memory stirred unwanted emotions, but Ashe shoved it aside.

They clicked the blade open.

A gunshot split the air deeper in the woods, followed by a wolf's yowl drifting through the trees. The sound crawled under Ashe's skin, driving their pulse into a hammering sprint and turning the edges of the forest into a blur.

"Focus," Ashe breathed. "He needs you."

Ryan's eyes were half-lidded. His chest barely rose.

With trembling hands, they made the first incision. The knife sank through singed fur and flesh. Ryan didn't move. Encouraged, Ashe carved an X into the wound to expose the embedded metal.

Then, they reached in.

A lightning bolt ran through Ashe's arm. The silver scorched their fingers. Nerves screamed. Tears streaked their cheeks, breath hitching hard. With a sob, they gripped the slug and yanked.

Crunch.

A shard of hipbone came out with the metal.

They hurled the silver deep into the woods, where it landed with a hiss like hot iron striking wet stone.

Ashe collapsed backward, clutching their hand and gasping as waves of fire shot through their arm. Ugly purple blisters settled where their fingers had touched the bullet. The world tilted sideways, and then went dark.

A heartbeat later, they jolted awake on the ground, lungs dragging for air. After a few breaths, they sat up, dizzy but present. They evaluated their work. The wound looked awful, but Ashe wasn't sure what else to do.

"Bet Renae's got a surgical kit in one of those pockets," they told Ryan, voice dry. The problem was Ashe didn't know where Renae's clothes were. And they definitely weren't going back out into the open.

They tore their own shirt and pants into strips, binding the hip as tightly as they could. "You better appreciate this; that shirt was a gift."

Once out of fabric, they looked at their work. It was the best they could manage for now. They slumped forward, resting their head against Ryan's fur. The faint rise and fall of his chest gave them just enough hope.

Then they looked up.

Beyond a ridge, a hundred yards away, four figures moved through the moonlight. Three wolves circled another figure. Ashe could make out Pines' wolf form and possibly Grace and Cole.

Please don't let that cry have been Renae.

The last figure looked too big for a man.

It stood hunched, limbs too long, torso bloated, head crooked at a wrong angle. Their stomach churned.

A wolf lunged.

The figure moved with impossible speed. Its claws lashed out, and the wolf was torn from the air, body twisting. It smacked into a tree with a sickening crack that echoed through the clearing like breaking bone.

"No!" Ashe screamed.

The change surged up inside them. This time, they didn't resist.

Their vision flared red, blood surging behind their eyes. Each heart-beat thudded like a war drum beneath their ribs. Bones fractured and reformed, tendons unraveling and reweaving. Skin tore, slick with sweat and something older. Power surged up their spine like fire on a fuse.

Ashe exhaled one final breath of humanity.

And the rage took hold.

Chapter 6

The scent of corruption stained the woods, thick rot clinging to damp bark. It was old and acrid, drifting in from every direction. Still, Pines knew the source was close. It made pinpointing the shooter's exact location difficult.

It had been years since Pines had smelled someone touched by Fäulung. The memory came unbidden. A boy of thirteen, the Macon pack refusing to believe such darkness could take root in a child. Pines forced the image aside.

The shots came quicker now, reckless and wild. The shooter had marked him as the threat.

The old wolf wove through the trees in a chaotic loop toward the assassin's position. The ground beneath him was treacherous, riddled with sinkholes and jagged stones. He slid under sagging branches, muscles bunching as he leapt over sprawling roots.

He wasn't alone.

Through the nascent pack bond, Pines felt Grace and Cole tracking from opposite flanks. The pack link wasn't yet strong enough for communication, but their emotional signals pulsed faintly.

Focus. Fear. Anger. Resolve.

Grace's presence was all edge, a predator's hunger sharpened to a blade. Cole's fear felt strong but unfamiliar. He wasn't accustomed to living in mortal danger. Still, his resolve burned steadily beneath it.

Another shot cracked past his ear. Pines slid behind a weathered boulder, crouching low, teeth bared. He scanned the treeline. A hint of motion caught his senses.

Between two spruce trees, half-hidden by a fallen log, a thickset man waited with his rifle. Mud streaked his elbows and stubbled jaw. His expression was flat, patient.

Pines sniffed. Sweat. Gun oil. Damp canvas. And something else, something fouler. Dark corruption coated the man's scent, an odor of putrid flesh left to spoil in summer heat.

A bullet punched into the clay inches from his flank, kicking grit into his eyes. Pines dropped low again. Pinned down. Vulnerable.

His pulse drummed in his ears.

One heartbeat.

Two.

Grace emerged to Pines' right, her red coat whispering through the trees like drifting smoke. She was breathing hard, making no effort to hide. The gunman jerked, swinging the barrel toward her.

Pines moved.

He burst from cover in a blur of fur and fury. Grace dove behind a pine tree just as the trigger snapped. Bark exploded around her, splinters slicing through the air. She yelped, rolled, and then sprang up, circling wide.

Pines hadn't wanted the others involved, but Grace had given him the opening he needed.

All four legs exploded into motion. He dropped all pretense of evasion and charged. He slammed into the man's chest, jaws locking around the throat. They tumbled backward into the hollow.

The old wolf bit down.

The throat gave way too easily, tissue parting like wet paper. Metallic warmth filled his mouth. A wet scream burst out, gurgling through blood and bile. Corruption flooded his nostrils.

His victim kicked wildly, boots flailing, but Pines twisted his head with brutal force. Windpipe. Artery. Cartilage. All gave way. The assassin gurgled once more, reaching feebly for his killer. His leg knocked the rifle, and he felt the burn of silver threaded through it, a safeguard the lesser Witherbound used so no Lycan could use it against them.

Pines shook until nothing was left to fight. Only then did he finally let go.

Grace trotted up beside him, panting, her red coat streaked with grime. From the far side, Cole crept forward. Ears twitching. Steps cautious. He leaned down to sniff the body, then jerked back, face twisting in revulsion.

Pines watched him carefully. The kid looked pale beneath the fur, unsteady. It was too much to witness in a single night. Too much to become part of.

Cole kept staring at the corpse, chest hitching, a soft whine escaping his muzzle.

The reek of corruption receded from the corpse.

But something else still lingered. The taint felt close, soaked into bark and root like cursed sap. Whatever controlled the assassin hadn't died with him.

And Pines could feel it watching.

Grace stiffened, lips curling, eyes locked on something beyond the trees. Her senses were sharper than Pines', more attuned to the unseen. He followed her gaze and arched his back, muscles coiled, facing the same direction.

Cole turned as well, tearing his eyes from the corpse. Confusion radiated from him in waves. He hadn't sensed the wrongness yet.

Ahead, the forest was black, not merely dark but layered and unnatural. The air hung still yet charged, as if waiting for the world to flinch. A curtain of oily shadow blanketed the slope, masking whatever stirred beyond.

A Specter might have followed the gunman to see if the job was finished. Or to step inside what was left and finish it themselves. Thankfully, only the strongest spirits could take a dead body. And Pines had never known one that would aid Tzelut.

Still, he debated veiling back to human. To grab the gun or call out to the darkness.

A breeze stirred around the wolves. Then, a sound.

Crunching leaves. Footsteps, deliberate and slow, coming from beyond the ridge.

A figure stepped from the deep dark between two maples. It moved with a broken gait, like something wearing human skin for the first time.

Arms hung loose at unnatural angles while joints fought against each movement. Bones seemed misaligned with every step, as if the body itself was trying to reject its occupant.

Standing over seven feet tall with massive shoulders, it revealed a ruined face when it stepped into the open: deep gouges, patches of raw scalp, one eye socket hollow. Its bare chest was mottled with scars, the skin pocked and stretched like it had outgrown itself.

Pines had scars of his own, gained through his years of fighting. That paled in comparison to the thing before him. Its face had been partially skinned. Exposed muscle and teeth showed through the ruin.

Revulsion crawled up his spine, but he couldn't look away. He knew that face.

Sebastian had once been a well known Alpha, a warrior of the Carolinas. At Moonmotes, the man had ranted about scorched-earth tactics, about purifying Gaia with fire and fang. His entire pack had vanished long ago, presumed dead in a raid gone wrong.

Yet here he stood. Dripping with malice.

"You still run with pups, old man?" Sebastian sneered. His voice oozed into their minds, bypassing ears entirely. "You were always weary, Pines. Always clinging to peace. While you hesitated, I bled for the cause."

Pines growled low. He sent a message through the pack link.

His name is Sebastian. He was a Lycan. He knows how we fight.

The link was still too new, too raw. More instinct than language. He wasn't sure how much they'd understand.

"Yes, my brother," Sebastian said aloud, his words sliding through the pack link like fingers through open wounds.

The other two wolves looked to Pines, confused and uncertain. Emotions rippled through the pack bond: dissonant chords of fear, disbelief, hesitation.

The old wolf didn't look away. He couldn't.

The thing stepped within fifty feet of the pack.

This can't be happening!

Lycans couldn't be touched by Fäulung. That was the law. The unbendable truth. They could falter or lose themselves to bloodlust or despair. But not this.

The scarred visage twisted into a sinister smile as it saw understanding in the old man's eyes.

"Yeah, it's as bad as you think."

"And it's **GOING TO GET WORSE**!" The last words came out twisted, barely understandable.

Bones cracked. Skin tore. The transformation was instantaneous.

But what emerged wasn't Lycan.

A full foot taller, even while grotesquely hunched. The spine jutted like broken ridges beneath mangy patches of blood-red fur clinging to its warped frame. Leathery gray skin stretched tight over twisted muscle, marked by faint scars that glowed dimly, sick lime green runes pulsing in the dark.

Arms dangled past its knees, the limbs too long and loose, ending in claws more like bone scythes than fingers. Viscous yellow mucus dripped from jagged, overgrown teeth. Black ichor oozed from open joints and seeping wounds. The surviving eye was shadow in motion, a pupil-less abyss brimming with ageless hunger.

Gaia, preserve us.

The monster leapt.

Pines barely shoved Cole aside in time. It landed where they'd just stood, dirt erupting beneath its weight. Grace and Cole fled into the brush. Pines took off in another direction. Leading the thing away.

The Banewolf—he refused to accept it as Lycan—was fast. Too fast. Trees blurred past as Pines sprinted. He didn't try a Full Tearing. The process would leave him vulnerable for seconds. And seconds meant death.

He needed to give Grace and Cole enough time to disappear. That was all he could do now.

Even if Pines could achieve full transformation, even if he threw himself into the fight with everything he had, he wouldn't win. He was nearly eighty. The years had taken their toll on his strength. His speed. His edge.

And Sebastian had gone missing in his prime, a brutal, relentless warrior even then.

A boulder crashed onto the path ahead. Pines skidded, narrowly avoiding another stone hurled with monstrous force. He twisted through the trees, lungs burning, just trying to survive.

Another impact crashed as rock chips peppered his back legs. He risked a glance. Sebastian, mid-run, scooped up a rock the size of a skull and hurled it.

At Grace. She had flanked around the Banewolf, trying to give Pines some breathing room.

Damn stubborn wolf!

The projectile clipped a young hemlock, splitting the trunk with a loud crack before veering off. Too close. Far too close. They weren't going to outrun it. Not all of them.

Pines pivoted hard, dug in with all four legs, and charged. The thing didn't expect it. The flicker of surprise on Sebastian's mangled face gave the mentor a jolt of grim satisfaction.

He ducked a sloppy swipe and lunged low, jaws locking around the creature's heel. The flesh was wrong. Rubbery. Oily. Unnatural. Like biting into tendon soaked in bile and smoke. Still, he yanked.

Sebastian roared. A wet, rattling bellow that made the trees tremble. He spun, claws raking through the air. One strike came within inches of splitting Pines' skull. The wolf readjusted, positioning his body directly behind the Banewolf to avoid the swipes, never letting go.

Realizing its tactic wasn't working, the Banewolf dropped to all fours and used its free leg to kick Pines away.

Claws raked down Pines' flank as he was flung backward. Flesh tore free in his grip with a ragged, sucking rip. Layers unraveled, sinew peeling in loose strands.

The Banewolf straightened, rising to its full, grotesque height. Its bulk shifted onto the uninjured leg with a wet, cracking pop. Tendons twitched beneath twisted hide. No blood leaked from the wound. Only a sluggish trickle of dark, tar-thick ichor, plodding down the ankle.

Pines' mouth burned. The taste of rot and venom seared his tongue. He spat the torn flesh onto the dirt and staggered back, stomach churning.

But the injury wasn't closing. That ankle, mangled and leaking, remained broken.

At least some of the rules still applied.

The old wolf struggled to rise. Pain flared through his ribs, the last blow having done more than just bruise. Something inside him was broken.

It snarled and took one wary limp towards Pines before turning to see it was surrounded.

Pines yipped, urging the others to run. The attack had been a distraction, a sacrifice to buy them time. But Grace and Cole ignored him, darting in from opposite sides, snapping at the creature's flanks. They aimed at the injured leg, trying to cripple it.

Run! Pines screamed through the pack link. The bond wasn't strong enough for full words, but maybe the urgency would carry.

No.

The reply struck him like a spark. Not just defiance but anger, blazing hot. Pines turned and saw Grace, eyes locked on the monster, her stance unshaken.

He blinked. A clear message from one so new.

Cole ran dangerously close to the Banewolf, barely dodging a swipe. Sebastian lurched, the wounded leg collapsing under his weight, dropping him to one knobby knee.

Grace bristled with excitement, already charging in as she leapt to sink her teeth into the exposed leg.

But the Banewolf was no fool. It had exaggerated its injury, drawing one in close enough to strike.

Pines screamed into the link, but it was too late.

The monster quickly swiveled, slapping the smaller attacker into a nearby tree. Grace hit with a *thwack*, then crumpled to the ground. Branches cracked, falling on top of her.

Pines rose, each breath a lance in his cracked ribs. Pain flared with every movement, but he didn't care. His eyes locked on Grace's motionless form. Buried in branches. Too still.

Then, slowly, he turned.

The Banewolf stood watching, head cocked at a grotesque angle. Black ichor dripped in ropes from its torn flank, hissing where it struck the soil. Its smile split too wide, tearing flesh at the corners to reveal jagged, uneven teeth that seemed to twitch with their own life.

A voice crept through the pack bond, damp and parasitic, rooting itself in the corners of Pines' mind.

Don't worry, I will guide and train those who survive.

"*Help her!*" Pines pushed the thought toward Cole, raw and desperate. Whether the young wolf understood or simply obeyed instinct, he bolted into motion, circling wide around the hulking beast.

Pines lowered himself into a crouch. Ribs flaring, limbs trembling.

This would be his stand.

The old wolf dropped into a low, braced stance, limbs taut like drawn wires and hackles raised. A ferocious snarl ripped free from his chest, raw and defiant.

He planted himself between the Banewolf and his wounded packmates. A wall of flesh and fury. A challenge.

He didn't care about tactics anymore.

This was sacrifice.

Across the clearing, Sebastian saw it in his eyes. That twisted smile spread wider. The monster dipped low, mirroring Pines' stance. Mocking him.

They both knew how this ended.

Gaia, take me home. Don't let me become that. Pines cast the plea into the soil, hoping Gaia would grant it. The ground thrummed beneath him, a low vibration of answer.

The Banewolf's head snapped away from Pines, attention broken. A blur of rage and muscle struck Sebastian with the force of a missile.

Ashe had arrived.

The Warhide met the Banewolf with bone-jarring impact, the force of it reverberating through the forest floor. Pines felt the vibration beneath his paws as nearby trees trembled from the shock.

The two figures tumbled in a chaos of limbs and blood, dirt swirling around them. Ashe crashed down on the abomination, teeth bared in a snarl. They tore into it without hesitation, claws raking its chest and stripping away rotted, corrupted flesh. Viscous, midnight-dark fluid sprayed in arcs across the trees, each drop sizzling where it touched the living wood. The frenzy was pure instinct. Rage, panic, and something darker.

Pines didn't wait.

He rushed in beside them. His jaws locked around the monster's thick wrist. The texture was like sinew soaked in tar, but he held fast, using all his strength to pin the arm.

Maybe now, with the two of them fighting as one, they had a chance.

Pines just hoped that Ashe wouldn't lose themself to the wild hunger that burned inside their wolf spirit.

One monster was enough.

Ashe tore into the Banewolf with fury, claws shredding flesh, eyes wild with rage. The thing roared. It fought back. Blood and shadow spilled.

And somewhere through the chaos, Pines felt it.

Gaia was watching. She was not done with him yet.

Chapter 7

The Banewolf didn't even glance Cole's way as he darted around it. Why would it? He hadn't landed a single hit.

Grace is hurt because of me. Pines is barely standing. Ashe is locked in a death match.

Grace lay crumpled beneath a snapped pine tree. One leg bent the wrong way at the knee, flesh already ballooning, skin stretched tight.

He didn't have time to wallow. Cole skidded to a stop, heart pounding as he looked for signs of life. Her breath came shallow but steady. He sniffed her body. No scent of torn flesh or fresh blood.

Still, that ruined leg made bile rise in his throat. He pawed at her, and she didn't flinch.

What do I do?

Cole couldn't shift back to human. He had tried before reaching Pines, but every attempt slipped away the moment he grasped for it.

Once, he had felt the change rising in him, almost breaking through, when a vision through Grace's eyes pierced his mind. Pines in danger, a flash of emotion and imagery that wasn't his own. The intrusion had struck him raw and overwhelming, and the transformation snapped shut.

Behind him, the sound of tearing flesh and snarling rage. Pines and Ashe were still fighting the monster.

I can't do anything to help with that.

He bent low, teeth latching onto a fallen branch. The bark was slick with dirt and old sap, rough against his tongue. He yanked hard. Muscles strained. The limb scraped and bumped across the forest floor before tumbling free of Grace with a dull, final thud.

He dropped it and turned back to her. She was still breathing, but barely.

Cole found it strange to care so much about Grace. She was only a wolf, yet there was more beneath the surface, a sudden kinship that made her feel as important as any human out here.

Cole let instinct take control. He leaned down and licked her muzzle gently.

Her whiskers twitched once.

Then, with a sharp inhale, Grace's eyes snapped open. She snarled and jumped to her feet, fur bristling. Cole leapt back, lowering his head submissively. Grace bared her teeth, scanning the area, but the fight was distant now. Slowly, she stopped growling.

Grace looked toward the distant fight, preparing to spring back into action. Her left hind leg was not touching the ground. She was in no shape to go back into the fight against the Banewolf.

Cole moved to block her, growling low. Grace crouched, ears flicking in surprise. She growled in return, but Cole would not budge.

Stay, he commanded through the pack link.

Grace blinked. Her body sagged, the fight leaving her. She sat hard, wincing as her haunch hit dirt.

Go, she sent back, along with urgent flashes: *Pines, Ashe, Banewolf. Urgency.*

It wasn't an order like his. It was a plea to go help since she couldn't.

He nodded once, then turned and ran.

*　*　*

The mountaintop boiled with chaos.

The Banewolf's matted fur blocked Pines' vision as he clung to its arm, jaws locked on the foul limb. Every muscle screamed in protest, but he didn't let go. Atop the beast, Ashe raked it open with fury.

The creature howled. The sound began as a rumbling bellow before spiraling into a glass-shattering shriek that drew blood from Pines' ears.

Pines tried to look at Ashe. They were in a trance of anger and aggression. Still tearing large chunks from the monster beneath them.

Ashe's Warhide form held fast, muscles locked in purpose. Even bloodied, they moved with deadly precision, deflecting some swipes and absorbing others with sheer brute endurance.

Pines' admiration of Ashe's resilience cost him. In that moment of distraction, Sebastian wrenched free and flung him through the air. He hit the ground hard. Vision spun. Limbs refused to move.

Through the blur, he saw the abomination twist with a savage heave. Ashe held tight, but not tight enough.

The Banewolf drove an elbow into Ashe's ribs, loosening their grip. In that split second of weakness, claws thrust up beneath their arms and dug deep before hurling them aside with savage force.

Ashe collapsed beneath the Banewolf's weight, their body crushed into the dirt. The Banewolf straddled the Warhide with clinical malice. Its claws sliced deep with horrifying precision, peeling them apart one deliberate cut at a time.

Let's see how you like it.

The Banewolf's voice oozed into Ashe's and Pines' minds. It wasn't thought, but a violation, dragging behind it a vision. In the shared space of their bond, Ashe's body flayed open, their skin peeled back in strips. Screams swallowed by the woods. The images lingered vividly, stitched into the folds of their awareness.

How could it connect to our pack link so strongly?

Pines tried to move, but each breath came shallow and ragged. Air refused to fill his lungs. Pain flared from his cracked ribs. Sharp. Electric. Unrelenting. His vision swam. Through the haze, he caught sight of

Ashe. They were still fighting. Rage guiding them.

But momentum had shifted.

Sebastian had the advantage now. He moved with cruel precision, deflecting Ashe's frantic strikes. Each counter was deliberate, punishing. He had the experience of fighting as a Lycan. And now he was dismantling Ashe, blow by blow.

The Warhide's strength was fading, cuts bleeding them out by degrees. Ashe's chest heaved, their breaths frantic. Panic clawed at them, Sebastian's psychic intrusion twisting their mind while pain dragged them under.

Through the pack link, fragments of emotions crashed together: Ashe's guilt at not being enough, Cole's fear he wouldn't arrive in time, Grace's throbbing pain. Beneath it all, Pines sensed something else. Someone trying to hide themselves from the link.

Slowly, the Banewolf raised its arm, savoring the moment. Its eye locked on Ashe with unholy glee, like a predator toying with wounded prey.

He's going to win.

They had gotten close. Ashe had carved deep gashes into the beast's torso. Parts of its entrails spilled through the wounds, slick and steaming.

For a moment, Pines almost believed they could have won. But now, even if the Banewolf eventually succumbed to its injuries, it had already succeeded. The pack was broken and scattered. They were too young. Too few.

The Banewolf had fulfilled its purpose. The Seer had warned him all the young pack members would be needed.

Pines saw Cole charging in. With no time left, the old wolf forced himself upright, legs trembling, insides on fire. One last strike. That's all he had left.

BOOM.

The monster's head exploded.

Chunks of bone and ichor sprayed through the clearing. The beast collapsed on top of Ashe in a twitching heap.

Pines looked behind the corpse to see Renae in all her naked human glory. She held the assassin's rifle in her hands, barrel still smoking. After a battle of wolves and monsters, the sight of a lone human in their midst felt almost unreal.

Muffled snarls came from beneath the dead Banewolf. Ashe was still pinned, but Pines could hear the confusion in their growls. Wild, unfocused anger seeking a new target. The Warhide was having trouble discerning friend from foe.

Renae stepped into Ashe's view and pointed the rifle down at the pinned Lycan.

"I'm your friend," her voice, like iron. She spoke slowly, never looking away from Ashe's eyes.

"I'm going to throw this gun down now because it's burning my hands. Don't let me regret it."

Renae tossed the weapon. It clattered onto the forest floor, but Pines' gaze locked on her hands. What he'd mistaken for smoke from the barrel was rising from her palms. Thin wisps curled off reddened, blistered skin.

The older woman stepped back, slow and deliberately, posture coiled tight. Ready to bolt or fight.

Ashe rolled free. Their eyes snapped toward each person, bloodshot and wild. They bared their teeth, a low growl building in their throat as they struggled to their knees.

The land around was still. Cole and Renae poised to defend themselves from their earlier walking companion.

Pines took a breath and Veiled. Back in his human form, he felt so weak, but it was the only way to access the calming bond.

Rising to his feet, the old man edged toward the injured Warhide. Ashe's unease pulsed through the bond. Pines stopped a few paces away, then extended his hand with slow, deliberate precision. Ashe didn't flinch, but their body tightened like a cable stretched to its limit.

The touch sparked something familiar, an echo of the connection they had shared that first night. It calmed the tremor running through Ashe's muscles.

Pines was one of the few who could push emotion so subtly through a direct link. He summoned memories of trust and peace, drawing on moments of calm he had known before. Images of his wife surfaced, but he kept them close. Those were only for him.

Ashe's teeth were still bared, flicking between Pines and Renae, but then their whole frame seemed to deflate. The fur melted away in patches, receding as the human form took over once again.

Blood trickled from a gash at Ashe's temple. Deep slashes marred their arms and chest. One side of their torso was smeared with ichor that was reddening the skin.

Pines glanced over and saw Renae sag with visible relief, dropping to her knees. Her hands clenched, the pain she'd been holding back finally catching up.

Cole ambled closer to the other three in wolf form. He was the only one without injuries.

That reminded Pines.

"Is Ryan stable?"

"I think so," Ashe said, their voice frayed and thin. They didn't meet Pines' eyes, barely able to lift their head.

"I bandaged him before I left. He was... still breathing."

The words dragged out, as if they weighed too much to carry. Their limbs trembled faintly. Eyes distant. Glazed.

Cole tugged at Pines' wrist, then turned and sprinted off in Grace's direction.

Pines exhaled. Rest could come later. First, they had to get off the mountain.

Regroup.

Survive.

"Yeah," he said quietly. "Let's gather the rest of our pack."

Renae shivered nearby, skin slick with cooling sweat and strain.

Pines looked from her to Ashe, then to the trees. His voice was low, edged with exhaustion.

"Then we find our clothes and get somewhere safe."

Chapter 8

The walk back felt three times longer than it should have. Every step carried the weight of the battle. Rocks in the path seemed to rise like boulders, while snapped twigs made them flinch at shadows.

Silence clung to them like a shroud, refusing to release its grip.

The usual chorus of insects had dulled to a faint whine, more funeral hymn than the wild songs of earlier. No hikers crossed their path. Nothing interrupted the quiet.

Cole was grateful for the emptiness. How could anyone explain their group? A limping wolf, three battered humans, one cradling an unconscious second wolf like a fallen soldier. And him.

After the fight, while Pines had tended to the injured wolves, Renae had taken a few patient minutes to guide Cole through Veiling back to human form. The process had felt strange and clumsy, like trying to remember how to walk. But now his two legs carried him forward without thought.

He had offered to carry Ryan, but Ashe refused, insisting it was their responsibility. When he bent to lift Grace, her growl made it clear that was not an option. All that was left was to walk and keep his mind away from what had happened.

From the bodies. The screaming. That *thing*.

He'd asked Pines if they should do something about the dead. Pines had only said he was making a call.

"Someone will handle it."

When Cole pressed, the old man added, "You'll meet them soon enough."

He was still only handing out breadcrumbs.

When they reached the gravel parking lot, Cole's knees buckled. His body had held together until safety, then betrayed him completely. He hit the gravel on all fours, retching violently as Renae moved behind him, her hand settling on his back with the kind of steady comfort that felt almost maternal.

He appreciated it, even though he hated the attention.

Even after his body emptied itself, it kept trying to purge more. Stomach muscles clenched, lungs ached. If he could have thrown up his guilt, his fear, the memory of that thing's mouth, he would have.

He locked eyes with a single piece of gravel, focusing on it like a lifeline, willing the spasms to stop. When they finally passed, he sagged onto his heels, trembling, throat burning. Shame flared hot beneath the bile.

No one else had broken down. Not visibly. They all stood like survivors of some ancient war. Bloody. Bruised. Silent.

We almost died! Ryan might die! What are we doing here?

Pines walked over, crouching beside Cole, careful to avoid the puddle. Renae eased back a few steps as he approached. Not far, not sudden, but enough to show she was not ready to trust him completely.

Cole caught it but said nothing. His own trust wavered too.

"No shame in it," Pines said quietly. "You shouldn't have had to go through what happened. None of you."

He paused, swallowing hard before he straightened slightly, his voice louder for the others to hear.

"There's no weakness in fear or panic."

He turned back to Cole, quieter now, almost a confession. "You didn't let the fear stop you. That matters. And I'm proud, guilty as hell, but proud to be the one Gaia chose to guide you five."

Cole didn't know what to say.

Ashe shifted Ryan in their arms and grunted. "You sure talk a lot for someone who hates talking. Can we finish this somewhere with A/C?"

Pines exhaled a short laugh and stood. He held out a hand to Cole. The younger man accepted, relieved to have the attention shift away, relieved not to stand as the example of failure anymore.

The old man gave everyone an address to head to. He promised it would be a place of safety and he'd explain what happened. Ashe laid Ryan into the back of the RAV4. The injured wolf didn't stir.

"Okay, I'll take Grace with me." Pines turned to Cole. "I need you to take Ryan's car."

Ashe, wearing Ryan's torn-up pants, fished into the pockets and pulled out the keys. Without a word, they tossed them to Cole. He snatched them midair and climbed into the bright yellow Dodge Charger.

Cole twitched at a sharp rattling noise. It took a second to realize it was coming from Ashe's RAV4. Something off in the hubcap, ticking in time as the car pulled onto the road.

Cole turned the key. The Charger's engine rumbled to life with a deep, aggressive purr that didn't match his mood at all. Techno music snapped on at full volume. The shrieking chaos of noise hit like a slap. His heart leapt into his throat. Hands shaking, he fumbled for the knob and silenced it.

He and Renae exchanged a nod as he signaled for her to back out first. She offered a quick smile, backed out, and led the way. They pulled out onto Bankhead Parkway, the glow of city lights ahead. The Charger handled like a dream, but it was too much. Flashy. Loud. This was the kind of car that got broken into outside the places he used to play.

He thought about plugging the address into the GPS, then dismissed it. Easier to follow Renae's little red sedan. Easier not to think too hard. With the adrenaline finally gone and his body beginning to unwind, Cole found himself drifting. For the first time all night, there was space to relax. Space to reflect.

He'd turned into a freaking wolf.

It had been... incredible. Seeing through the beast's eyes. The simple joy of running on all fours. The primal awareness. It was unlike anything he'd ever experienced. He'd remember that feeling for the rest of his life.

But the euphoria hadn't lasted. Ryan, barely conscious. Grace and Renae, rattled and hurt. Ashe, running on fumes. Pines, worn down to the bone. Everyone had been pushed to the edge. Scarred. Shaken. Close to dying.

Everyone except him.

Cole. Perfectly fine. Whatever that meant.

But what could he have done? Maybe if he had pushed Pines for more information earlier, Cole would have been better prepared.

Renae turned onto Memorial Parkway. They were heading north now, toward the Tennessee border. Cole watched her car ahead, steady and small in the dark.

She'd been smart. Sharp. She hadn't known anything more than he had going into tonight, but she'd handled herself like a pro. Maybe it was experience. Or maybe she'd always been that capable. He was sure a twenty-year-old Renae would've been just as dangerous. And if she hadn't reacted in time...

They'd all be dead.

Well, maybe not Ashe.

Their werewolf form was terrifying. Ashe had torn the Banewolf apart with their bare hands.

What would it be like to be a werewolf? Would I be that strong? That fast? That brutal?

Would I even want to be?

His phone buzzed in his pocket, dragging him out of the spiral. Cole dug it out and glanced at the screen.

Rebecca.

A surge of emotions hit all at once. Regret. Affection. Worry. Their last argument hadn't gone well, and he'd spent most of today convinced it was the end of something important. Last night he said something he shouldn't have. A cruel jab about being the one bringing in money, about how she could make it easier if she only did more. The taste of it was sand the instant it left his tongue, but he hadn't pulled it back.

Worse, it wasn't true. She was grinding through double the college course load, trying to graduate early just to help support them. She was going to back his dream.

Three years together. A partner he treasured. He didn't want to lose that.

"Hey," Cole answered. The rest caught in his throat.

"Hey." Her voice was gentler than he expected. Relieved, maybe. But there was something else beneath it. Tightness. Frustration.

A few moments passed before she continued.

"Are... are you okay? Are you at a gig?"

He could lie. Just say yes, keep it simple, and avoid everything messy.

But he knew where that road led. He'd seen it play out in his parents' house. Secrets and silence. Each building a wall neither could climb. Now they barely spoke. Their marriage had become an arrangement neither wanted to abandon, but neither wanted to nurture either.

He and Rebecca had promised not to do that. Honesty, even when it hurt.

"No. I met some people up on the mountain. I'm just heading over to one of their places now." He hated how vague it sounded, but how could he explain the night without sounding insane?

Maybe this was what being Pines felt like.

"Oh... okay," she said, hesitation bleeding through. "I'm here at the house if you want to talk. I've been waiting. I got worried."

Cole's heart dropped. "Um, I gotta meet at this house, but then I'm coming straight home." He cut off what he expected her next question would be. "I don't know how long, so don't wait up. But I want to talk too. I'll make some breakfast."

A pause. Then her voice softened. "Okay, I guess. See you in a few hours." Another beat. Then, teasing: "Breakfast better be damn good. And no eggs."

Cole smirked back at the private joke. "One egg."

"No!" she laughed. "You left so much shell in the last one I thought it was crunchy on purpose."

"Fine. Half an egg," he laughed back. Her laughter, even through the static of the speakerphone, grounded him. It felt real. Human. Something to hold on to and not let go.

They bantered a little longer until the road ahead curved onto gravel. Renae had turned off onto a dirt path lined with leaning trees. A crooked **No Trespassing** sign hung from a low branch. Beyond it, a modest house peeked through the shadows, flanked by two aging trailers.

"Hey, I'm here. Gotta go. Love you."

"Love you," she said softly, then paused as if wanting to add more before hanging up.

Cole pulled up beside Pines's van. Before he could step out, the passenger door creaked open. And a very naked, very toned woman with dark red hair stepped into the night breeze.

She moved with an easy confidence, unbothered by the cold or her nudity. Porch light caught in the mess of her curls, casting soft light across her mocha-toned skin. She stood like she belonged here.

Cole froze. Blinked once. Then again.

She was stunning. Not just in how she moved or looked, but in something deeper. Something familiar. Recognition clicked.

He closed his mouth with an audible click of teeth, then scrambled to pull off his shirt.

"Here," he said, offering it out. "Uh... you look cold."

She took it without hesitation, tugging it over her head with clumsy, almost childlike motions. Cole tried, and mostly failed, to keep his eyes on her face.

When she finally looked up, he met her gaze. Her eyes were amber, bright and intent.

No. Surely not?

"Grace?"

She tilted her head slightly, then nodded. "Yes. Cole."

Behind them, Pines stepped out of the van, walking over to them.

"Good. You figured it out," he said. "You can catch the others up while I get the first aid kit for the wolf."

Cole looked Grace up and down, scanning her for injuries. She looked down at him, confused by the attention.

"The other wolf," the old man said as he stepped back into view of the others. His silhouette was framed by the porch light.

"Everyone, get inside and rest." He looked at Renae. "Get Ryan out of the SUV and put him on the dining room table. Ashe, I'll need to check you too."

Without waiting, he turned and followed a fading path to a large metal workshop hidden behind the house.

Grace walked beside Cole with a slight limp, each step stiff from the ambush. As they rounded the van, Ashe appeared, carefully cradling Ryan's unconscious wolf form. Renae held the front door open, both of them focused on getting Ryan inside.

"Hey, uh..." Cole gestured to the woman at his side. "This is Grace."

"Oh. Oh, holy shit," Renae sputtered, almost releasing the screen door.

Still in the doorway, Ashe spun at the name, eyes going huge. "That's so cool!" they blurted. "Grace, you look amazing and uh... human? What the hell?"

Grace just nodded.

"Hold on," Ashe said, disappearing into the house with Ryan still in their arms.

The rest followed.

Inside, the house was small and worn but lived-in. A cramped living room blended into a narrow kitchen. The walls were lined with aging paneling, cracked and faded, and the air carried the heavy scent of dust and age. There were only a few chairs, a floral-patterned couch, and a round table barely large enough to hold dinner, let alone a large wolf.

Ashe laid Ryan gently on the table, the wolf's body covering nearly all of it.

They turned and pulled Grace into a tight hug, pushing past the ache of their own injuries. Grace's eyes went wide, darting toward Cole, then Renae. She stood frozen in surprise, offering no hug in return.

Ashe noticed and backed off, awkwardly rubbing their ribs.

"Sorry," they said quietly, glancing down. "Didn't mean to..." They let it trail off, then looked up and smiled. "Still. You gotta admit, this is pretty cool."

Cole and Renae nodded, smiling at Ashe's excitement.

"I'm happy," Grace said, her face neutral.

Light sparked in Ashe's eyes at those two words.

"No way, and you can talk! I can't believe it."

"I learned from humans when I was a pup." Grace's voice was steady and precise, offering nothing more. Her tone precluded any further inquiries.

Ashe glanced at Grace's bare legs, then at Cole's shirtless torso. "Ugh. I'm finding us all real clothes," they muttered, hiking up the waistband of their oversized jeans. One hand clutching the sagging fabric, they disappeared down the hall, flipping on lights as they went.

Cole, Grace, and Renae settled onto the couch, Renae deliberately taking the middle seat. She was positioning herself as a buffer, and honestly, he appreciated it.

Pines returned carrying two metal boxes. One was white, marked with a red cross. The other was a beat-up army green tin, etched with strange, curling symbols. He set them beside Ryan and got to work cutting away the makeshift bandages.

"Cole," he said, his voice low. "Help me."

The dried blood clung stubbornly to Ryan's fur. The wolf stirred under the touch but did not wake.

Ashe returned in borrowed clothes and tossed an outfit to Grace. Then they narrowed their eyes at Pines.

"Why do you keep so many women's clothes in the back room?"

Pines grunted. Not an answer. Just noise.

Instead, he uncapped a plastic bottle filled with thick, blue-green sludge and handed it to Cole, along with clean cloths and a handful of Q-tips.

"Wherever a wound doesn't look right, use this. If it is black or oozing, use it generously."

The stuff smelled strange. Sweet, almost floral, with an undertone of something earthy. Cole didn't ask what it was. He just nodded and started working.

If he hadn't been able to help in the fight, then maybe this was something. He could clean wounds. Stop the bleeding. Ease pain.

He tended Ashe's injuries while Pines focused on Ryan. When they finished, Cole turned to Pines.

"You too," he said.

Pines waved him off, but Cole didn't move.

"If it is important for us to be taken care of, then it should be important for you as well."

For a moment, Pines didn't respond. Then he sat down.

Fresh lacerations marked his shoulder, overlapping older, half-healed scars. Cole worked in silence.

With everyone tended to and Ryan asleep again, the group gathered in the living room and took whatever seats they could find.

Pines looked them over, his expression unreadable. He let the quiet stretch. "All right. Let's talk."

Chapter 9

He looked them over. Faces pale in the low light, eyes dulled by exhaustion and something heavier beneath. Tension hung in the room, quiet but crackling. They all wanted answers. Deserved them. But he hesitated.

All must endure, or none will. That was the vision The Seer had given him, a truth binding their lives to one another and to the land itself. Pines had nearly seen it fulfilled that first night they stood as a pack.

Pines wasn't sure how much he was ready to share. Not yet. The ambush had shaken more than bones. No one was supposed to know about the newly turned pack.

He doubted spies were among them. His detection glyphs should have caught anyone possessed by a dark spirit or infected by Fäulung.

But those who served Tzelut were clever. Their grip on mortal affairs ran deeper than the Lycans ever had. They didn't always need a sniper's bullet. Sometimes it was an eviction notice. Sometimes a careless drill into sacred ground. A fine paid, the papers signed, and the world kept turning. And all the while, the land grew a little more bruised, a little more broken.

If they ever discovered what The Seer had told Pines...

That thought twisted cold in his chest.

"I'll give you what I can for now," Pines said quietly.

Renae leaned forward, her expression caught between fury and exhaustion. "You should tell us *everything*, Pines. You keep saying 'later' or 'soon.' We've earned more than that. We *need* answers."

Pines gave a slow nod, the weight of her words settling onto his shoulders.

"You're right. You've earned more. But not every question can be answered right now. Not because you don't deserve them, but because some things are still unclear. And others... aren't safe to talk about yet. We'll get there. For now, I'll tell you what I can."

Grace sat beside Renae, arms wrapped tight around herself. Her amber eyes stayed fixed on him, sharp and unnerving. She looked down, flexing her fingers. Testing them. Still unsure whether they were hers.

How much the wolf would comprehend, he didn't know. But she would. In time.

Knees cracked as he stood. Eyes stayed on him as he paced to bleed the nerves from his limbs. When he turned, the silence of unspoken years hung heavy on his shoulders.

"Gaia has chosen you. Call her the Earth. The pulse beneath stone. The breath between storms. The name doesn't matter, only her purpose. Primordial creation. Life.

"Each of you carries an ember of her essence inside. Sometimes she stokes that spark, but only when needed. He looked away for a moment, then met their eyes again. "This isn't a curse. Not something caught in blood or passed with a bite.

"You were born this way. Every one of you."

He let the silence settle for a moment, heavy and reverent.

Ashe stared at him, motionless. The others listened, but something in Ashe's eyes made it clear. Those words had landed differently. When they finally spoke, their voice was quiet. Measured.

"But how did you know it was time to find us?"

"We have allies," Pines said. "Some can see fragments of what's to come. And sometimes, we feel it. A pull. A thread in the dark. Gaia guides us when she can."

Renae narrowed her eyes. "So what does being chosen mean? What are we supposed to do?" Her voice hardened. "I'm fifty-six. I'm not some hero in a prophecy. I'm not your weapon!" Her voice tightened, each word honed to a point. The fury hadn't broken loose yet, but it was close to the surface.

His jaw clenched. The old guilt was rising again.

"This world doesn't stay in balance anymore. Not on its own. Humanity builds, burns, and blinds itself to what's breaking beneath it. Spirits weaken. Old protections fade. And something vast, hollow, and hungry presses in from the dark."

"And it's growing. Adapting. Watching. Whispering at the edges of things."

He forced himself to meet their eyes: Renae's guarded, Cole's confused, Ashe's attentive, Grace's unreadable.

"Lycans exist to resist. To remind the world that nature is not tame, that it still carries teeth and claws. We are guardians, we are messengers, and when there is no other choice, we are executioners. When factories poisoned the Tennessee River, a pack nearby brought the smokestacks down, stone by stone. When the rich son of a billionaire took his rifle to hunt the last of the white rhinos, we hunted him instead."

He looked at Renae, then back to the others. "I don't know why you weren't awakened sooner," he said, voice low. He tried to keep the edge out of it, but some of the truth bled through. "I don't know why Gaia chooses one soul over another. I only know she has her reasons. Reasons we aren't always meant to understand."

Renae's face reddened. Her voice sharpened, brittle with emotion. "What if I don't want this?" This was the rawest he'd seen her, even when he had found her before her First Tearing.

"What if I just stand up and leave?" She was talking to Pines, but the words were meant for the others. The frustration was clear, but there was something deeper beneath it. Wounded pride, maybe. Or an old grief that hadn't found a place to go.

Ashe turned toward Renae, silent but clearly stunned. The idea of rejecting Gaia's gift, of walking away, had never crossed their mind.

Outside, a branch scraped sharply against the living room window. Everyone flinched, then relaxed, embarrassed.

Pines walked around the room, letting the others linger on what Renae said. His next words were set in iron.

"You've been marked by the spirit of the Earth. I don't have a better way to say it. You can walk out that door, and if you tell me to, I'll leave you be."

"However, if you leave and choose not to pledge to protect Gaia from her enemies, we in turn will not work to protect you. Unfortunately, you have been marked by Gaia. There is no hiding from it now. The mark is on you, and others will see it. They'll smell it on your skin. Hear it in your blood."

The weight of his words settled.

Renae held her breath. Fingers clenched into the fabric beneath her, knuckles paling with the strain, but she said nothing.

Pines grunted. He didn't want fear to be his tool. But truth had sharp edges.

"Not everyone who sees that mark will greet you kindly. Some will want to control you. Others will try to destroy you. And a few... will want to drag you into things far worse than death."

"Looks like that's already happening," Cole muttered, more to himself than anyone else. His own words seemed to surprise him.

Pines turned to him. Renae gave a slow, bitter nod.

He nodded back. "It is. That ambush wasn't chance. They got there before I could take you to Gaia herself. And honestly, she normally does a better job of explaining than I ever could."

Pines thought back to the ambush. The existence of a Witherbound Lycan disturbed him deeply. He had been taught, like all elders, that Gaia's chosen were immune to Fäulung's direct influence. There had been stories, rare whispers, of Lycan unknowingly serving Limbs of Tzelut. But never had he heard of one outright infected. When tried before, it either failed or killed the Lycan outright.

But sharing that now risked scaring the pack away. And they were needed. They were supposed to stop what was coming, though Pines still didn't know how.

Ashe leaned forward, eyes bright with need. "So we were supposed to meet her? Can we still?"

They showed none of the hesitation etched on the others' faces. Even Grace looked uncertain. Whether she was afraid or simply confused, Pines couldn't yet tell.

"In time," he said. "The Wildlands are sacred. Only Gaia's servants can enter. But the Monte Sano path may be compromised. And there isn't another way nearby, I trust."

Ashe's face sank, and Pines felt the weight of their hope falter. He hated how many delays this journey already had.

"It won't be long," he promised. "I'm sending another pack to scout the area. Once they give the all-clear, I'll take you to her myself." He paused, then added, "I'll also try to arrange a meeting with the other local pack. They're younger, like you. You might get clearer answers from people chosen in this millennium."

Cole and Ashe let out a laugh. Brief and possibly forced, but real enough to matter.

Pines softened. "I know this is a lot. Most new Lycans have time to adjust. You don't have that luxury. But you still have choices. Not about being Lycan. That part is done. Gaia doesn't unmark someone. But you get to choose how to live with it."

Golden light slipped between the blinds, striping the worn floor in narrow bands. Dawn had arrived without fanfare, and its quiet presence seemed to remind them all how deeply tired they were. The buzz of adrenaline had drained away, leaving only soreness and silence. Pines felt it too, but the sight of morning brought a strange, small relief.

The long night was ending. They were still here, and that would have to be enough.

"There's more you need to know," he said after a moment. "But not today." He glanced over to where Ryan lay resting. "I still need to tend to your packmate. Make sure his leg heals cleanly."

He looked back at them. The words hung like smoke in the air. "You all need rest. Time to heal, mentally and physically."

The quiet didn't hold. Protests started almost immediately. Too many questions left unanswered. Too much fear clawed at the edges of their understanding. Voices overlapped, a dissonant mix of frustration and confusion.

Pines raised his hands, his tone steady but final. "I know. But even if you weren't wounded, battles like last night leave scars unseen. If you don't tend to them, they fester. Just like any wound."

That silenced most of them. Cole exhaled and leaned back in his chair, eyes unfocused, somewhere far off.

Across from him, Renae still hadn't moved. She said nothing. Whatever argument still burned behind her eyes would have to wait.

Pines let the silence take root. He had done what he could for now.

Chapter 10

The sun was setting, the fever of the day finally broken. A summer rain had passed, but overcast clouds still dimmed the evening sky. Ashe had spent most of the day drifting in and out of sleep, dodging the worst of the heat.

The nice thing about losing their regular paying job was that it afforded them an alternate sleeping schedule. Even if it was the only thing they could afford right now.

They had been picking up freelance graphic design work from home, yet the past few days left them too frayed to concentrate. The dreams only worsened it, the supernatural and the ordinary twisting together until they could no longer tell them apart.

After the mountain and the meeting at Pines' place, the group had scattered back to their lives. Pines had told them they were safe. The assassins were gone, and if they'd known where to strike, it was because Sebastian had known the site to enter the Wildlands and had been waiting.

Ashe had given Cole a ride home from Pines' house. He'd been in a rush, talking about needing to make breakfast, and asking Ashe if they knew how to keep eggshells out of the pan.

He'd been good company until he'd asked why Ashe's engine kept making a "wonking" sound. They'd glared at him, and the rest of the trip passed in silence. Except for the wonking and the damn front rim's persistent rattling.

Pines had asked if Grace could stay with anyone until he figured out a setup for her. He stressed the importance of the wolf-turned-human having as much interaction with other humans as possible for the next few months. While she would need to turn back from time to time, it was important she learned the human form.

"She gets her time to learn how to be human," he'd told them, "and then you all will learn to be the wolf."

No one seemed eager to jump at the opportunity to babysit. Pines' eyes never left Renae during the request, and after a little back and forth between the two, she reluctantly agreed. Renae and Grace had left together, with Renae promising the others this wasn't a permanent arrangement.

Ryan had slept through Pines' entire monologue. Still, Ashe thought he already looked much better after the meeting. Pines had promised Ryan would be able to turn back to his human form when he woke. He would also fill Ryan in and make sure he got home safe.

The group had exchanged numbers and agreed to keep in touch if anything surfaced.

Before Ashe had left, the pack leader had given them the task of Veiling to the wolf form. If they could manage that, he'd said, turning back human would be easy. Then he handed them dried herbs and a stick of sidewalk chalk, like some kind of budget ritual kit. Ashe had stared at the supplies, unimpressed.

The others hadn't gotten homework.

It bothered Ashe that the others had been capable of Veiling with little issue. Even Grace had shifted to human form that first night, right there in the van on the ride back. It seemed backward: Ashe could become the Warhide but couldn't run with the wolves. What did that say about them?

The previous nights had followed the same pattern. Ashe would wake up, shower, scroll through job boards while eating ramen, and then maybe watch TV or put on some music.

Once night fell and they were sure no one was watching, Ashe slipped into the fenced backyard. Then they sprinkled the herbs and drew a partial moon on the concrete deck. Sitting in its center, Ashe willed themself to Veil.

For hours, they sat still and focused. The wolf spirit stirred, just out of reach. The change never came.

Tonight would be different. It had to be.

Ashe stepped onto the back deck as the last light bled from the sky. The herbs were already scattered, the chalk moon redrawn. They settled into the center, closed their eyes, and reached for the wolf.

Ok, we can do this.

They breathed deep, trying to empty themselves the way Pines had described. Release joy, release love, offer it to Gaia. The wolf spirit stirred, closer than before. Ashe's skin prickled. Something was building.

Almost. Almost there.

Their phone buzzed in their pocket.

Ashe's eyes snapped open. The sensation scattered like startled birds.

"No, no, no..." They pulled out the phone, ready to silence it and try again.

Kyle's name glowed on the screen.

Ashe stared at it. The phone buzzed again in their hand, insistent.

Four days. It had been four days since the fight at their parents' house. Four days since Kyle had hugged them in the dining room and promised to be their roommate next year. Four days of silence because Ashe hadn't known what to say.

What do I even tell him?

The phone buzzed a third time.

If they didn't answer, he'd worry. He'd probably drive over. And then what? Explain the chalk circle? The herbs? Them naked in the backyard trying to turn into a wolf?

Ashe answered.

"Hey." Their voice came out rougher than intended.

"Hey yourself." Kyle's tone was light, but something tight ran underneath it. "You alive over there?"

"Yeah. Yeah, I'm fine."

"Uh-huh." A pause. "Because 'fine' people usually answer texts. Or, you know, exist."

Ashe winced. They had been ignoring his messages. Not on purpose, exactly. They just hadn't known what to say that wasn't a lie or insane.

"Sorry. It's been... a weird few days."

"Weird how?" Kyle's voice sharpened. "Did Mom call? Did she say something? Because I swear to God, if she—"

"No. No, it's not that." Ashe cut him off before he could spiral. "I just needed some space. To think."

Silence on the other end. Ashe could picture him in his room, probably sprawled on his bed with his headphones half on, chewing his lip the way he did when he was trying to figure out if someone was bullshitting him.

"You'd tell me if something was wrong, right?" Kyle asked. Quieter now.

I almost died. I turned into a monster. There's a wolf spirit living in my head that wants me to hunt and kill.

"Yeah," Ashe said. "I'd tell you."

"Okay." He didn't sound convinced. "Because you know I'm here. Whatever happened with Mom and Dad, whatever they said after that doesn't change anything. Not for me."

Ashe's throat tightened. "I know."

"Good." Another pause. "You eating?"

"Yes, Kyle."

"Real food? Not just ramen?"

"...Mostly real food."

"Ashe."

"I'm fine. I promise." The lie tasted like chalk on the deck. "Can I text you tomorrow? I've just got some stuff I'm working through."

Kyle sighed, long and theatrical. "Fine. But if I don't hear from you by noon, I'm showing up with pizza and a lecture."

Despite everything, Ashe smiled. "Deal."

"Love you, weirdo."

"Love you too."

The call ended. Ashe sat in the circle, phone still warm in their hand.

The wolf spirit was gone. Not hovering just out of reach, not stirring with hunger. Just... gone. As if Kyle's voice had chased it back into whatever corner of Ashe's soul it lived in.

They tried anyway. Closed their eyes. Breathed deep. Reached for the calm.

Nothing.

Ten minutes passed. Twenty. The wolf didn't stir.

Ashe opened their eyes and stared up at the overcast sky. The clouds had thickened, swallowing whatever stars might have offered light.

"Fuck."

They stood, brushed chalk dust from their pants, and walked back inside.

***

Swallowing their pride, Ashe sent a message to the "No Pines" text group. They asked if anyone could help them Veil. Ashe promised pizza and a personalized drawing for anyone who showed up.

Renae replied quickly, saying she had her hands full with Grace.

Cole apologized, saying he was still at work but could come by tomorrow.

Then Ryan answered: "I'm free tonight!!! OMG YES. Let's WOLF OUT!!!" The words were followed by two wolf head emojis.

Ashe groaned aloud. They needed help. Ryan could probably provide it, but still—ugh.

That's not fair. I've only really talked to him once, and he was apologetic about what he said.

"Shut up, brain. I don't want to be logical," Ashe muttered to themself.

They didn't care about being fair. Not now. Objectivity just made it hurt more. People like Ryan always found a way to make them feel like a freak.

A darker voice answered. Look at you. You're a twenty-three-year-old nonbinary werewolf. You are a freak.

They hated how smoothly the thought slid into place, and worse, they could not tell its source. Their own voice, the wolf spirit's, or something new waiting to torment them with what they already knew deep inside.

They'd been struggling with their identity for over a year already. This only deepened the isolation. It sharpened the doubt.

The old whispers seeped in. Fast. Disjointed. The ones that came when everything felt too heavy. Their breathing caught in their throat, shallow and uneven. A cold sweat broke across their skin. Fingers tingled. The edges of the bedroom blurred for a moment, as if the world had pulled slightly away.

And with every breath, every crack in control, the Warhide edged closer.

Pines had warned them not to take werewolf form until he returned. He'd said the Wolf Spirit could overwhelm them. Could take control entirely.

Ashe stared down at their phone. One more thought slid in, soft and poisonous.

Maybe that wouldn't be so bad.

Ashe focused on their breathing, steadying each inhale. Slowly, the panic began to loosen its grip.

If they were ever going to embrace this life, they had to learn to Veil. And the truth was, a big part of them wanted to. If Ryan could help, they'd let him.

"Suck it up. It's going to be fine." They typed out their address and told Ryan to meet them in a couple of hours.

"Coolio," was the one-word reply.

Ashe sighed and stepped into the shower, hoping the water would carry away the weight of their thoughts.

They heard Ryan's car five streets away. The bass rattled the windows before it even pulled into the driveway. Ryan stepped out dressed head-to-toe in camo, complete with a matching hat, that same stupidly charming grin from the other night plastered across his face.

"What up, Enby!" he shouted, one leg still inside the car.

Ashe blinked. "What?"

"What up, Enby?" he repeated, a little less confident this time. "That's the term, right? I've been learning."

Ashe gave a tight smile. "Yeah, but... that's not quite how it works."

"No? What if I say—Whaaaat's up my enby?" He stretched the words, grin widening.

"Ew." Ashe wrinkled their nose, but a soft snicker gave them away. "Just stick with the first one."

He shrugged. "Alright. Get in and let's go wolf out."

"Shhh! My neighbors!"

"Yeah? You think they're really gonna put two and two together and figure out you're a werewolf?" Ryan looked amused.

"Even if you screamed, 'Ahhhh, the transmorphication is taking over!'" He fake-howled. "AWOOOOOOOO." Ashe glanced around, alarmed, but no one responded.

Ryan didn't stop. "If anyone saw anything, they'd probably just close the blinds or call the cops. Come on, I know a good spot."

"Transmorphication?" Ashe shook their head. "Look, why don't I just follow you?" They didn't like the idea of being stranded without their own vehicle.

"Because I drive fast, and that thing won't keep up," Ryan said, jerking a thumb at their SUV. When he saw Ashe's face darken, he quickly added, "Besides, I'm the fragile one. Remember? Sexy Latino, soft bones..."

Ashe narrowed their eyes. The tone was too flirty, too smooth. It made their chest tighten. They looked away, pulse ticking upward. This wasn't what they'd wanted when they asked for help.

"I'm gonna go get the herbs and chalk," Ashe muttered, walking to their front door. Maybe they could just go back inside. Lock the door. Pretend this never happened.

"Won't need 'em," Ryan said, a spark of mischief in his eyes.

"Fine," Ashe groaned, walking back to the sports car. They cast one last look at their home, then their SUV, and lowered themself into the passenger seat.

Ryan swung in and fired up the engine. Techno-pop blasted through the speakers in an assault of sound. The yellow sports car tore onto the road, tires screaming against the pavement.

The drive was a blur of speed and pounding music. Ashe dug their nails into their thighs, every muscle drawn taut as Ryan weaved through traffic. The pain worked to focus them away from the lack of control.

By the time they reached the darkened greenway, their face was pale and sweat had soaked through their shirt.

"My bad," Ryan said, finally turning down the music.

The gate was closed, but the chain hung loose and unlocked. Ryan stepped out and pushed it open with a rusty groan that carried too far in the still night.

Ashe leaned forward, watching as they rolled in. The parking lot beyond lay in deep shadow. No overhead lights. No movement. Only the distant dim light of streetlamps, their glow failing to reach the park's edge.

Multiple paths branched out ahead, winding through the trees like veins disappearing into dense underbrush. Off to the side, an empty playground sat still, the swings shifting gently in the wind. Next to it, a fenced-in dog park stood deserted, its gate creaking back and forth with each lazy gust.

Ashe had been here plenty of times. But at night, stripped of sunlight and sound, the park felt different. The paths they knew by heart felt unfamiliar, and the silence had turned watchful.

"Maybe this isn't the best idea," Ashe tried one more time to back out.

"Nah, it's perfect," Ryan said. "No one's here. We've got the place to ourselves."

Their phones buzzed at the same time.

Ashe glanced down. A new message from Pines: the meeting with the other pack was happening tonight. The Huntsville Pack was already on its way down the mountain. The meeting time was set for midnight, and Pines made it clear that showing up on time was a sign of respect. The address came through next: Full Moon Brewery near downtown.

"It's already 10:10," Ashe said, checking the time. "Should we just head over there?"

Ryan glanced toward the back seat, a flicker crossing his expression. For a second, he looked genuinely disappointed.

But then he rebounded, smiling too big.

"No way, Enby," he said, climbing out of the car. He jogged toward one of the trails, waving a hand over his shoulder. "Come on, this won't take long!"

Ashe stayed seated, staring at their phone as concern settled over them. This meeting wasn't just a formality; it was a chance at acceptance. Maybe even a kind of family. But how would they look to a new pack as a Lycan who couldn't even Veil?

They looked toward the back seat, curious about what had caught Ryan's attention.

A picnic basket. An actual woven, cartoon-looking picnic basket sat nestled on the seat. Two fluted glasses rested carefully on top. Surely it wasn't meant for them. More likely, he had been on a date and forgotten to take it out.

Ashe blinked, then turned back to the window.

Ryan was already halfway down the path, his camo blending too well with the trees and gloom.

"Shit," Ashe muttered. They swung over the hood of the Charger and sprinted into the dark after him.

Chapter 11

With every step deeper into the trail, the sounds of the city faded, replaced by the whisper of wind through leaves and the steady rhythm of their footsteps.

The path narrowed as it wound through denser trees and deeper shadows. The smell of asphalt and exhaust thinned, replaced by earth and wild mint crushed beneath their shoes. The city's hold weakened here, step by step.

Ashe caught a subtle hitch in Ryan's stride, his pace faltering when he pushed too hard. The strain flickered across his face before he forced it away, a reminder that even a Lycan's body had limits.

Dropping into a slower pace, they followed the slope toward a narrow stream. Overhead, the trees creaked and sighed, the only companions to the quiet flow of water.

Every few minutes, Ashe checked their phone, each glance a grain dropping into the hourglass of their anxiety. When they reached a clearing by the stream flanked by two mossy boulders, Ryan finally stopped. Seeing the screen check again, he reached over and gently plucked the phone from their hands.

"Don't worry, we aren't gonna be late." His voice was unusually soft. "We aren't too far away, and this is important for you."

He gestured for Ashe to sit, then settled across from them on the opposite boulder.

"I've done this a few times now, and it's been easier every time." Ryan looked straight into their eyes, his expression unusually serious. "I think your problem is you just need to loosen up."

Ashe stared, waiting for more. But Ryan just held their gaze, as if he'd dropped some ancient wisdom and expected applause.

A dry, disbelieving laugh slipped from their throat.

"That's it?" The words came out sharper than intended. "You got anything else up there?" Pointing to the top of his head, they continued, "I know I need to be relaxed and free of emotion to catch the wolf."

"Ha!" Ryan barked, springing to his feet. He strode toward Ashe, who instinctively shifted into a guarded stance. He either didn't seem to notice or simply didn't care.

"See, that's the problem!" he said, pointing a finger. "I never said *no* emotion. Do I look like I'm suppressing anything?"

Before any answer could come, Ryan Veiled. Fur burst from his skin, claws shredding his pants at the seams. His shirt clung awkwardly to his shifting frame while his limbs shortened and contorted. In seconds, the transformation was complete.

A large wolf now stood before Ashe, still half-draped in his camo shirt and hat. The sight was ridiculous. Ryan tried to trot around proudly, but the oversized shirt snagged on his paws. He tumbled, yelped, and rolled with a heavy thump into the stream.

Ashe broke into laughter as the wolf fought with the wet shirt, flailing and twisting until he finally freed himself. He trotted over, dripping, tongue hanging out, tail swaying proudly. He still wore his white briefs, now stretched and awkward, tail poking through a single leg hole.

A satisfied little "woof" escaped him as he strutted over with exaggerated flair.

"Lick me and you're getting muzzled," Ashe warned.

Ryan stopped just outside arm's reach and gave himself a vigorous shake, spraying droplets in every direction.

Annoyance gave way to a wave of emotion that brushed against Ashe's thoughts. Light and warm, the feeling tinged with playful pride. And beneath it, something more tender.

Through the wolf's eyes, Ashe saw themselves bathed in moonlight, glowing. The image hit harder than expected. For a heartbeat, it was intoxicating to be seen with that kind of awe.

But underneath the surface, something else stirred, an emotion the wolf was holding back. Something more... intimate. Not wanting to press, they forcefully pushed the connection aside, letting the link fade. They hated how easily the bond ignored permission, how quickly it blurred what belonged to them.

A buzz hummed from the torn pants nearby, but they both ignored it.

"So if it's not about suppressing emotion," Ashe asked, "what *am* I doing wrong?"

The wolf sat. Eyes closed. Fur melted back into skin. Ryan reformed slowly, face scrunching with discomfort.

Ryan blushed when he noticed his underwear had dropped to his ankles during the second Veiling. He quickly pulled them up, looking away from their gaze.

"So, uh... it's not about shutting off your feelings. It's more like... offering them. The good ones. The stuff that makes you happy—that's what the Wolf Spirit is reaching for."

He picked his shirt up from the stream bank, wrung it out, and laid it across the rock to dry.

"You said you're trying to *catch* the wolf spirit, right? But it's not something to trap. It doesn't want to be chased. It wants to be welcomed."

Ashe couldn't help the long, skeptical look. "So you're telling me I haven't been *happy* enough to Veil?"

"Well... yeah," he said, rubbing the back of his neck. "Sorry. That's how it worked for me. Cole said it was the same for him."

Looking down, his expression dimmed. "I had a better plan for this. But it was gonna take longer than we've got. Look, just try."

With a shrug, they began to undress. Hands moved on instinct, but tension flexed through them with every layer removed. Standing naked in front of Ryan felt... wrong. Too exposed. Vulnerability didn't come easy, and certainly not this kind.

Maybe with the others it wouldn't feel so loaded. But Ryan? He had a way of looking at them that lingered. Too confident. Too close. It wasn't overt, but it was there.

Pulse quickening, they hesitated. The air rasped too cold against skin that wanted armor. Each breath scraped like glass through a throat that wished to stay silent. But this was the price.

Fine, I can do this.

Setting their jaw, they stepped forward, shedding the last of their clothes without flinching.

If this doesn't work, they thought darkly, *maybe I'll Warhide out and eat him. That'll make me happy.*

The thought brought a small, defiant smirk to their lips.

Naked beneath the low clouds, Ashe approached the stream. The gentle rush of water filled the quiet. Summer air passed over their skin as they lifted their arms, welcoming the wolf.

Time loosened, and sound stretched. The stream's gurgle warped into something distant and dreamlike. Wind curled around them, threading through hair and breath with a quiet insistence.

Happy, happy, happy. I'm happy.

It was there. A quiet ember of joy Ashe had kept protected from the rest of the world. Small, steady, buried deep beneath everything else.

Okay, let's stoke the flame.

Memories of their brother surfaced first. Kyle was stubborn, impulsive, and fiercely loyal. Their bond had grown tighter over the past year, especially as things in Ashe's life collapsed. They had each other's backs. Always.

One special moment came into sharp focus.

It was late, and Ashe had been pulling up to their parents' house to do laundry. Headlights washed across a frozen figure.

Kyle. Mid-sneak out.

Ashe's headlights pinned him like a spotlight in some prison escape movie.

He didn't move. Maybe he thought if he stayed perfectly still, he'd somehow disappear. But he was hard to miss in a yellow-orange shirt so bright it practically issued a warning to passing planes.

Ashe turned off the engine and got out. Without saying a word, they looked away, pretending to find something very interesting in the distance. Walking right past him, they even brushed into him slightly, still acting like he wasn't there. Kyle stayed perfectly still, a statue of guilt.

They continued inside, never mentioning the encounter.

Weeks later, a band shirt arrived in the mail, signed by every member of Ashe's favorite group. Kyle never explained how he got it. The only note read: *"Thanks for ignoring me."*

Ashe smiled, the memory blooming.

The Wolf Spirit stirred again within Ashe, the pulse of something older than Huntsville, older than blood itself. This time it answered the softer call. Not rage, but happiness drew it near. They nurtured the memory like kindling, feeding that ember of joy, trusting in Ryan's words.

Don't chase it. Invite it.

Letting the feeling open like an outstretched hand, the spirit approached the offered calm, touched it briefly, and vanished.

Time snapped back. Sound crashed in. The scent of water, wet earth, their own breath dragging hard through their body.

Ashe opened their eyes.

The world was different. Taller and brighter than before. Ryan was bent over them with a smirk of self-satisfaction.

"I told you, I freaking told you."

Blinking, they looked down. Four furred legs, steady in the grass. Darker than Ryan's form, leaner, built for speed rather than bulk.

It had worked. A brief howl slipped free. A sharp, wordless claim of triumph.

The world was impossibly alive. Smells layered one atop the other: rain in the soil, distant pollen, the faint metallic tang of the stream. Every sound rang with intention.

It wasn't the wild, intoxicating rush of the Warhide. The surge of power and dominance still called to them. This was something else. Something steadier. The wolf form didn't burn like fire, but it filled them like breath. And for now, that was enough.

Before Ryan could say a word, Ashe bolted into the woods, leaping over roots and rocks with effortless speed, carried by sheer exhilaration. Wind blew the fur on their face. A squirrel darted past. They gave brief chase, not out of hunger, but for the sheer joy of motion.

Breath heaved in and out. The run stripped everything else away. It could've been minutes or days; they couldn't tell. They didn't care.

Coming back near the stream, they drank deeply from the stream. Nearby, Ryan was sitting fully dressed, typing on his phone. They padded back toward him, tail wagging with loose contentment.

Too focused on his phone, it was only when they gave a playful growl that Ryan looked up. His face lit up at the sight.

"I *knew* you could do it! Told you I'd show you how."

The joy stuttered. His words rang hollow, and they stopped short, ears twitching. Those final words stole the victory. Ryan had offered advice, but the breakthrough had been theirs. Hard-earned and deeply personal.

It felt like everything good in their life was always soured in some way.

A low, unimpressed woof escaped their throat.

"Oh, right. You're gonna need to turn back," Ryan added, unfazed. He was too wrapped up in *his* accomplishment to feel Ashe's frustration.

He launched into a rambling explanation of how he'd done it, describing the shift in mindset and the sensation of grounding into his human self. They half-listened, already reaching for the feeling of normalcy. Compared with the elusive Wolf Spirit, returning felt far easier to grasp. They focused, and the change began.

Eyes open, they watched their body rise and twist. Bones cracked and skin folded, reshaping Ashe to their full stature. It was fast, but brutal. Their whole body felt yanked inside out and snapped back again. When it ended, Ashe was kneeling, human again, breath ragged and muscles aching from the effort.

Ashe was smiling. Despite the ache, the Veil had been theirs.

Ryan was already running toward them. Still naked, Ashe had just enough time to flinch before his arms wrapped around them in a full-body hug. A jolt ran through them, skin crawling from the sudden, uninvited contact.

Then he kissed them.

Not a question. Not a pause. He just *took* it, as if it was owed.

The contact sent confusion fluttering through their pulse before fury flooded them, sudden and unrelenting. This wasn't tender or romantic but invasive, a violation that left their skin burning where his lips had pressed. The taste clung, sour with sweat and arrogance, leaving them struggling to breathe it away.

"You're amazing," Ryan whispered. Eyes closed. Lips still too close.

Ashe struck, shoving him harder than intended. He stumbled back, confusion breaking across his face.

"You... what? It's fine to have feelings. If I stepped too far, I mean... I guess I'm sorry?"

"You *guess*?" Ashe's voice was a knife. "You *GUESS*?"

Arms hung rigid, fingernails digging into their palms. The soft warmth of the transformation was gone now, scorched away by betrayal.

"You unbelievable *asshole*," they growled. "You took everything that was supposed to be good about tonight and made it about you."

Through the bond, something reached for them. Regret, maybe. Or just self-pity. They slammed it shut.

Muscle surged beneath Ashe's skin, warping unnaturally as if their very flesh was trying to escape the rage burning inside. With jagged bursts, their spine cracked back. Not enough to fully shift, but enough to mis-align their silhouette into something off, something wrong.

A scream caught in their throat and collapsed into a ragged snarl. Teeth had thickened, sharpened, now plainly visible as their lips curled back. At the knuckles, fingers cracked forward, twisting unnaturally. Nails blackened and swelled into crude claws that halted just short of splitting the skin. Coarse, dark hair erupted down their arms and chest, failing to mask the heat that pulsed beneath.

Raw. Furious. Near-feral.

Neither fully human nor wolf.

Ryan's eyes widened in horror. "Wait... Ashe... what are you..."

Power flooded out from them, twisting the air around their new form. Ashe turned on their transgressor, eyes glowing with something ancient and wrong.

"I just got caught up in the moment," Ryan stammered, backing against a tree, hands raised. "I was happy for you. I thought you'd be happy too!"

Ashe lunged.

One hand clamped onto Ryan's shirt. With frightening ease, they lifted him. Fabric tore beneath his arms as he kicked and gasped. He clawed at Ashe's wrists, but it was like grappling stone.

"Please don't eat me!" he cried, eyes wild. "I'm sorry. I'm *so* sorry!" His words split the night, sharp and frantic, and Ashe caught the reek of fear pouring off him, hot and salty on the air.

This didn't feel like fully crossing into Warhide. Not yet. The fury still burned, close and scorching, but the shift had halted just short of the edge. The hunger to hunt, that primal pull, pressed hard against them but had not overtaken. Still, the sweet tang of fear, the sight of him cowering, weak and exposed...

Not yet. But it was close. So close.

Releasing their grip, Ryan landed hard on his tailbone with a grunt. His hand shot to his hip as he winced in pain, scrambling backward across the dirt toward the stream. His eyes never left their face, wide with horror. He wasn't sure if he was staring at a person or a blood-thirsty monster.

They looked at their arms and body. This had to be what Pines had been when Ashe hunted him. He had talked about it afterward. *Grayskin.* An unstable middle ground between humanity and beast. Born of emotion, raw and volatile. He had warned that it would take a great deal of time to learn and longer to master.

Every muscle in their body trembled with the strain of holding it. Eyes closed, they forced a slow inhale through flared nostrils.

In. Hold. Out. Again. And again.

The breathing exercises helped, but the Grayskin form fought against their control, wanting to surge back into full rage. Gradually, the trembling began to subside, though the effort left them drained.

A text alert on their phone cut through their concentration, reminding them of the meeting. The sound pulled them back to the world around them, and they strained to put the wolf back in its cage. Their body deflated and collapsed in pain from so many transformations in such a short time.

Ryan scrambled to collect Ashe's clothes. "I'm sorry," he repeated, voice small. "Really."

"I don't want to talk about it." Their voice was scraped raw, hands unsteady as they took the clothes. Their chest ached. Every nerve throbbed.

Idiot. They'd seen the signs and pretended not to. Thought silence would kill it. Thought patience would make him stop. Stupid for not driving. Stupid for not running away at the picnic basket. Stupid for standing there, stripped bare, with nothing between them and him but their own shaking hands.

Ashe pulled out their phone. The screen lit up, showing it was after midnight. Their thumb hovered over the group chat, Ryan's voice cutting in before they could accuse him of more.

"You were figuring out the wolf thing," Ryan said, words picking up speed. "You were gone a while, but c'mon. They won't care. What werewolf gives a shit about time?"

Pushing their attention away from him, they scrolled through the group texts.

He had messaged that they'd both be delayed, but nothing more. No explanation. No context. Ashe's fingers flew across the screen.

"OMW."

Dressing hurt. Every limb burned with residual strain. Beside them, Ryan said nothing.

Without a word, they emerged from the woods.

The treeline gave way to the paved walking track. The trip back was taking longer. Ryan's limp was worse now, his hip clearly bothering him. Ashe's own body felt like it had been pulled through a shredder. Every step sent dull throbs through bone and sinew.

A notification buzzed from Cole.

"Something's wrong. Get here now!"

Adrenaline wiped away the pain. Ashe took off in a sprint, lungs burning with each stride. Behind them, Ryan cursed and started running too, but Ashe didn't hear him. All they could hear was the echo of the kiss, burned into skin that still crawled.

Chapter 12

Pines stood in the Nashville night, smoke clinging to his throat. What had been The Seer's brownstone was now little more than a charred husk. Music still drifted from bars a block away, laughter spilling out of neon doors, but this place stood silent, gutted, its windows black holes swallowing sound.

He'd waited until nightfall, then slipped past the yellow caution tape.

How does someone who claims to see all possible futures not see his own house burning?

He crawled through a blown-out window, bricks blackened and split by heat. Ash drifted in loose spirals, peppering his face as he slid inside.

The floor groaned and cracked beneath his boots. A kidney-shaped table lay warped and collapsed, brass legs twisted like broken bones. Orange shag carpeting still smoldered at the edges, coughing up a sweet chemical sting. One lava lamp had burst, its wax cooling in neon clumps across the floor.

The walls told the rest of it. Vinyl sleeves melted to plaster, their colors blistered into gray pulp. Posters of rock gods curled into themselves, faces burned away until only blackened silhouettes clung to velvet backdrops. The Seer's shrine to sound and excess was now a mausoleum, the entire decade entombed.

"Well," Pines muttered, "that's one way to close the seventies."

Edging deeper into the ruin, a new scent caught his nostrils, crawling into his nose and settling in his chest. The same corruption that had clung to the sniper on Monte Sano.

Fäulung. The Rotting Essence.

Witherbound agents of Tzelut had been here. They knew the Seer. They had touched this place. Pines wasn't prepared for a showdown with the corrupted. Most humans who carried the Rot never amounted to more than husks, their bodies leaking the stench of decay but no real strength. It took years steeped in that poison for power to take hold, and by then there was nothing left of the person inside. Whatever will they once had was long gone, swallowed and replaced by Tzelut's hunger.

But even a newborn husk could swing a silver blade, and one slip in a place like this would end him.

His boots whispered through debris. He sifted rubble, overturned scorched cushions, checked the kitchen, the stairwell. A basement door hung by a single hinge. Every corner promised ambush, corpses, or movement. His ears strained for the scrape of metal, for breath that didn't belong. Only silence answered, and silence felt worse.

Once, he thought he saw a hand beneath a charred beam. Bracing himself, he pulled it free and found nothing more than a mannequin's shriveled remnant, its melted grin mocking his urgency. In the upstairs hall, blackened footprints led into a bedroom, only to vanish at a collapsed wall. Pushing through smoke-stained drapes, he found himself staring at open air where the bricks had fallen away.

The place was a tomb, but not for the Seer. The spirit was gone. Dead, fled, or playing both sides, hard to tell with a spirit that old. An entity claiming to remember the Renaissance probably thought betrayal and salvation were just different verses of the same hymn. Either way, he wasn't getting answers here.

Turning his back on the ruins, he headed for his van. His lungs ached from the smoke. On the walk back his mind ached from the questions.

The Seer had warned him: keep the new pack alive, or the entire Southeast would go fallow. Plants shriveling to husks, animals fleeing in blind panic, even the Wildlands scored open as if Gaia herself had been slashed across the cheek, sap running like blood from the wound. He pictured rivers black with sludge and orchards sagging with fruit that split and festered on the branch. Even then, his imagination barely brushed what would truly come.

Nashville's neon bled into the mirrors as he pulled onto the highway, heading for Chattanooga. One of the honored elders lived near Lookout Mountain, running Rock City with his family. He was also one of the last few he could trust right now to give him honest answers.

The hills closed in as the road grew darker. Fresh air clawed through the open window, drowning out the van's tired rattle and leaving him with his thoughts.

Not that the thoughts were kind.

Maybe the Seer hadn't been compromised. Maybe the elders had. Half the Moote were too busy politicking to smell the rot under their feet. They'd rally for Gaia's defense one moment and then urge caution with the next. He used to be one of them. He'd hated the endless promises and favors needed to push action they should have taken anyway.

Had Sebastian been right before he went missing? Lycans were supposed to be Gaia's fist, not this limp hand they'd become. If the council had shown Sebastian a shred of support, would he have ended up the twisted monster Pines had put down on Monte Sano?

Now he wasn't sure who deserved bullets more: Tzelut's agents or the Lycan too proud to admit the world was burning.

His pack deserved better.

If they survived.

Tapping the wheel, he debated calling them. Tell them not to meet the Huntsville pack yet, not until he'd sorted the Seer's disappearance, not until he knew which way the knives were pointing.

He picked up the phone, thumb hovering over Cole's contact. The app erased numbers after they were entered. A small mercy of modern technology. For once, the world made protecting his people easier. He almost smiled at the thought, but the weight of what he was about to say kept his jaw set.

If he warned them now, maybe Ashe could...

Headlights flared white.

An eighteen-wheeler barreled through the intersection, red light screaming in its wake. Pines had time to mutter, *"Shit"* before the world detonated.

Metal shrieked. Glass burst. The van folded sideways with bone-snapping violence. His chest hammered against the seatbelt, his head ricocheting against the window. The phone flew from his hand.

For a moment, silence. Then voices, distant, shouting if he was okay. Shapes blurred at the edge of his vision.

The smoke of the Seer's house still burned in his nose. Gaia's warning still drummed in his ears.

And then—nothing.

Chapter 13

The brewery sign read "CLOSED AT MIDNIGHT", but several cars lingered in the parking lot. Cole was the first of the pack to arrive, but unease kept him from going in alone. He sat in his car and began writing out some notes he had been working on.

His relationship with Rebecca had stabilized, though tension still simmered between them. He still hadn't told her what was happening. Pines insisted on secrecy, and while Cole understood the need, it didn't sit right. Telling her everything might be reckless, but keeping her in the dark felt worse.

In his notebook, Cole had divided a page into two stark columns. On one side he'd written: "Things to Tell Rebecca". On the other: "Reasons to Break Up." It wasn't the most mature approach, but it was honest. Every comic, movie, and childhood story had taught him the same lesson.

Secrets didn't protect people. It left them blind to danger.

It left them exposed.

And Rebecca was already seeing through the cracks. Cole was usually eager to share new friends, new bands, and where he was going next. Lately he had been vague, careful not to lie outright. Tonight, he could tell she was putting the pieces together, and he knew he had to decide.

Headlights flashed in his rearview mirror, snapping him out of thought. Renae's sedan parked beside him. Switching off his engine, he threw the notebook on the passenger seat and stepped out into the muggy night air.

Grace stepped out first, her form-fitting black leather catching the glow under the parking lot lamps. She moved with deliberate precision, each step measured, her weight rolling lightly on the balls of her feet. Her eyes swept the lot in quick, practiced arcs, head tilting as if testing the air. Even in human skin, the predator showed in the way she claimed the surrounding space.

Cole gave her a small nod, which she returned with a barely perceptible dip of her chin. Renae was still in the car, speaking to someone over the phone. Standing there, he was unsure whether to break the silence.

"Good to see you again," he ventured, immediately regretting the stiffness of his voice.

She turned slowly, a faint smirk curving her lips.

"Thank you," she replied simply. Her eyes narrowed as she looked him up and down. It was unnerving.

"We're working on her manners," Renae offered lightly, circling around the hood of her car.

Cole looked away and wiped sweat from his brow. The summer air hung thick and still, broken only by a faint breeze carrying the hum of distant crickets.

As the wind shifted, so did Grace. Her nostrils flared, and her eyes narrowed. The wolf in her had stirred, sensing something just out of reach.

Alert. Listening.

"Rot and blood," she murmured, the words barely audible, yet they seemed to carry the stench themselves. Her focus remained fixed on the brewery doors.

The air around Cole thickened, the breeze turning from relief to warning. The wolf within him stirred, its focus drawn to Grace's words. Shadows bled heavier at the edges of his vision, pooling dark in the corners. Unease crawled up his neck, and with it came a treacherous flicker of excitement, sharp enough to twist his stomach.

"They're werewolves, right?" he forced a nervous chuckle. "Maybe they have a fresh kill inside. Roasted pig or something. Dinner, maybe?"

Even as the words left his mouth, he felt foolish. Grace's amber eyes found his.

"No," she said flatly. "Human rot. And Lycan. The scent of who hunted us lingers." Her expression hardened as she turned to Renae, waiting for confirmation that the threat was understood.

Renae's expression hardened. "Text Ashe and Ryan. Now." She rushed to her trunk, throwing it open.

He fumbled for his phone, sent the message, and got a curt "OMW" in return.

Grace stood locked in place, staring fiercely at the building. Challenging it to reveal its secrets.

Cole stared bitterly at the Full Moon Brewery. He tried to tap into the wolf without giving it ground. He only wanted its senses, not the form. Just enough to glimpse what she saw.

The squat brick building had once been a school, now repurposed and rough-edged, with a corrugated awning casting jagged shadows. On one side, a pair of tall glass doors served as the main entrance. On the other, a wide, roll-up metal door clearly meant for deliveries. High, narrow windows served for airflow more than sight, giving the place a fortress-like air.

Renae had stepped up behind him, snapping him out of his thoughts. There was something different about her shirt, stiffer and bulked in places it hadn't been a moment ago.

"We should just go, right?" his voice wavered. "If something's wrong, we should let Pines handle it. If it's a misunderstanding, he can explain it."

Renae slid a fresh magazine into her 9mm with practiced ease. The click echoed through the lot. Too sharp. Too unnatural in the quiet.

"Pines isn't here," she said. "If someone in there needs help, we need to know. We'll wait for Ashe and Ryan to get here. Then we will go in."

They sat on the edge of Renae's trunk while Grace maintained her watch. He called Pines. It rang and then went to voicemail. He texted. Nothing.

The silence grated. Pines was still their only real link to this world, and once again, he'd gone dark. No answers. No updates. It was starting to feel less like secrecy and more like control.

Time dragged, and Cole couldn't hold his focus on the looming unknown. His gaze slid back to Grace. The faint creak of leather marked her restless movements, limbs taut with unspent energy.

Curiosity got the better of him as he whispered to Renae, "Why the Matrix getup?"

Renae glanced sideways, lips twitching in amusement. "She liked that I had clothes from prey taken on previous hunts. She asked if she could wear it until she earned her own."

"She won't be able to get out of that outfit quickly. What if she needs to, you know, wolf out or something?"

"I never had trouble." Renae smirked and winked at the younger male, clearly amused at his discomfort.

Grace looked their way, confusion flickering across her face as she examined her outfit. She recognized the humor in Renae's tone, but the meaning slipped past the newer human.

"Wait. *Your* outfit? Not your kid's or something? You actually wore that out in public?"

Renae faced back toward the brewery, momentarily distant.

"I used to go to a lot of raves back in the day. Back then, it was more Goth than glitter. That's actually where I met Jay." The name snagged in her throat. Her smile dimmed, voice thinning into silence.

Missing the change in tone, he focused only on the words said.

"Is Jay home now? Did you tell him what happened to you?" Excitement pitched his voice too high.

Grace whirled at the loud voice, amber eyes flaring in irritation. He flinched, quickly mouthing an apology. Satisfied, she refocused on the building.

Renae's voice lowered further. "Jay was murdered a while back." She didn't wait for a response, continuing softly, "You didn't know. It's fine. But if he were alive, I'd have told him everything."

She glanced briefly at her phone before adding quietly, "We never kept secrets."

They'd been standing in the parking lot for far too long. Ashe and Ryan had still not shown. Grace began pacing with barely contained impatience. Renae's hand tightened around her weapon, frustration visible in every motion.

He was still weighing what to do when a muffled boom rolled out from deep inside the building. The windows bowed under the pressure, glass trembling but not breaking, as dust sifted down from the awning in a slow gray curtain.

Grace reacted before the sound had even faded. She lunged forward, feral and sudden. Renae followed close behind.

Cole hesitated for half a second, scanning the quiet street for any sign of help. With no deus ex machina appearing from the skies, he steadied himself and sprinted after the other two.

Chapter 14

The smell hit Cole before the sight did.

The citrus tang of hops still clung to the air, sweet and almost refreshing, but beneath it was something far more rancid. Blood, excrement, and smoke mingled, staining his nostrils. Somewhere deeper in the building, something was burning.

Grace slipped inside first, silent as breath. He instinctively reached for her arm, not even sure what he meant to do. Hold her back? Keep her safe? But she shook him off without looking, already locked in.

Renae moved next, pistol drawn, eyes alert and determined. Cole lingered on the threshold a moment longer before forcing himself to follow, silently promising he would be more helpful than he'd been on the mountain.

Inside, a small dining room stretched out before them, dimly lit and wide, the kind of place meant for laughter, drinks, and shared arguments about house specials.

Now it was a slaughterhouse.

Tables lay overturned or shattered; chairs splintered into jagged pieces. Bodies sprawled everywhere, none appearing to have tried to escape. They'd either been taken completely by surprise or had made a hopeless, desperate stand.

Blood splattered walls in chaotic patterns. Limbs and entrails littered the floor, tangled in grotesque piles. A lone fly buzzed in slow circles over its fresh feast. From the dripping faucet nearby came a hollow tap, an unsteady beat that marked the silence of the dead.

Moving slowly and fighting nausea, Cole's gaze fell upon a man slumped near the bar, mouth forever locked open in horror, strangled by his own intestines. He looked away sharply, breathing through his mouth.

Focus.

He couldn't let panic overtake him. Instead, he fixed his attention on Grace.

Grace had kicked off her heels the moment they'd entered, leaving them by the door, choosing stealth over fashion. Now she walked as if nothing here could touch her, stepping barefoot through congealed pools of blood, each stride leaving a dark print behind. Her nostrils flared, pulling in the air. Where he saw only carnage, she was gathering information. The scents told her what his eyes could not.

Grace glanced back quickly, ensuring her pack was with her, then fixed her gaze on the bar lining the back wall. At its far end stood a pair of red double doors, the kind that swung both ways.

With deliberate care, she knelt and pulled a splintered pool cue free from a body pinned to a shattered table. She tested its balance, reversed it, and held the jagged, blood-darkened point forward, as a makeshift spear.

Renae shifted smoothly into position beside Grace, gun lifted and ready. Cole stayed a few steps back, wishing he could match their calm. His eyes darted nervously from shadow to shadow, each dark corner hinting at motion.

Spotting the splintered leg of a barstool, he picked it up and gripped it tight, taking comfort in the pressure against his palm. The slight pain anchored him, distracting from the nightmare around him.

Grace stilled, head angled toward the doors as muffled sounds bled through. She moved to advance, but Renae's hand found her shoulder, gently holding her back. She made quick hand motions: herself first with the gun, Grace to follow close behind, Cole to guard their flank.

Crouching low, Renae eased one door open, its hinges creaking faintly. She peered into the darkness, saw something the others couldn't, and moved swiftly inside. Grace followed without hesitation.

Cole scanned behind them, heart thudding as he searched for any sign of movement. Nothing. He itched to look inside but knew getting distracted is how they got you in the movies. However, the silence from Renae and Grace was unnerving. It felt too still. Finally, overwhelmed with curiosity, he crept toward the double doors, breath held, and peered through the narrow gap.

The room was deceptively large, lit by flickering fluorescent bulbs that filled the space with a cold, buzzing hum. Massive copper brewing tanks lined the room, their surfaces reflecting distorted fragments of light. Pipes snaked across the ceiling, disappearing into dark recesses.

The smell was overpowering, remnants of hops drowned beneath smoke and scorched metal. At the far end, one tank had violently ruptured. Jagged copper fragments punctured nearby walls, and thick, oily residue splattered the floor and equipment around the blast site. Four bodies lay crumpled at its base.

"Cole, we need you." Renae's voice echoed urgently through the space. Without hesitation, he rushed forward and knelt beside her.

Up close, the damage was even more horrific. Three bodies were clad in black tactical gear, riddled with deep lacerations and severe burns. Dark, viscous fluid seeped slowly from their wounds. Not quite blood, something else entirely.

The fourth victim was different. He'd clearly taken the full force of the explosion, his face and chest reduced to a mass of charred, melted flesh. He wore casual clothing like those outside, but any further identification was impossible.

Renae pressed two fingers to the man's neck, then glanced quickly around. Spotting a first-aid kit mounted on a far wall, she sprinted toward it.

Cole scanned the room nervously for hidden threats, his senses overwhelmed. The injured man groaned weakly, bloody bubbles forming around his nostrils. Renae returned swiftly, tearing open gauze packs with practiced hands. She took Cole's palm and pressed it firmly against the worst of the wounds on the man's chest.

"Keep pressure here," she said, her voice calm but urgent.

He complied, fighting revulsion as heat radiated into his hand, flesh squelching beneath his fingertips.

Grace prowled the room silently, checking the bodies for signs of life. A sudden grunt, followed by a wet and visceral thud, made Cole tense. Looking up, he saw Grace standing over one of the corpses, her pool cue buried deep in the man's eye socket.

Cole recoiled, trying to shift as far away from Grace while maintaining pressure on the burned man's wounds.

"What the fu..." The rest of the word caught in his throat as Grace yanked the cue free. Impaled on its tip was something black and squirming, slick with oil, writhing and emitting a sound like boiling insects. As they watched, the mass shriveled, collapsing inward.

Grace calmly sniffed the end of the cue and gave a disdainful snort, flicking the deflated remains aside.

"Smelled like Banewolf."

The memory of the creature on Monte Sano dried his mouth. "Were these things the same as what attacked us before? The one Pines said he'd never seen?" The question spilled out, directed at no one and everyone, born from a desperate need to understand.

Renae's expression darkened. "I don't think so. But that..." She gestured at the dark goo sliding from the bodies onto the floor. "We should stay clear of it, just in case."

She turned decisively to Grace. "Empty their pockets. Take everything but phones. We don't want to risk being tracked, but maybe we can piece this together later." Renae quickly finished bandaging the injured man, who lay limp, breath ragged. "We need to get him out of here and to a hospital."

Cole instinctively reached for his phone to call 911, but Renae gently caught his hand with bloodied fingers, shaking her head.

"Think it through," she said softly. "What do you think happens to us if ambulances and police arrive and see this?"

Swallowing hard, he nodded, slipping the phone into his pocket and moving to help lift the injured man. The body felt awkwardly heavy, burned flesh sticking to his skin. He refused to look down, focusing instead on Renae's calm instructions.

Grace, having methodically stripped valuables from the corpses, discovered her borrowed leather outfit lacked pockets. Without hesitation, she began stuffing the scavenged items into Cole's front and back pockets. Her movements were quick and clinical, yet her touch felt invasive. He flinched but remained silent, tightening his grip on the wounded man and focusing on the task at hand.

Halfway across the brewing room, the injured man's eyes shot open, wild and terrified. His limbs jerked weakly against their grip. Renae leaned closer, murmuring soothing words to calm him. He fixed his eyes on her, his charred lips cracking and splitting painfully as he tried to speak.

With great effort, a whisper emerged, ragged and desperate.

"Missed one."

Then he fell limp again, consciousness slipping away, leaving Cole to wonder helplessly if the man had surrendered to exhaustion or death.

Moving as one toward the double doors, Grace took point, pool cue raised like a Spartan spear, her body taut, eyes sweeping for threats. She confirmed Renae, and he were ready, then pushed through.

Grace slipped into the dining area, nudging one of the swinging doors wide. Behind her, Renae walked backward through the opening, holding the burned man beneath the shoulders as Cole supported his legs.

A deafening boom tore through the air.

Renae was ripped off her feet, dropping the man as she collided with Cole. He let the body drop and caught her on reflex, stumbling backward into the brew room. The wounded man hit hard, and the doors swung halfway shut before catching on his limp body, jamming partway open.

A pained grunt escaped the man's throat, but he didn't move.

Another blast roared out. Grace spun, diving behind the bar just as the wall above her shattered into a hail of splinters.

Easing Renae beside the wall, Cole crept toward the partially ajar door and leaned just enough to see down the hall.

A lone figure advanced with slow, confident strides. His silhouette was broad, his frame armored in black tactical gear. The flickering LED wall lights stuttered against his form. He held a double-barrel shotgun cracked open, ejecting two steaming shells before sliding fresh ones in. With a sharp flick, the weapon snapped shut, the sound clean and final.

His whole body went cold. The wolf in him surged, wanting blood.

"No," Cole muttered. Rushing the gunman would get him killed.

Grace peeked over the bar, her amber eyes flaring. She ducked again just as a third blast blew a fresh crater in the bar's siding. Wood and tile scattered across the room.

"Thought there were four of you," the gunman called out, voice thick with mockery. The sound was distorted by the acoustics and a lingering ring in Cole's ears. Still, he sounded cruel. Certain.

"Don't suppose you'll make it easier on me and step out?" The gunman chuckled, but the laugh twisted, catching in his throat, crumbling into something wet and raw.

Renae coughed in Cole's arms. The back of her shirt was torn to shreds, holes punched clean through. For one heart-stopping second, he thought she was dying in his hands. And again, he was doing nothing to help.

But no blood had seeped through.

Tearing the fabric away, he saw a slim black vest embedded with metal. Relief came fast and sharp. She'd come prepared for a fight. But why? They were supposed to be meeting a friendly pack.

And she'd told them she was a retired professor. What kind of professor owns a bulletproof vest? He touched one pellet and hissed in pain, yanking his finger away and shoving it into his mouth.

"Silver?" he mumbled around the burn.

The doubt could wait. For now, he rolled her onto her side and found the quick-release. The vest came loose with a metallic clatter, silver balls coming loose and rolling in scattered directions. Renae's skin was flushed where the silver had struck, but not pierced. Her breathing came rapid but steady.

Cole exhaled shakily. The tension didn't leave him, only shifted. She was alive. But she was hurt. And once again, he'd been unable to stop it. It seemed he could only catch people after they fell.

She blinked at him, gave a faint smile. "Just winded," she rasped.

Trying to sit up and failing with a soft grunt, Renae pressed the grip of her 9mm into his hand.

"I need... a minute," she whispered. "Help Grace."

Cole nodded, fingers tightening around the pistol. His heart pounded in his ears. Standing, he pressed his back to the door, and listened.

Footsteps approached, slow and deliberate. Glass shards crunched under the gunman's boots.

A quick glance revealed the man advancing at a casual pace, shotgun trained on the bar, waiting for Grace to break cover. He wasn't in a hurry. He was enjoying this. Cornering them. Toying with them.

Cole's grip tightened. Grace was exposed. Renae was down. He needed to take action.

The gunman stopped just short of the bar.

"Fine," he called out, voice thick with venom. "I'll drag you out by your little wolf tails and skin you alive. Always wanted werewolf-skin boots."

Gritting his teeth, Cole counted the thousands of ways this could go wrong. Every scenario he imagined ended with him dead. But he wasn't going to watch anyone else fall while he stood on the sidelines.

With a grunt, he shoved hard into the door. It swung open, knocking the wounded man aside. He jumped over the injured man and launched himself into the dining room.

The gunman turned. Cole raised the pistol and fired.

Gunshots cracked through the room. One caught the attacker in the shoulder, spinning him partially as he roared in rage or pain. The shotgun came up.

Cole dove just as it thundered, the blast shredding floorboards and tile where he'd just been. He hit the gore-slick tile hard, sliding across it, curling into himself. Making himself smaller. Harder to hit. He rolled behind an overturned table, the rush of blood in his ears drowning out everything else.

The gunman re-aimed at the bar.

But Grace was already moving.

She launched her broken cue like a spear. It struck the gunman in the gut with a soft, squishy thud. The shotgun fired wide as he staggered; the recoil caused the weapon to slip from his fingers and hit the floor.

Never pausing, she vaulted the bar and sprinted at the man, her bare feet skidding through blood. The man reached for the cue embedded in his torso, crying out in pain as he tried to rip it free. Grace never gave him a chance, leaping onto his back, arms wrapped around his head.

She screamed as she twisted.

A sharp crack echoed through the room. Then another.

The gunman's legs buckled. Grace never let go as he collapsed to his knees, riding him down as he fell face-first onto the blood-slick floor. She held fast, waiting. Her eyes glowed as the last tremor left the body. A sinister smile widened across her face, deepened by the shadows around her.

Cole staggered at the rush of satisfaction through the pack link. The joy of a successful kill bled into him. Grace met his gaze, unashamed. He let the pistol slip from his hand, arms trembling. Not knowing what else to do, he ran his palms over himself, searching for wounds.

None.

Somehow, again, he was fine. Resting his head against the overturned table, he tried to steady himself. Across the room, Grace moved through the wreckage, eyes alert, scanning for anything left waiting in the dark.

Through the doorway, Cole spotted Renae stirring. She crawled to the burned man, checked his pulse, then looked up.

"We need to move," she said, voice sharp. "He needs a hospital. Now."

Cole turned to scoop the man up, but Renae raised her hand, gesturing toward her weapon. Realizing this, he spun, dashed back to the table where he'd taken cover, and grabbed it. She took it back with a silent nod and holstered it.

Rejoining them, Grace cleared a path through the wreckage. Cole and Renae lifted the burned man carefully between them. As they turned toward the exit, something nagged at him.

Looking back at the gunman's corpse, unease crawled up his spine.

"...Is he bigger?"

The other two didn't hear him or were too focused on potential danger to look at a corpse. But it still nagged at him. Earlier, the man had seemed close to Cole's size. Now, his body sprawled unnaturally, bulked and bloated. Easily over three hundred pounds. Worse, something moved beneath the skin. Slow, rhythmic pulses.

Cole frowned as they passed closer to the corpse. Blinking lights and paranoia must be playing tricks on his mind. Now wasn't the time. He turned back and focused on the injured man in his arms.

They had to get out.

The harsh scrape of wood against tile echoed from behind them, stopping them cold. Before they could turn, a heavy oak table hurtled out of the darkness and struck Grace hard, knocking her sideways before slamming into the entryway with bone-jarring force. A thick piece of the base jammed into the doorframe, sealing their only exit.

Renae set the man down and ran toward her injured packmate. Cole pivoted fast, muscles tightening as his mind raced to make sense of what he was seeing.

The scattered debris of bodies was gone. Bloodstains still painted the floor, but the corpses had vanished. Only tattered scraps of clothing fluttered in the air.

Only one body near the bar remained. The gunman.

Or what had been the gunman.

Where his corpse had been now loomed a heaving, shifting mound of flesh. A grotesque amalgam of human forms melted together, features fused without logic or mercy.

Arms jutted out at strange angles. Some limp. Some twitching. Others slowly folded back into the mass. Legs kicked, struggling for purchase on the slick tile. Ribcages surfaced and vanished beneath the multicolored patches of skin. Rising and falling out of sync.

Without warning, an arm tore from the bulk. Long and bent at unnatural angles. Another arm gripped it halfway down, fingers half-melted into the flesh, fused at the wrist like wax pressed into warm clay. The held arm twitched violently as the fused one clenched tighter, guiding its reach like a puppet limb. Together, they stretched impossibly far across the floor and snatched a corpse from near the entrance, dragging it with a wet scraping sound that rattled through Cole's teeth.

The corpse disappeared in jerks and shudders, pulled into the mass.

A new limb pushed through the surface. Fresh fingers twitched blindly. A dozen mouths moved, muttering in a low, unintelligible chorus. Then, all at once, they screamed.

"Tzelut consumes. Submit or be unraveled from within."

Tongues slid from the mouths, tasting the air in anticipation of the feast to come.

Chapter 15

"Faster, please," Ashe urged, clutching the passenger seat as Ryan's Charger tore down the road. Every turn rattled their bones, nausea climbing their throat.

Ashe checked their phone. Still nothing from Cole or Renae. Guilt gnawed at them. They'd chosen the Veil over the meeting, and now others might be paying for it.

"Tell them fifteen minutes," Ryan said, his grip tightening until the wheel creaked.

"They're not responding." Ashe's voice came sharper than intended. "We should've left sooner."

Ryan flinched but didn't argue.

He jerked the wheel into a hard turn, speeding onto I-565 at more than twice the recommended limit. The Charger fishtailed, tires shrieking before they caught.

Ashe almost said it. I'm not mad at you; I'm mad at myself. But the words caught behind clenched teeth. Because they were mad. And the worst part? Even now, they were ready to spare someone else's feelings. Someone that...

Bile rose, a sour blend of motion sickness and the lingering toll of too many shifts in too little time.

"I don't think we're supposed to shift that much, that fast."

"Yeah," Ryan muttered. "First time I double-shifted, I puked and cramped up hard." He glanced at them. "Didn't think you'd go full Hulk right after I tried to celebrate with you."

"You kissed me, you asshole." Ashe rolled the window down, sticking their face into the rushing air. "Shut up and drive."

"Just don't vomit on the upholstery. This baby was my graduation gift."

"Fancy present for passing sixth grade."

The car hit a bump, jarring Ashe so hard they yanked the assist handle clean off. They shared a look. Mutual irritation. Mutual restraint. They both turned away, one focusing on the road, the other on not puking up their dinner.

The bright yellow Charger skidded into the lot, tires screaming in protest. Ashe had the door open before the engine died, already scanning: every car, every window, any movement in the dark.

The brewery loomed ahead. Red brick, low and wide, outlined in the jittering glow of streetlights. Ryan stepped up beside them, posture relaxed, his eyes drifting casually toward the sign overhead. Full Moon Brewery.

"Name's a little on the nose," he said.

Ignoring him, Ashe swept across the parked cars again. No others. No blood. No bodies.

"They said they were going to wait for us," Ashe said quietly. Something stirred deep within them. A restless awareness. The Wolf Spirit, excited by the potential danger ahead.

Muffled impacts rattled the walls inside. It could have been gunfire or machinery; either way, Ashe's chest pulled tight.

"What's that?" Ryan whispered, pointing toward a figure walking backward, dragging something down the building's side. Ashe rushed to the Charger's trunk and pulled out a golf club, the only weapon available. Ryan followed, snatching another.

"Drop it!" Ashe shouted as they closed the gap.

The figure halted mid-step, shifting just enough to reveal his bloodied face.

"It's me," Cole rasped, barely holding himself upright. His shirt clung damp to his frame, streaked with dust and fluids Ashe couldn't identify.

"Renae and Grace. They're inside. It's bad." His words came in choppy bursts as he struggled to catch his breath, barely holding back the fear pressing at the edge of every word.

Before Ashe could reply, a blast shook the building. One of the upper windows shattered, glass bursting outward in a deadly spray. Cole instantly shielded the burned man with his body.

They looked up, and for a heartbeat it wasn't glass but claws. The Banewolf loomed above them again, savage strikes descending in merciless arcs, raking through flesh, tearing them open over and over. The night blurred, breath caught in Ashe's throat, and their body locked in the memory.

Ryan hit them from the side, the impact jarring them back into the present. Both Lycans landed on the hard-packed earth as large shards sliced down in a razor rain.

"Don't kiss me," Ashe groaned into the grass. Heat rushed to their face. They'd frozen. Cole hadn't. Even Ryan hadn't.

Ryan's face also burned with equal parts anger and embarrassment. He looked toward Cole, but the other man stayed focused on the injured man, checking for signs of life. The musician finally looked up. His arms and face were laced with fresh cuts, blood trailing down his jaw.

"Go help Renae and Grace," he said. "I've got him. Just go."

Shoving Ryan away, Ashe scrambled to their feet, sprinting in the direction Cole had come. Ryan hesitated, then followed.

The rear door hung open, swaying on its hinges. Ashe slipped inside, blinking against the sterile light. The air hit them like a slap. Burnt grease, scorched herbs, and the raw-metal tang of cooked flesh.

They were in the kitchen. Counters gleamed. The sinks were dry. Not a plate or smear of sauce anywhere. Every knife was magnetically mounted in a perfect line. Cutting boards leaned precisely. Pans hung in symmetrical rows. The condition of the room didn't sit right. Too clean for what was unfolding.

One heavy double door stood along the wall labeled Brew Floor. Another door on Ashe's right was unmarked. Pantry, maybe?

Muffled pops sounded through the wall, each one setting Ashe's pulse racing.

They crept toward the brew floor door, then paused.

Ryan still hadn't entered. He stood just beyond the exit, pale, shoulders drawn tight, eyes locked on the door ahead. Ashe moved back toward him, forcing steadiness into their voice.

"Get ready."

"Are you going to turn?" His eyes darted from the door to Ashe, like he was weighing which one to fear more.

Ashe paused, teeth catching their lip. "I think I should."

Ryan swallowed hard, his gaze lingering on them too long. "Then I probably shouldn't be near you. Pines said if you're not fully in control..."

He didn't have to finish. The fear hung unspoken between them. Fear of whatever was inside. Fear of Ashe.

"I'll go around," Ryan added quickly, already stepping backward. "Try to find another way in."

Disgusted, they turned away from him. "If you see Renae or Grace, get them out."

With barely any hesitation, Ryan turned and disappeared back into the dark.

"Damn coward," Ashe exhaled. They worked to put him at the back of their mind. The door loomed ahead, with the muffled sounds behind it growing sharper. Each one carried the weight of something alive trying to stay that way.

Reaching inward, they stoked the heat where the wolf lived. It surged up. Wild. Furious. Hungry. It pressed just beneath their skin, muscles tensing with readiness.

So was Ashe. But a sliver of fear cut through the heat. What if they couldn't pull back? What if the Warhide took over?

They let go anyway.

But it broke.

Agony tore through them. Muscles locked. Nerves screamed. Ashe hit the floor hard, gasping, legs too weak to stand. Earlier turnings had cost them too much. Their body couldn't take another shift.

Still trembling, they gripped the edge of a counter and hauled themselves upright. Vision swam as a scab from the fight with the Banewolf split open, soaking their shirt in fresh blood.

A scream ripped through the brewery.

Ashe staggered forward, not whole, but moving anyway. They shoved through the brew floor door, half-running, half-bracing for whatever waited on the other side.

The room stretched out like a cavern. Massive copper vats rose like ancient statues, their sides streaked with condensation and grime. Harsh lights shimmered across slick tile. Pipes twisted overhead, steam hissing faintly from joints.

The scent hit next. Not hops. Not yeast. Just scorched metal, smoke, and burned flesh.

Ashe's chest tightened. Bodies lay crumpled near the far wall. Some were wrapped in tactical gear, armor partially melted to their bodies. Others fused to the floor. The air pulsed with the weight of death.

What did this?

Every step felt like a gamble as they crept toward the corpses. Muscles twitched, knees threatening to give. Ashe wasn't ready.

Then the doors to the front room slammed inward.

Renae stumbled through the breach wearing only a bra and torn jeans. Shoulders hunched. Eyes wide. One hand gripped a pistol. The other was locked around Grace's waist, half-dragging her into the brew room.

Grace was barely upright. Blood streamed from her side in pulsing bursts, soaking through shredded leather pants and pooling beneath her with every step. Her eyes were glassy, lips parted in a grimace of pain she couldn't voice.

The gun flashed as Renae fired blindly into the darkness of the other room. Shadows danced in twisted shapes, each shot deafening in the enclosed space. But underneath the shots was a cry. No, not one cry, but dozens, each voice distinct in its agony.

The pistol clicked dry.

There was no time for hesitation. Ashe surged forward, legs still unsteady, and caught her other arm. Grace's weight collapsed against them. Together, Renae and Ashe dragged her behind the nearest brewing tank, footsteps slipping in the spreading blood.

The injured Lycan groaned as they lowered her. A raw, guttural sound, half-human and full of pain.

Renae turned a red valve. Beer hissed out, washing over Grace's wounds in a foaming rush. The black ichor that seeped from her slashes sizzled violently, washing away in a foul, sulfurous steam. Grace screamed once, sharp and raw.

"You need to do a Full Tearing. Now."

"What?" Ashe blinked, breath catching. They didn't understand what Renae was saying.

"Warhide, we need your werewolf. Right now!"

Ashe's muscles seized at the very thought. Their legs trembled under them.

"I... I can't." The words slipped out small, ashamed.

If they hadn't wasted time at the park. If they hadn't collapsed trying to force the shift. They could have helped.

But now...

Renae scanned the room, desperate for anything. Anything that could be used in place of claws or fangs.

"What the hell is happening?" Ashe asked, tension tightening every syllable.

The dining room doors flew open. Hinges tore free and screamed across the floor. Through the broken door frame, something poured in.

"That," Renae simply replied.

A wave of bulging, roiling flesh crawled forward in lurching spasms. Limbs sprouted in mismatched pairs from its sides only to be swallowed again, vanishing into the heaving surface. Skin split wetly across its bulk, revealing raw muscle and twitching nerve clusters that writhed beneath a coating of blood and bile.

It moved without symmetry or design. A pulsing patchwork of knuckles, teeth, eyes, and mouths that never stopped shifting. A dozen eyes blinked out of sync across what might have once been a spine. Its entire front writhed in confusion, limbs snapping in and out of place like it couldn't decide what it wanted to become.

"That's wrong. That's just wrong," Ashe gasped. Their voice felt borrowed, too small in the face of what stood before them.

"I've emptied two magazines into it and nothing!" Renae shouted from behind, still bent over Grace, scrubbing the last of the black sludge from her wounds.

Evidence of gunfire marked its surface. Puckered burns and punched-in holes stippled the creature, the flesh around them charred and raw. But something felt off. The skin near each wound twitched, as if recoiling from the damage itself, steaming where it met the air.

It reminded them of Ryan's injury on the mountain.

Already though the damage was vanishing. Tissue bubbling, rising anew. Obscene in its eagerness to return.

"We'll unmake you. Nerve by nerve, name by name," the mouths moaned, speaking as one chorus of stolen voices.

A deep sickness crawled through them as the blob reared and whipped a malformed limb toward them. The appendage bristled with far too many fingers.

They stepped forward and swung. The club collided with a heavy crunch, shattering a mess of knucklebones fused into something neither hand nor claw. The broken pieces hit the floor and twitched, spasming like parasites cut from a larger host.

Out of the corner of their eye, Renae hauled Grace upright and dragged her toward the back wall. She snapped open the plastic spigots on several sanitizer drums marked ETHANOL. Clear liquid sheeted over the amber spread and ran fast across the tile.

Looking back at the thing, they saw it had jerked away, only to split itself open again. The ruined limb slurped inward, swallowed whole, and in its place emerged something less formed. An appendage more tail than arm. Dragging black slime as it thudded wetly to the floor.

It came again, faster this time. Ashe ducked low. Air tore past their face, stinking of rot and meat. Their legs buckled, barely catching themselves. Only adrenaline kept them moving.

"Back away, Ashe!" Renae barked, digging frantically through her pockets. "Get clear of the liquid!"

Most of the floor was already flooded, the beer spreading fast, leaving only a few dry patches between islands of foam.

Ashe flung the bent golf club at the approaching mass. It struck the creature's surface and sank halfway in before the thing let it fall, splashing into the sticky pool below. Turning away, they bolted, legs screaming in protest. Needles stuck down their spine, but fear shoved them forward.

Can't fight it. Can't outrun it. Just get out. Just move.

The blob surged after them, howling. Every mouth screamed vengeance. Renae didn't hesitate. She flicked her lighter and hurled it into the pool.

Flame roared to life.

A blue blaze leapt across the ale-soaked floor, hissing and crackling, racing toward the center of the room. The creature lurched away but couldn't escape the spreading flames. Blues turned to reds and oranges as fire climbed up its limbs, poured into its wounds, filled its mouths and scorched the twitching tongues. Its shrieks turned shrill, tangled in dozens of competing throats.

Ashe staggered back, dropping to their knees, stunned by the overwhelming heat. Their lungs locked as smoke and fire closed in around them.

"Move now!" Renae coughed, yanking Grace toward the door.

The brewery's copper tanks glowed orange in the rising heat. Fire crawled up their sides, the metal groaning and warping under the intense temperature.

The Wolf Spirit refused to let Ashe stay down. They could feel its howl inside, nudging them forward. Ashe pushed up through the heat. Muscles seized. Fatigue fought adrenaline.

But they rose. An unsteady phoenix in the flames. Not reborn, just refusing to fall.

Ashe stumbled into the kitchen just in time to hear Grace cry out, her sleeve glowing orange as smoke wafted from the fabric. Renae shoved her through the doorway into the grass, then dropped beside her, beating at the smoldering cloth.

Then the world cracked. The blast took everything.

Air. Sound. Direction.

There was a brief sensation of weightlessness, then Ashe was thrown through the door. They hit the ground hard, rolling across dew-slick grass.

For a moment, nothing but white flashes and ringing—screaming or metal or their own thoughts, impossible to tell. Their body thrummed with static. Nerves misfired. Limbs didn't feel like they belonged to them anymore. They couldn't remember which way was up.

Had they already died?

The ground was cold and wet against their cheek, with the rest of their body numb. Ashe doubted the afterlife would be so bland, so they let that sensation pull them back to consciousness.

Smoke drifted above, gray against a flickering sky. Debris clattered down like broken bones. The brewery was belching fire from the collapsed rear wall. The door they'd just escaped through no longer existed. Charred bricks and broken beams blocked the way.

The monster's muffled screams still leaked from inside.

Firelight surged behind the wreckage, its glow rippling against the night. The brewery hissed and groaned. Pipes burst within. Steam rose from the ruin.

Renae reached them first. Grace followed, limping, arm wrapped in cloth. Ashe pushed upright, temple throbbing but still alive.

"Thanks." The word came out broken, barely audible over the ringing of alarms.

"You're the one who came in to save us," Renae said, placing a steady hand on their back. "Let's see if we can make it to the parking lot."

The three moved slowly, picking their way across the back lawn. Every step jarred Ashe's bruised frame. The cool night air hit their face, a shock after the searing heat.

Grace stumbled again. Ashe moved to her side instinctively, watching the way she clutched her arm, how pale she looked under the soot.

She didn't speak for a long moment. Then, with amber eyes still forward, she muttered, "Thank you."

The words felt practiced, distant, like something she'd been told to say rather than something she meant. Ashe didn't respond. Just stayed beside her, steps in sync.

At the edge of the lot, Ryan stood waiting, waving them over.

"Cole took that guy to the hospital," he called out. "All the other doors were locked, so I stayed out front in case you needed anything."

It sounded reasonable. But hesitation showed in his stance. The way his eyes slid away before finding theirs. His voice was steady, but there was an unspoken apology under it.

Not answering, they let their gaze hold him steady, the tension between them loaded and unfinished.

Ryan's expression faltered. He rubbed the back of his neck, looking elsewhere.

Renae was too focused on Grace to notice. But Grace glanced between the two of them, eyes narrowing slightly, reading something she didn't name. Ashe turned away before she could say anything.

"We need to go," Renae muttered, already scanning the street. "Before the fire department shows up. We can't be here when..."

A sound cut her off. From inside the building, a deep, grinding rumble shook the ground.

The front wall of the brewery groaned, bowed outward, then gave way with a thunderous crack. Stone, metal, and glass erupted in a violent spray across the lawn. Where the door had been, only an open wound remained. From the gap, something heaved itself into the open.

The blob.

Smaller than before, maybe half the size it had been inside. But still enormous. Still breathing. Body charred, chunks of flesh sloughed off whatever surface it brushed. What remained was a blistered landscape of blackened hide and exposed meat, vivid pink and oozing.

Ryan stepped back. Then again.

"Jesus Christ," he shouted, turning toward his car. He didn't look back. The Charger's engine roared to life, tires squealing faintly as he whipped it around.

"Stop!" Renae called after him, voice cracking. But it was already too late.

Ashe saw the shift in her face, her age more apparent now as shock collapsed into something colder. The reality of his choice. He was leaving them, three injured people, alone.

They weren't surprised. Just exhausted. Tired of him choosing the worst moments to show everyone exactly who he was.

Renae blinked hard and shook it off.

"We can't leave this to responders," she said, voice steady again. Too steady. "We need to end it." Her eyes flicked to her car. "I've got more bullets in the trunk. Get Grace to safety."

It was a lie.

Not the bullets, but the plan behind it. Renae knew it wouldn't be enough. Her face didn't flinch, but the grip she had on control wavered for just a breath.

They didn't say anything. Didn't need to. They made peace with what came next.

"I'll tear it apart," Grace growled, her voice scraping low, somewhere between human and beast. Muscles shifted beneath her skin, stretching the scraps of her leather outfit until the seams split.

"I'll join you," Ashe said through clenched teeth. Their body screamed in warning. Bones ached. Tendons burned. Something deep within whispered that if they tried to shift, it wouldn't just hurt. It would break them. Damage that wouldn't heal right, but it didn't matter.

That thing had to die. They planted their feet and rose tall. If this fight ruined them, so be it.

The blob writhed violently, turning itself inside out. Patches of its blackened skin peeled away, smothering lingering flames. Beneath it, fresh meat churned. Tendons stretched with bones poking outward at impossible angles. Long cords of sinew dragged across the pavement, searching.

That thing. Its shape. Its sounds. It was carved into them now. It would haunt every quiet moment, every dream. However long they had left, it would never be far. The only thing they could do was prevent it from haunting someone else.

A roar cut across the lot.

He came back. The thought hit before Ashe could stop it.

A yellow blur tore through the night and smoke, headlights slicing the haze. Ryan's Charger vaulted the curb at full speed, metal screaming as it scraped pavement. He didn't swerve. Didn't slow. Ashe caught a glimpse of him behind the wheel. Face pale, mouth twisted in a soundless scream.

The impact crushed part of the blob beneath the hood. Black fluid exploded upward in fat jets. Bone fragments rattled across the lot. A mangled limb slapped against the windshield and stuck there, twitching, clawing at nothing.

The Charger kept moving, plowing the mass backward until it struck the crumbling wall. Metal and brick came down together, burying car and creature beneath the wreckage.

Then—stillness.

The brief reprieve was cut by the monster's death throes. Not loud. Not shrill. But low and wide, a sound that seeped into the marrow.

Both Lycans moved without speaking, transformations cut short before they could finish. The Charger's horn blared, drowning out the sirens building in the distance.

On the driver's side, Ashe yanked hard. The door bent but didn't open. Grace drove her fingers into the seam and pulled until the metal gave with a shriek.

Smoke billowed out.

Inside, Ryan lay slumped across the seat, blood running from his temple. His shirt had scorched and melted to one shoulder, fused to the skin. Without hesitation, Grace grabbed him under the arms and hauled him clear just as heat crept toward the front tires. Ashe dropped beside her, dragging his legs across the grass.

Behind them, the blob convulsed. Its outer layer peeled away in sheets, too blistered to hold shape. It slapped uselessly at the wreckage, twitching against the crushed metal. Then, slowly, it collapsed with a wet sucking groan. One last ripple. Then nothing.

Grace dragged Ryan about twenty feet back and laid him down with surprising care. She brushed ash from his face with the back of her hand, fingers softly caressing his forehead. A strangely tender gesture in the chaos.

"Brave," Grace said, voice low.

She looked up at Ashe, eyes rimmed with soot, something unreadable behind them. A question. Or a challenge.

"Yeah, my hero," Ashe muttered, bitterness slipping out before they could stop it. But the words felt slightly hollow.

He had come back. Driven straight into the heart of the thing. Risked everything, knowing full well what was waiting. Guilt settled in Ashe's chest. Someone could be heroic and still be insufferable.

The way Grace looked at him, eyes full of awe and something gentler, made it clear her opinion differed from Ashe's.

Ashe knelt beside him. Ryan's eyelids fluttered open.

"Idiot," they said softly, with only a bit of heat behind it.

"Saved your ass," he croaked, then hacked out a coughing fit.

Renae's car crunched over broken glass as it pulled alongside. No one needed directions. It was time to disappear.

Ashe opened the front door while Grace half-carried Ryan into the back seat. He groaned with each motion, burned shoulder jerking. As he sank into the seat, Ashe caught it. A smirk twitched at the edge of his mouth.

Grace slid in beside him, filthy, torn, and bleeding, but her eyes clear.

Eyes locked with Ashe's as she reached to pull the door shut. There was no smile. No words. Just a stare heavy with intent. Possessive. Protective.

He's mine.

Ashe blinked once, slow. Then shrugged.

He's all yours.

They fell into the passenger seat as red and white lights lit the lot's edge. Firetrucks raced closer, the responders blind to what still waited in the ruins behind them.

"Hold on," Renae said, white-knuckling the wheel. The car jumped the curb with a jolt.

Ashe's head swung back into the seat as they hit the street, tires shrieking. The city blurred past. The engine roared forward, masking the final groan of the brewery as it crumbled into itself.

"You were right," Ryan rasped from the back, eyes locked on the flames consuming his car.

Ashe turned. "About what?"

"We should've taken your car too."

Chapter 16

The phone dinged again.

Cole groaned and dragged the covers over his head, willing the world to stop vibrating long enough for him to sink back into sleep.

He'd already called in sick to the post office. Driving a mail van half-awake and sore from a supernatural firefight felt like a quick route to the obituary page. His music students would have to wait too. He canceled every lesson for the day with vague excuses, knowing full well that "gift from Gaia" didn't qualify for sick leave or hazard pay.

Another notification chimed against the nightstand. With a sigh, he rolled over to grab his phone.

And found himself staring directly into Rebecca's face.

She didn't speak. Arms crossed, fists tight beneath her sleeves. Her hoodie hung loose at the shoulders, but her whole body was braced, tension laced through every inch. Her eyes were on him, a quiet burn of worry tangled with something sharper.

It had to be later than he thought if she was already home.

"How long...?" he mumbled, still pulling himself out of sleep. "Have you been there the whole time?"

"Long enough." Her voice was even, shaped by effort. Not cold, but measured too precisely to be casual. "The hospital called. Your Uncle Owen made it through surgery. They said he's stable."

He sat up slowly, the sheet dragging across his lap. "Thanks."

Rebecca didn't move. "You told me your parents were both only children."

Rubbing his eyes, he forced his brain into motion. The room still felt heavy, but the space between them had thinned.

"He's not really my uncle," Cole said. "Just a friend who needed help. I didn't want him to get in trouble." Even as the words came out, they tasted off. Too cautious. A truth forced into the shape of a lie.

Rebecca's mouth drew tight. "Was this friend from the other night? From the group that keeps lighting up your phone?" Her voice stayed level, but her chest rose faster, breath shallow and clipped. "Or is this another friend you're not going to tell me about?"

He opened his mouth, but she cut him off.

"Was it his blood? On the clothes you threw in the outside bin?"

He winced. His body was fine now, all trace of the wounds gone. Gaia had seen to that. But the shirt still held dried blood in the seams, and the memory of the thing in the brewery still scraped against the back of his thoughts.

She planted one foot forward, shoulders squared, though her hands betrayed her, fingers curling into fists that trembled against her thighs. He had seen this before, the way she rehearsed pieces of a speech to stay calm, but the cracks still showed, raw emotion bleeding through.

"You've been lying to me," she said. "Or avoiding the truth, which is the same thing. I know something's going on. You come home in torn-up clothes. You won't look me in the eye. You talk in half-sentences. You smile without meaning it." Her voice cracked, just slightly. "I'm not stupid, Cole."

"I know," he said quietly. Her words burned because she was right.

She tossed his notebook onto the bed. "Maybe this will help. Have you made your decision yet? Or are you still weighing the pros and cons of staying with me?"

He opened his mouth, then closed it again.

He'd been waiting for a moment that didn't exist, a perfect time where everything could be explained without anyone getting hurt. He'd become what he hated about Pines: someone who decided which truths were too much for others to carry.

She deserved answers.

"You're right," he said. "Let me grab a shower. I'll meet you in the dining room."

He meant it and tried to show it. She left the room without replying.

Swinging his legs off the bed, he checked his phone. The pack chat was still active. Ryan had asked if someone could pick up Grace. He didn't feel comfortable with her tending his injuries. She'd been watching over him since the fight, too close, too often. It was becoming suffocating.

No one had acknowledged the request. Instead, the thread had already moved on to debating the attackers' identity and what the hell they were supposed to do next.

He quickly checked one contact, confirming what he already knew—still no word from Pines. Cole shut off the screen. If everyone else was still breathing, the rest could wait.

Steam curled in the bathroom, fogging the mirror and softening the ache in his ribs. He stayed in the shower longer than usual, hoping it would delay the inevitable, but all it did was replay the night.

He'd spent so much energy resenting the fact he hadn't gotten hurt during the Grove ambush, like it was a mark against him, proof he hadn't done enough. But after fighting that skin-stitched monster in the brewery, after bleeding and almost dying, he didn't feel any better. No great transformation followed. No clarity. No reward.

What stayed with him wasn't the pain. It was getting the man out while Grace and Renae held the thing off. The creature had locked onto the burned man the moment it sensed he was still alive, and it had taken everything they had to rescue him.

But they had. And now the man was going to live. That wasn't glory. It wasn't a badge. But it mattered. And that was enough.

Clean-shaven and a little less grimy, Cole pulled on a faded Velvet Revolver shirt and black gym shorts. He glanced in the mirror again. His hair was still a mess, his eyes still sunken. But at least he didn't look like a zombie.

Rebecca sat at the dining room table, fidgeting with a sleeve of fast food crackers, snapping them one by one. The black-and-gold table, rescued from the side of the road, still wobbled on its cinderblock leg. It had borne their weight since. So had their relationship. Now Cole wasn't sure either would hold.

She didn't look up when he walked in. Her fingers worked methodically down the sleeve, cracking, stacking. Her leg bounced under the table, heel tapping against the floor in the rhythm of a hummingbird.

He hesitated in the doorway.

Should have done this earlier. After the Grove. Before the brewery. Before all of it.

Sitting across from her, he said, "I'm going to tell you everything. And then... if you still want to be here, I want that too. But if you don't, I'll understand."

Rebecca didn't nod. She didn't blink. The only reaction was her thumb snapping into the edge of another cracker until it split.

So he told her. Everything.

The night in the grove. The First Tearing. Pines. Grace's injuries. The horrors at the brewery. The pull of the Wolf Spirit deep in his chest. How it changed him, reshaping everything he thought he understood.

He left out the part where Grace had been naked at Pines' house. Some details didn't help anyone.

Rebecca didn't interrupt. She barely moved. Every so often her brow would twitch, or her hand would tighten on the table. When he finished, she leaned back slightly, arms crossed, fingers digging into her sleeves.

"Are you on drugs?" She studied him like a stranger across a distance, voice pared down to the bone. Not sharp. Not angry. Only weary.

Cole gave a bitter laugh. "God, I wish. That would make all of this easier."

He'd seen too many musicians burn out. Selling thousand-dollar gui-tars for fifty bucks just to get high again. He had sworn never to be one of them. He kept clean for her. For them.

She scanned his face, still trying to find the lie. Her jaw tensed, then eased. Then locked again.

"I'm not lying to you," he added.

Her voice was quiet, but her tone had changed. "That's not what I'm worried about now."

He exhaled and stood, stripping off his shirt and shorts in one mo-tion. Rebecca raised an eyebrow. Her lips parted, then pressed together again. Her eyes narrowed. Not in amusement, but wariness.

"If this is some last-ditch romantic gesture," she said, "you're about to get dropkicked."

He gave a tired smile. "Just... wait."

The Wolf Spirit was already close. It had been waiting, pressing just under the surface since the fight. Cole reached for it. There was no fear. Only a pulse of warmth. A shared breath. A hunger beneath his ribs that wasn't rage but need.

He Veiled.

There was no warning. Just bones shifting, skin folding, the sound of tendons pulling tight like guitar strings being tuned too far. Fur spilled from his arms. Joints bent backward. He hit the ground on all fours, paws digging into the thin rug.

Rebecca moved back a step. One hand braced on the chair, the other raised just slightly. Not enough to fight. Just to anchor herself. Her mouth parted, her pupils not tracking him at first. She blinked once. Then again.

He sat, tail curling close, trying to look as non-threatening as a su-pernatural werewolf could manage in a dining room.

She rubbed her eyes. Full-on cartoon disbelief. Cole, still in wolf form, gave a soft chuff. She didn't laugh, but didn't scream either.

Eventually, the pull of the woods came. The Wolf wanted out, but Cole dragged it down. The return to human form came slower. Each joint resisted. Fur slid from his skin in reluctant threads, clinging before finally letting go.

It had hurt coming back. Ryan had warned him a second shift so close to the first would feel worse. But this felt different, as if the Wolf Spirit itself resisted his return to human skin. When it ended, Cole sat shivering and naked.

Rebecca had returned to her chair. One hand on the table, the other gripping the edge. Her posture might as well have been carved from marble.

She didn't look at him. Her gaze stayed fixed somewhere past his shoulder.

"Why?" she asked, her voice barely above a whisper.

"I don't know," he said. "We were told it was a gift. Pines said... Gaia chose us. But I didn't ask for this. None of us did."

"And that gift means getting hunted? Fighting monsters? Killing people?"

He didn't answer.

"It's been a week and you've almost died twice." She didn't yell. But her voice carried a tremor that said yelling was close. "Tell Gaia or Pines or whoever you have to that you're out."

"Renae tried that already, and all she was told was she'd be hunted down one way or another." He exhaled. "And... I don't think I would walk away even if I could."

It was the first time he'd said it aloud. It felt true. He could help people. He could make the world right.

Rebecca's eyes flicked toward him, then away just as quickly. She pressed her hand to her mouth, thumb resting against her bottom lip.

"You realize how insane that sounds," she said finally. "You aren't a fighter, and you are going to get yourself killed."

Her voice cracked on the last word, and she blinked hard, shaking her head as if she was trying to clear it. Rising slowly, she took tentative steps toward him. Whether she was afraid of him or for him, it was difficult to tell. A warm hand lay on his chest, and she stared up into his face, her eyes large.

"I can't just sit here and wait for the day you don't come back," she said, voice just above a whisper. "And I'm not stupid enough to pretend this won't end that way."

She stood a moment longer, motionless, torn between the door and the space they'd shared. Then she nodded once. Slow. Mechanical.

Her body moved before her mind caught up. The warmth of the hand left a cold spot as she gathered her things. Rebecca moved with the focus of someone trying not to think too hard about what came next.

Cole watched her, every motion feeling final.

"I don't know what to do with this," she muttered, almost speaking to herself. "What I saw. What I feel."

He stepped in front of her and rested his hand over hers. She flinched, but didn't pull away.

"I love you. And I get it. This might be the line for you. But whether you stay or not, my feelings won't change."

She didn't respond, but her fingers curled gently into his palm. Her eyes were red. She looked at him finally, and he saw something on her face shift. Not forgiveness. But something close.

She pulled her hand back. "I'll call you. In a few days. I just need time."

He nodded.

She finished packing, walked to the side door, then paused. "I still love you," she said. Then she stepped outside.

The door clicked shut. He stood there a long time, listening to nothing. Cole drifted into the garage and the makeshift studio where his guitars waited. He sat with fingers brushing the strings, but the notes came out hollow. Every melody unraveled before it took shape.

The music was gone.

He rested the guitar on its stand, buried his face in his hands, and let the tears come. He hadn't saved anything. He had just told the truth. And now all he could do was wait, hoping it had been enough.

Chapter 17

The house perched atop the hill looked too clean.

Ashe sat in the driver's seat, hands resting on the steering wheel, unmoving. When the group had agreed to meet, Ryan had offered his place as a "comfortable locale." Cole and Renae had already agreed before Ashe had checked their phone. Arguing about it now seemed petty.

The gate code glowed on their screen. They should punch it in. Instead, they sat there, Kyle's face swimming up unbidden.

Yesterday, he'd said he was coming over. Ashe had tried to put him off. Too sick. Not enough sleep. When he didn't text back, they'd hoped that meant he'd let it go.

He hadn't. Shown up anyway, soup in hand, stubborn as ever.

One look at Ashe. The bruises mottling their arms. The way they held their ribs. The split along their temple. The container hit the floor.

"What happened?"

They'd tried to deflect. A fall. A stupid accident. But Kyle saw through every word, eyes going hard.

"Were you jumped? Was this because of..." He stopped himself. But Ashe knew. *Because you came out. Because someone decided to make you a target.*

The truth would have been easier to tell, somehow. At least that kind of violence was human.

"I'm fine. You need to go."

"Like hell."

"Kyle. *Go.*"

They'd pushed him toward the door. The look on his face as it closed. Confusion collapsing into hurt, then something worse. The quiet certainty that Ashe was hiding something. That after everything, they still didn't trust him.

The soup had sat on the counter until this morning. Ashe threw it out without opening it.

Protecting him, they told themselves. But sitting here now, staring at a rich kid's gate while their brother thought they'd been hate-crimed and wouldn't talk about it. It felt less like protection. More like another wound they'd handed him to carry alone.

They punched in the code. The gate slid open with mechanical grace, chains and gears clicking beneath the well-oiled surface.

The landscape beyond was manicured, but only just. Broad lawns rolled toward the private road, a sculpted first impression that frayed on closer inspection. Edges were uneven with clover creeping through the grass.

Rows of ornamental trees flanked the drive, shaped into near-spheres, though wayward branches disrupted the perfect spheres, reminding Ashe of the skin-blob monster. The mulch beds were tidy but faded in patches, and weeds poked through the seams. One of the topiary bushes leaned, its shape unintentionally abstract.

As the Rav crawled forward, asphalt gave way to over-designed basalt cobblestone. Glittering grey shards that caught the sun and bounced the heat back into Ashe's eyes.

"At least the engine finally shut up," Ashe muttered to themself. The strange knocking noise had stopped yesterday, which probably wasn't a good sign. Pines had better get back soon so he could repair the damage done to their car.

But they hadn't heard from him in days. Not since the last vague message saying he'd check in soon.

Renae said he was probably lying low, but that didn't sit right. He genuinely seemed to care about the five new pack members. He might be gruff and avoid questions, but Ashe doubted he'd ignore his pack on purpose.

Especially after what happened at the brewery.

Or maybe they were wrong. Maybe they'd misread him. Another bad judge of character in a long string of errors.

They pulled up to the four-car garage with no other vehicles around. The A/C had given up yesterday, so waiting in the car for the others to show wasn't an option. Grabbing the stack of pizzas off the passenger seat, Ashe stepped onto the sunbaked stone and tried not to admire the house.

Multicolored stonework gave the outer walls an expensive, earthy sheen. Wide arched windows lined the facade, and the double front doors rose like the entrance to a fortress. Too big. Too polished. Simply too much.

Ashe took a breath and started up the path. In the corner of their eye, something streaked across the lawn.

A red wolf.

It chased a squirrel through the open field, the smaller animal darting in frantic zigzags. The wolf matched every turn, limbs stretching with fluid precision, until it lunged. It pinned the small rodent and, with a decisive snap, provided a quick death for the small prey.

The beast inside Ashe surged, teeth bared in excitement. It wanted to be there. Running. Chasing. Killing. It wanted to tear through fur and bone and taste triumph.

It wanted to kill... the wolf.

Ashe recoiled inwardly. That wolf was Grace. Their packmate. And the instinct hadn't just wanted to run with her. It had wanted to hunt her.

"You and I are going to need to work a few things out before I let you back out," Ashe muttered under their breath.

They rang the doorbell, half-expecting some butler in coattails to answer and look down on them like a roach on imported tile.

No answer. A second passed, then a click from the speaker.

"Hey Ashe, doors open." Ryan's voice. Flat. Unwelcoming.

Balancing the pizza boxes on one arm, Ashe pulled the front door open and stepped inside.

Inside, the house echoed. The foyer stretched wide beneath a vaulted ceiling, but each room Ashe passed was hollow, marked only by sealed boxes and the absence of photos, furniture, or life.

Eventually they found the formal dining room, the first furnished space in the maze of emptiness. Setting the pizzas on an immaculate rosewood table, Ashe noted how the deep brown surface shimmered with veins of purple and red, polished to a soulless sheen.

There was no cushion of give as they sat in the formal dining chair. Minutes passed with no one in sight. Paranoia crept in. Why hadn't anyone greeted them? How could Ryan afford all of this?

Crypto bro came to mind. That'd track. People like him always seemed to land soft. Meanwhile, Ashe had just emptied their bank account to pay for the pizza now on the table.

A blur passed by the front windows, then the door creaked open.

Grace walked in, drenched in sweat and completely nude. Ashe turned away fast, eyes fixed on the table. The woman didn't acknowledge it. She gave a curt nod and padded toward the stairs, muscles moving fluidly beneath her skin. She looked unbothered. Entirely self-assured.

Even with her injuries, there was a sense of wholeness about her, a quiet confidence. Standing next to her made Ashe feel incomplete.

Twenty minutes passed in silence. Ashe scrolled aimlessly, their thumb drifting across a cracked phone screen. This was feeling a bit like payback for arriving late at the brewery.

The front door opened again. This time it was Renae and Cole, arms loaded with canned drinks, laughter fading as they stepped inside. Trailing behind them came a third figure, hunched beneath a black hoodie and heavy sweatpants.

Jericho.

The burned man they'd rescued from the Full Moon Brewery.

Before Cole left the hospital, he'd slid the brewery survivor his number.

A couple of days later, Cole had texted the group saying Jericho had escaped from the hospital. Not checked out. Escaped. The doctors had insisted on monitoring him. He'd insisted on being anywhere else.

Renae demanded to go with Cole to pick him up. She wanted to ensure the younger Lycan was not alone in case this was another trap.

As they entered the dining room, Jericho lowered his hood. His face was a map of ruin. Scarring crawled across his jaw and temple, skin bubbled and warped, his mouth locked in a permanent half-snarl. One eye was a pale, milky haze. The other stayed sharp and dark. Patches of his beard were gone for good. His body moved stiffly, each step a reminder of what motion used to feel like.

Even with accelerated healing, Ashe remembered what Pines had said: some wounds never close clean. Fire and silver leave marks that never fade.

The sight bothered Ashe deeply. It wasn't just the damage. It was how quiet he was. How hollow he looked inside all that ruin.

Jericho nodded once in Ashe's direction, then eased into a chair, hands braced against the wood, shoulders trembling with the effort. A few seconds later, Ryan appeared from the upstairs hall, Grace in tow and now wrapped in a silky robe.

"Sorry," Ryan said. "I was on the phone with the cops. Had to report my car stolen after they found it in the wreckage."

He looked directly at Ashe. The words weren't sharp, but his eyes were. Walking past everyone, Ryan took a seat at the far end of the table. Grace followed, perching beside him, her gaze locked on his face with a soft sort of reverence.

Ashe forced a smile. If he wanted to blame them for the car, fine. Let him.

"Let's go ahead and eat," Renae said, pulling open one of the pizza boxes. She grabbed a slice and, seeing no plates, dropped it directly on the table before cracking open a canned soda.

The others followed her lead, except Jericho, who sat still, hands resting on the edge of the table. Cole offered to grab Jericho something, but the burned man shook his head.

"Wouldn't stay down," he rasped.

Ryan bit into a slice, talking around the food. "Anyone gotten ahold of Pines?"

Ashe glanced up from their uneaten slice. "I tried before I got here. Still going to voicemail." They scanned the table, hoping someone else would contradict them. Heads shook.

"It's not like him," Jericho said, his voice rough but steady, drawing every eye at the table. "After what happened on the mountain, and how important he said you all were... he should be checking in."

The room went still. Several people stopped mid-chew.

Jericho looked around the table and frowned. "What? He didn't tell you about the vision?"

That got a ripple of confused reactions.

"What vision?"

"From whom?"

"What are you talking about?"

Jericho held up both scarred hands. "Pines said my pack was supposed to watch over you until he got back. That's all I knew. He was worried that Tzelut's agents might discover what you are. If you stayed quiet, maybe they wouldn't find you."

He coughed hard, a wet, tearing sound, and Cole passed him a napkin. Jericho spit into it, then pressed it to his mouth, wiping away the green-red mucus that settled on his lips.

Cole ducked into the kitchen, quickly returning with a red plastic cup of ice water and a stack of paper towels. Jericho took them wordlessly, sipping carefully.

Ashe caught the embarrassed look and realized Ryan probably hadn't expected anyone to find the Solo cups. Maybe they were leftovers from parties he hadn't wanted to clean up after, or remnants from a different life before the fancy house.

Jericho paused to breathe, fingers curled tight around the cup. Everyone waited. The food sat forgotten.

"I don't know what The Seer told him," he said at last. "Only that something was coming. Something big. It would wound Gaia so deeply the land might never recover."

A long silence followed.

"Who is Tzelut?" Cole asked.

Jericho took a shallow breath, his good eye steady on Cole. "Tzelut isn't a person. It's not even really a spirit. It's a rot."

He shifted in his seat, the movement making his scarred skin twitch. "There used to be balance. Gaia gave nature life. Nature spirits moved through the wild, tending to her creation. But when humans stopped living as part of the earth and started carving it up, something else started feeding. Greed. Rage. All the ugliness people pretend they don't carry."

He coughed once, then continued, voice low. "Tzelut was born from that. The worst parts of mankind given form. It crawled up from the roots and sank into the bones of the earth. Now it spreads through anything that lets it in. People. Animals. Even places. It twists them. Uses them."

He glanced toward the window, distant. "It doesn't just want death. It wants to repurpose. Corrupt. Make the world unrecognizable. So that nothing sacred survives."

The words settled over the table like a weight. Ashe could see it in everyone's faces. The same realization hit them all at once. They weren't just dealing with monsters. They were dealing with something that wanted to unmake everything.

Ryan stood abruptly, pushing his chair back with a screech. "And this seer guy said we're supposed to stop that?" he snapped.

Jericho's good eye didn't waver. "Pines never said you were supposed to stop it. Only that you were important."

"Come on," Ryan continued, more frustrated. "We've barely learned how to shift. Most of us don't even know what we are." His voice was growing sharper now. "We've known about Gaia for, what, less than two weeks? How the hell are we supposed to fight something that eats corpses and grows arms out of its stomach?"

"Hit it with a car," Grace said, her eyes daring anyone to argue.

Ryan cracked a grin, despite himself.

If Jericho looked annoyed at the outburst, he didn't show it. He simply let the room settle before continuing. "That skin job you fought at the brewery was a limb of it. A piece of Fäulung. You feed it your fear, your pain, your guilt... and it gives you power. But it always takes more than it gives. And eventually, there's none of you left."

Multiple voices rose at once. Questions, denial, fear disguised as outrage. Jericho tried to respond, but another coughing fit overtook him, violent and deep.

Ashe's phone buzzed against the table. They looked down and froze.

PINES – INCOMING CALL

"Quiet," Ashe said quickly, sliding the phone to the table's center and answering on speaker.

The voice on the other end was strained and panting. "Ashe... listen... I don't have much time."

Ice slid through Ashe.

"They got me," Pines said. "I escaped, but I'm still being followed. I'm hiding out now."

No one at the table spoke. Even Jericho covered his mouth to control his hacking.

"Uh... what can we do?" Ashe asked. Their voice felt small, thin. But the others had gone still, waiting, and they didn't want the silence to stretch.

"Are all of you safe?" Pines asked. "I heard the Huntsville Pack was attacked."

Jericho's gaze dropped to the table. His face was unreadable beneath the scars.

"We're okay," Ashe said. "Where are you? We can come get you."

There was a pause. They couldn't hear anything except the shallow, uneven breaths over the line. Then, faint movement. Followed by a rustling wind.

"It's not safe to come to me," Pines said finally. "Are you all together?"

"Yeah," Ashe answered. "We're here now."

"Good. Tell me where you are. I'll come to you."

Jericho waved at Ashe from across the table and shook his head slowly.

Ashe muted the call. "What?"

"Something's wrong," Jericho whispered. "Tell him you're at his house."

He doubled over in another coughing fit, spraying flecks of blood onto the pristine table.

Ashe waited until it passed. Then, unmuted, careful to keep their voice neutral. "We're at your place; we didn't know where else to go."

On the other end, Pines exhaled a deep, shaky breath. "Good. Good. You need to come back up to Monte Sano Mountain."

He rattled off an address. Cole punched it into his phone without comment.

Ryan had quietly moved closer, now seated beside them. Grace stood behind him, brows knit in concentration. Everyone wore the same expression.

Worry. Fear.

Renae leaned forward. "We can be there. But I'm still recovering. I can barely move. Could you come here instead?"

The line was quiet. For a moment, Ashe wondered if it had disconnected.

Then his voice returned. "It'll take me a few days to get back to town. You should be healed by then. Meet me at the address. I have to go before they find me."

The call ended.

No one moved. Ashe stared at the dark screen, willing it to light up again with some explanation. Some correction. Anything.

Cole's jaw was tight, his hands flat on the table like he was bracing for impact. Renae had gone still in a way that reminded Ashe of Grace. Predator-still, calculating. Ryan glanced between them, waiting for someone else to say what they were all thinking.

Grace was the only one watching Jericho. Her amber eyes tracked his face, reading something the rest of them couldn't see.

The silence stretched until it hurt.

Jericho broke it. "Even if they knew where he lived, they couldn't strike the house directly. There were wards on this property. Old ones. His first suggestion should have been to meet there."

"So something happened to him," Ryan said, turning toward Renae. "What do we do now?"

Jericho doubled over again, coughing harder. Scabs along his neck split open, and blood welled up through the fresh cracks. Cole moved quickly, catching his arm and easing him back into the chair.

"Cole," Renae said gently, "can you help him lie down somewhere?"

Cole nodded and helped Jericho up, steadying him under the shoulder. Ryan joined them, leading the way to a room down the hall.

When the footsteps faded, Renae turned to the others. Her face was set.

"We can't trust anyone but the five of us. Do you both agree?"

Grace nodded immediately. Ashe followed a beat later, slower.

Renae's voice softened slightly. "When Cole and Ryan get back, we'll make a plan. Everyone gets a say. We work as a pack. That means setting some things aside."

Ashe glanced down the hall, then back at her. They nodded again. More firmly this time.

Ryan was still a problem, but not the kind they had to fear. He didn't understand Ashe. Ashe didn't understand him. But he'd thrown himself into danger for the rest of them. Ashe hadn't forgotten that. Cole and Ryan returned, and all five sat close to each other.

Renae glanced at each of them in turn. "Pines told us we were either for Gaia or we would be left out alone." She hesitated, breathing in deep. "I still don't know what I'll choose. I have been screwed over by people like Pines and Jericho."

Different expressions crossed the group, each reacting to Renae's harsh words.

The older woman pressed on, her voice softer now. "But I won't leave you. I'm in this for us. We figure out what the hell is going on and stop what's coming after us. I don't think we will ever be safe until we do that."

"We also need to find Pines and rescue him," Cole said. "Even if you don't like him, he cared for us, and if he is still alive, I'm not going to abandon him."

Ashe agreed. They understood Renae's resentment, but the old man was their guide into this new world. They weren't going to let that go.

Renae nodded, though a bit reluctantly.

"Here's everyone's chance to walk away," she said, gesturing toward the front door. "If you don't want to be part of this, there's the exit." She studied each person, who in turn gave their assent.

The last was Ryan, who just smirked. "It's my house."

Taking that as agreement, Renae said, "Okay, let's figure out what we need to do."

Ashe was still afraid of what lay ahead. But under the weight of that fear, something solid had taken root. Not hope exactly. But the quiet certainty that these people wouldn't leave them behind.

Since coming out. Since everything had changed, it had been hard to imagine anything like a sense of belonging again. But here, maybe, there was the beginning of something close.

Chapter 18

Steam hissed from the poker as it plunged into flesh.

The rod glowed faintly orange at the tip, sizzling through skin and muscle until it struck bone. Pines screamed. Again. And this time he didn't bother to muffle it. He had no dignity left to preserve.

The thing standing over him had broken him days ago.

Or maybe it had been weeks. The overhead light was always on, with no windows to mark the passage of time.

Stupid old man. The thought was worn thin from repetition.

After telling Jericho's pack about the mess on the mountain and that he'd be sending some new pack members to meet, he had taken off for Nashville. He remembered The Seer's brownstone burned to the ground, the scent of Fäulung still in the walls. He should have turned back then.

Instead, he got on the road south. While turning off I-24, a semi-truck had t-boned his van. The impact had crumpled metal and bone alike. If not for Gaia's touch, he would have died on the spot.

He remembered the red light. The glass in his mouth. And the voices. They hadn't been asking if he was okay. They had been dragging him out of the wreck.

When he came to again, he was a slab of meat in a cold grey room. His naked body shivered. Pain and cold made thought impossible. His vision was blurred, but he was able to make out a deformed figure standing in front of him. Its body shape was wrong, and it reeked of decay.

Pines had first thought it was Witherbound, a piece of Fäulung. It would have made sense, seeing what they had done to the Banewolf and the same scent in Nashville.

However, when the figure stepped closer to him, it had sneered, showing two three-inch hooked fangs. Those fangs weren't just for piercing. The back of the fang was edged, as sharp as a box cutter, meant to rend the flesh of those who struggled.

This was a vampire. Pure alien evil.

Pines' vision cleared as he worked to focus his mind. He had seen this one in old photos. Had heard its name mentioned in council meetings. *Lugh the Judge.*

This was not one of Tzelut's tools. It was something older. Something that tolerated Tzelut because their hungers briefly aligned. And while vampires were supposedly immortal, time always took its toll.

The irises were milky white, and parts of its flesh had fallen away, exposing dried muscle and blackened bone. One arm hung shriveled and limp, the other missing a finger. He wore stained purple scrubs that barely concealed the emaciated form beneath.

"I require your cooperation," Lugh had said the first day. Then he drove a blade into Pines' forearm, nearly severing the bone. It had never left Pines' side until he gave it what it wanted.

All it had asked was for the pin to Pines' phone. It was a small request, and after hours of nonstop pain his mind had broken for just a moment. He relented and gave the eight-digit number.

The day he met his wife.

He could still see her. Red dress. Borrowed heels she'd complained about all night. The way she'd laughed when he spilled wine on his only good shirt. That laugh had saved him more times than Gaia ever had.

And now that date, that memory, belonged to the thing standing over him.

Since then, it seemed the creature was just having fun. It had stopped asking questions once it had gotten what it needed.

Tears welled in Pines' eyes as he stared up at the stainless-steel ceiling.

He lay on a rough surface, possibly jagged stone. The silver metal restraints attached to the slab had been set to just barely touch his skin if he moved.

He did not know where he was; he could not sense the spirit of nature. The absence was worse than the pain. Like being buried alive in a place Gaia couldn't reach. All he could feel was cold and torment.

The poker pulled free with a wet slurp.

The Judge set it down on a side table. The point still glowed faintly, blackening the wood where it touched.

Then he turned and gently brushed Pines' face with his malformed hand.

"We have the first names of your new pack," the vampire said. "All I need now are surnames. Give me that, and I'll leave you alone for one full hour."

It even tried to smile. The gesture only made Pines shake harder.

First names were bad enough. But surnames meant addresses. Records. Families. It meant leading this thing straight to five people who didn't even know what was hunting them.

He tried to hold onto his wife. The crooked smile she got when she knew she had already won, when his defenses had failed and he hadn't even noticed. But she was fading, slipping away as the vampire leaned closer, its breath cold and rotten against his cheek. The memory scattered like smoke.

Steeling himself, the Lycan turned away from his torturer. He didn't risk speaking as he feared what would come out of his mouth.

Pines would die on this table before he gave them that.

He hoped.

"Oh, I am sorry, wolf. I have not done an adequate job of domesticating you. I promise I will redouble my efforts to make up for my leniency."

The vampire picked up a hooked blade from the table. A modified utility knife.

It began to cut.

Long, deliberate swaths from Pines' upper arm, down past the elbow. Skin parted under the blade, the edge whispering through flesh. There was no elegance in it. Just pain, raw and unrelenting.

Pines screamed until his throat bled and sound gave out.

Then he kept screaming in silence.

Chapter 19

Ryan's house became their den. None of them said it out loud, but no one wanted to be alone. Their host offered his spare bedrooms, but only one had actual furniture. Unfortunately, that room was currently occupied by Jericho. When Grace announced she'd be sharing the main bedroom with Ryan, he promptly suggested that maybe Cole and he should take the bed instead. Ashe and Renae volunteered to stay downstairs in the vacant den.

While discussing their next steps the previous day, Cole had tossed a blood-soaked plastic bag onto the table. It held the items Grace had scavenged from the bodies at the brewery. Digging through the mess, he'd found a direct deposit slip from a private security firm.

The name meant nothing to the pack, but when they brought it to Jericho, the burned man nodded grimly. He said the firm worked exclusively with Dum-Prot Land Inc. The same development company the Huntsville Pack had already flagged.

According to Jericho, they'd quietly purchased several parcels of land that had once been state-protected. Forest tracts, wetlands, zones once labeled sacred or endangered, were slated for upscale housing.

He also let them know he'd reached out to the Birmingham pack. Once they finished whatever they were tangled in, they'd send help north. Jericho figured reinforcements might arrive in a few weeks.

The group tried to press him for more, but Jericho clammed up. He warned them not to dig further. Not yet. If Dum-Prot Land was behind the attack on his pack, then they were very dangerous. He stressed Pines had wanted Ashe and the others to stay low when he left and Jericho wasn't going to go against his wishes.

Later that night, Ashe started poking around online. Dum-Prot's website was polished, filled with drone shots of pristine homes, happy families, and lush green lawns. Their page boasted of "community-forward construction," "sustainable integration," and "luxury that lasts." They listed dozens of current projects across Madison County, but no specific addresses or site maps.

Buried at the bottom of the page was a quiet ad for a part-time graphic designer in Dum-Prot's Huntsville office. On a whim, Ashe sent in an application. Pines' and Jericho's warnings about keeping a low profile were fresh in their mind. But really, what could be safer than a corporate job? Either way, they didn't expect to hear back, yet the chance to slip a foot inside the company was tempting.

Searching beyond the company site, Ashe found most of its press was pure fluff. Puff pieces from local outlets that read like they came straight from the same PR firm. Each praised Dum-Prot's environmental ethics and employee wellness initiatives. Ashe skimmed them with growing disgust.

But buried on the second page of search results was something different. A short editorial from an environmental watchdog group. It criticized Dum-Prot for acquiring large tracts of land around the North Alabama Nature Preserve, as well as parcels once managed by the state conservation office. If they really cared about sustainability, why were they edging in on critical biodiversity zones?

The next morning, the group rose early, finished the last of the pizza, and finalized their plan. Ashe and Renae would head to the Madison County records office to uncover actual locations tied to Dum-Prot Land. Cole, Ryan, and Grace would return to the Grove Pines had shown them, hoping to spot anything the Huntsville pack might have missed.

Cole initially protested, insisting someone should stay and watch Jericho. But Ryan reminded him that Jericho was probably the safest among them, tucked away in bed, surrounded by silence and a ten thousand dollar security system. They were the ones who still needed protecting.

As Ashe and Renae were preparing to leave in Renae's small hybrid, Ryan jogged up and tapped on Ashe's window.

"Hey, we need your keys," he said, eyes lowered.

"Use one of the other cars," Ashe replied, a little too defensively.

"Cole's girlfriend has his, and Grace's ran off chasing a squirrel halfway through a U-turn."

The last thing Ashe wanted to do was hand someone else their keys. Especially to Ryan.

"You've got a four-car garage, and not one backup muscle car or tricked-out pickup?"

"Sold them." Ryan's grin faded.

A set of keys bounced off his chest, and he caught them with practiced ease. Both he and Ashe looked over to see Renae already walking toward the RAV4's passenger door.

She glanced back at Ashe. "Ready when you are."

**

Both groups pulled out, splitting at the intersection. One headed toward the chaos of the city. The other toward the mountain's silence.

Ashe couldn't help feeling a little envious of the latter. The Wolf Spirit grew restless in their chest, scraping against the boundaries of flesh and patience. They feared it might soon force its way free.

The morning air hadn't yet succumbed to the swelter of the Alabama sun, but the SUV was already stuffy. Even without A/C, Renae hadn't complained. She simply rolled down the window and let the wind stream through.

"My first car was a Chevy Chevette, which was basically a metal box with an engine. This is a luxury car in comparison," Renae had explained.

As they drove, their conversation drifted to life before the First Tearing. Renae asked the right number of questions and knew when to let a silence speak for itself. Ashe found themself opening up more than expected and regretted not having talked to her sooner.

Truth be told, Ashe had avoided bonding with Renae. She was nearing sixty, and Ashe had grown used to hostility from older people since coming out as nonbinary. It wasn't fair, but the fear had hardened into assumption. They'd told themself it was protection. Prejudice as armor, protection with a cost.

The bruised RAV4 rolled into the courthouse's underground parking. Ashe turned off the ignition, only for the engine to sputter and rattle like it was trying to escape its own bolts before finally stalling out. They leaned their head against the wheel and muttered a quick prayer to the gods of combustion that the SUV would still start when they returned.

They had ten minutes before the building opened to the public. Renae quietly pulled her pistol from her waistband and stashed it in the glove box. Ashe watched her, brow raised.

"Why didn't we just break in at night?" they asked.

Renae gave them a sideways look. "Do you know what kind of security this place has? Whether it's alarmed? Patrolled? Can you pick locks, or were you just going to rip the doors open with brute force and murder everyone you saw?"

"I probably could," Ashe muttered.

Renae shot them an exasperated look.

"Okay, okay, I get it," Ashe said, blowing out a raspberry. "So what's our cover? Are you working for the city commissioner, and I'm your stylishly disheveled intern?"

"We're two citizens looking at public records," Renae said, already stepping out of the car.

"That feels kind of... underwhelming," Ashe replied, following her toward the entrance.

"Exactly," Renae said. "You'd be amazed what passes under the radar when everyone's too bored to look."

The courthouse was an eight-story structure with glass panels forming a boxy skeleton around a vast atrium. Passing through the metal detector made Ashe feel slightly more at ease, though their nerves remained taut. For a moment, they'd imagined something more sinister. A supernatural scanner humming with hidden energy instead of a machine built to catch guns and knives.

They followed Renae toward the elevators, Ashe admiring her confidence. Shoulders squared. Steps precise. She moved as if she belonged. Especially in her navy slacks and matching blazer.

Ashe, on the other hand, was wearing a white tank top with a hole in the hem and purple capris that had seen too many washes. They'd also skipped a shower, not understanding how Ryan's fancy shower turned on. No wonder Renae kept walking a few paces ahead.

On the third floor, they approached a simple wooden door labeled "RECORDS." Renae opened it without hesitation, and Ashe followed close behind.

She had been right. All it took was a polite request and a valid ID. The woman behind the desk, with a nameplate that read **LINDA,** showed them to a side office and handed over four cardboard tubes filled with maps, permits, and zoning documents.

"Dum-Prot Land, huh?" the woman said as she set down the last tube. "That's been a popular request lately. Are they under investigation?"

Renae kept her expression neutral. "Oh? Other people asked for these?"

"Couple different folks over the past few weeks. Environmental groups, I think. Maybe some lawyers." Linda happily shrugged. "None of my business, really."

After she left, Ashe caught Renae's eye. "Popular request," they whispered.

"Jericho said they were looking into the company," Renae replied, but her jaw had tightened. "Let's see if there's anything interesting."

They divided the tubes and got to work, scribbling notes on locations, red flags, and anything that felt out of place. But now every sound from the hallway made Ashe's shoulders tense. Every time footsteps paused outside their door, they glanced up from the documents.

The government worker returned twice: once with additional files they'd requested, once to check if they needed anything else. Each time, Ashe felt her eyes linger a beat too long. Was she memorizing their faces? Taking note of which documents they were focusing on?

"She's watching us," Ashe muttered during Linda's second visit.

Renae barely looked up from a zoning permit. "She's doing her job."

But when Ashe glanced toward the doorway twenty minutes later, Linda was standing at the far end of the hall, pretending to organize files while stealing looks in their direction. Their eyes met for a split second before she quickly turned away. They kept her in their peripheral vision, just in case, but forced themself not to overreact. Maybe Renae was right, and she was just bored. Still, Ashe never turned their back.

After a couple of hours, the lines and signatures on the documents started blurring together. Ashe leaned back in the office chair and glanced at their phone, scrolling messages out of habit. One new email caught their attention: **HR@Dum-Prot_Land.com.** Ashe blinked.

"Huh," they said aloud.

Renae looked up from her stack. "What is it?"

"I just got a request to schedule an interview for the graphic design position. For today."

Renae raised an eyebrow. "They want to schedule an interview on the same day they received your application?"

"Maybe they're desperate," Ashe offered, though they didn't believe it. In Huntsville, where competition was high and design work scarce, the hiring process was usually glacial. That uncertainty had been one of many reasons they'd considered leaving town after being let go from Marshall Space Flight Center.

Now, a company was pressing for a same-day interview. It made Ashe's skin itch. Their instincts screamed it was bait, something set and waiting to snap.

But the counterargument slipped in just as quickly: it was a part-time position. Who would set a trap for something that trivial? If Dum-Prot had any idea who they really were, they doubted they would have reached Ryan's. And that sliver of logic, flimsy as it was, was enough to make them keep reading.

"What do you want to do?" Renae asked. Her voice was neutral, but Ashe caught the tension beneath it. She wanted intel. But she didn't want Ashe walking into a trap.

"I'm already confirming the time," Ashe replied, clicking through the scheduling link. "One-thirty."

Then they looked down at their clothes.

Renae took one look at Ashe, then at the clock and sighed. There was no time to go back to Ashe's house. With the same quiet efficiency she applied to everything, she walked to the window and closed the blinds. Then she began undressing.

"Come on," Renae said, motioning toward the documents. "We still need to photograph the rest of these before we return them."

Double-checking to ensure Linda wasn't getting a show, Ashe followed Renae's lead. They made a mental note that if they were going to do spy stuff in the future, they were going to need a fancier wardrobe.

***

Sweat gathered at the base of Cole's neck despite the cool air running through the small car. The last time they were on this mountain, it had taken Pines, Ashe, and Renae working in tandem to keep the pack alive. He hoped that returning during the day would make things less dangerous.

At least Grace was with them.

He glanced at the back seat. She sat with her eyes wide, scanning the trees and ridgelines with quiet reverence. Her posture was looser than he'd ever seen, her shoulders slack, chest rising and falling with ease.

She was coming home.

"Do you live up here?" Cole asked, hoping to coax more from the quiet wolf. It couldn't be easy being away from her home in a strange new body.

"Yes. My den is there," she said, pointing toward a deep wooded stretch farther up the mountain.

"I didn't think wolves lived around here anymore," Ryan said, peering out the window.

"I live here," Grace corrected, the words firm.

"I think he means wild wolves aren't exactly common around here," Cole offered. "Were you born up here, or did you find this place later?"

Her reply came without hesitation, though something frayed beneath the surface. "Taken."

Both men turned to face her. She didn't meet their eyes. Her gaze stayed fixed on the scenery outside. When she spoke, it was in a flat tone, but underneath, the words came from a place that hadn't healed.

She told them about her life before Monte Sano.

Taken from her den as a cub. Stolen. Not adopted. Not rescued. A man had kept her in a pen behind his house. A zoo in name alone. His yard was lined with cages full of other wild animals, either bought or captured.

"It smelled like old beer and rotting meat," she said. "People laughed at us. Took pictures. Tossed food. Sometimes rocks. I was too scared to growl."

Cole's teeth ground at the words. Ryan had gone still beside him.

"One night he came home drunk," she continued. "Said we hadn't earned enough. Opened my cage. Hit me." There was a pause. Her eyes remained locked on the treetops outside the car, but her voice slipped a little.

"He always hit the ones who didn't make him money."

Cole wanted to say something, *anything*. But nothing would have helped. His gut twisted, heat rising to his face. Not from shame, but from the weight of her survival pressing down on the car's interior.

"I bit him. Got away. I ran until my legs gave out." She stopped. The hum of the road filled the space for a moment. Cole looked in the rearview mirror and saw that her eyes were no longer wide but had narrowed in bitter fury.

"Didn't know where to go," she murmured. "I slept under parked cars. Coyotes hunted me."

She blinked slowly. "I forgot what clean water tasted like."

No one spoke.

"You're here now," Cole spoke, unsure if the words were meant for her or himself. "You made it out."

Grace said nothing more. Whatever had opened inside her, she let it close again. The other two didn't push. But Cole noticed, as the silence settled in, that Ryan quietly reached back and took her hand. He didn't say a word. Just held it the rest of the way up the mountain.

When they reached the trailhead parking lot and looked for an open spot, they managed to slip into a space just as another car backed out. Though it was late July, the canopy kept the air cooler than expected.

Dressed in loose clothing and ready to Veil, they stepped into the woods. Unlike the tense stillness of their last visit, the forest now hummed with motion. Birds flitting between branches. Insects droning in the undergrowth. A chorus of life.

A pleasant scent of damp earth and green settled in Cole's chest. The trail bustled with weekend activity. Hikers chatted as they passed, couples stopped for selfies by scenic overlooks, and the occasional trail runner jogged by with a polite "on your left."

Grace studied each passerby with narrow-eyed interest, giving each a quick sniff as they passed. At first it had been funny until a red-faced woman noticed Grace leaning too close to her husband and threatened to "start somethin'."

With practiced ease, Ryan defused the tension, offering a compliment, a joke, and just enough Southern charm to make her laugh. He gently caught Grace around the waist, and the three Lycans slipped away before the woman could reconsider.

Again, Ryan dominated the conversation on the trail, rambling about childhood four-wheeling trips and romantic hikes that ended in disaster or laughter. Cole watched Grace drink in every word.

The developing dynamic between them unsettled Cole, though he couldn't pinpoint why. Ashe had mentioned Grace's sudden attention toward Ryan after the fight, and now Cole was witnessing it firsthand. Her intense focus on Ryan felt different from normal human interest.

She looked human. Right now she was human. But Grace had lived as a wolf for years before her First Tearing. What did she understand about human relationships? About boundaries, consent, the slow build of genuine connection?

Was Grace's interest in Ryan instinctual? Or was it real human emotions she was still learning to navigate? He realized he had no framework for this. They were all too new to know about Lycan traditions around human relationships. Were there protocols? Taboos?

If Ryan noticed her piercing stare, he didn't show it. Perhaps he just didn't know what to do with the attention. Cole had heard him say before that women hit on him all the time, so maybe this didn't register as anything unusual.

Cole's mind was still turning over Grace and Ryan's dynamic when he would have walked straight past the turnoff. The spot where Pines had led them off the main trail was nearly invisible in daylight.

But then he felt it. A tug low in his chest. Something unseen pulled at him, drawing him away from the path and into the unknown. He veered without hesitation. Grace followed immediately. Even dulled in her human form, her memory of this terrain ran deep.

Voices called from the trail behind them, warning them to stay on the marked path. Good Samaritans with good intentions. But no one followed. The shouts faded, swallowed by the trees.

Even the sounds of nature seemed to stop. As if the birds and insects had chosen to remain behind with the humans. Only the occasional snap of a twig or crunch of leaves broke the silence ahead.

Still, Ryan continued his stories, rambling about a place nearby he used to go to that had a mysterious hole that ran down for miles. His voice never lost the casual energy from the trail.

They hiked along rugged terrain, guided by the pull in Cole's chest. It was hard to gauge how long they had been going before he felt it. A presence behind the trees. Eyes without a face. Watching.

Ryan's voice trailed off mid-sentence. He looked down and focused on his footing. Even Grace, who should have been at ease here, clutched the hem of her shirt, ready to Veil the moment something shifted.

Yet this didn't feel malevolent.

It felt like a sentinel. Watching them. Weighing the strangers in its territory. As they moved deeper into the woods, the presence thickened. Choking the three with invisible hands.

The tug in his chest vibrated with something else. Memory, maybe? A flicker of the first night the pack had gathered on the mountain. But this wasn't the pack link. It was messier. Older. Primal.

Another memory flashed. Cole's voice lifting into the trees, Ashe calling him The Indigo Jay, their smile lighting up something inside him. That feeling of being recognized and heard. Joy and serenity, tangled together.

The song started softly. A whisper against the hush. It was one of his most popular songs. About running from your problems only to find they've circled back to greet you. He'd written it before he had fans, before he had studio time, before he believed he could make this a career. It had been the turning point.

Behind him, Ryan's voice joined in. The chorus lifted together, two melodies woven into the quiet. Cole glanced back to find Ryan smiling as he harmonized. He'd never said he listened to Cole's music. Maybe he'd downloaded it out of curiosity.

The final note lingered long and strong. Cole poured everything into it. Grief. Love. Trust. He didn't know who he was singing to. Maybe the land. Maybe something beneath it. But the forest listened.

Then the world stirred.

A single bird chirped. Then another. Then dozens. A ripple of sound swept outward, a bright, urgent rustle that pulled the rest of the woods out of hiding.

"They welcome us," Grace said. Her arms spread, her face open and radiant with the returning soundscape.

Ryan, more cautious, leaned in close. "What just happened?"

"I don't know," Cole whispered, a tear slipping down his cheek. "But listen."

Ryan began to protest, but Cole shushed him and pointed into the trees. He followed Cole's finger, and his jaw went slack.

The birds weren't just singing. They were singing Cole's song.

Chapter 20

The building looked harmless.

A squat, three-story square wrapped in tan and white brick. One corner glinted with reflective windows, angled toward a deep blue pond surrounded by hemlocks and pines. From a distance, the reflection from the windows created an illusion of wilderness, as if the building were nestled in nature.

Ashe had to admit it was a pretty cool effect.

The RAV4 sat parked toward the back of the lot, close to the main road. Renae and Ashe had both argued about whether parking up close or further away made more sense. Ashe had won, mostly by virtue of being behind the wheel.

Now the two pack members sat in the afternoon heat, trying to evaluate the threat before them. There were no signs of danger. No sign of rot bleeding from the bricks. No stench of decay, no guard patrols or cameras tracking their every move.

Just silence and the low buzz of air conditioning units.

But Renae stayed tense, her fingers tapping the door in a slow, erratic rhythm. The older woman continued the argument that Ashe shouldn't go in alone.

"You coming in as my mom?" Ashe countered. "Making sure I do well in my job interview."

Renae gave them a flat look but didn't dignify it with a reply.

Ashe was afraid that if they didn't do this now, they never would. With a steadying breath, they opened the door. Summer heat hit them like a collapsing wall.

Renae slid into the driver's seat and reached out, gripping Ashe's arm. "Yell if you're in trouble. I'll drive through the damn building if I have to."

Ashe nodded and stepped free of her hand.

The burner phone they'd picked up on the way here lit up, and Ashe dialed Renae's number. She answered without a word and held up the screen in acknowledgment. With the call active, Ashe slipped the phone into the bottom pocket of the tight blazer.

The walk to the entrance dragged under the afternoon sun. The decision to park far had seemed clever, but the lot's pale pavement reflected the heat like a griddle. Sweat gathered quickly at the small of their back.

A dozen conflicting feelings churned. Pines possibly being kidnapped. The Wolf Spirit's constant pull, scratching to be released. The uncertainty of walking into the mouth of an enemy alone.

And beneath it all, the fear they weren't strong enough. That they couldn't protect the people they'd grown close to.

Hunt. Protect. Kill. The Warhide stirred beneath the surface.

"Breathe," they whispered. Shading their eyes, they focused on their surroundings.

At each end of the lot stood crape myrtles in full bloom, their white blossoms spaced with uncanny symmetry. The surrounding mulch was dark, uniform, and placed without gaps or weeds. Every branch trimmed. Every patch of shredded bark arranged.

Nature tamed by man.

But real nature wasn't orderly. Ashe knew that from their own garden. Real soil bred rot, insects, decomposition, and life. Weeds always found a way in. Trees dropped limbs, and animals dug through bushes, leaving dead patches behind. Nature was stubborn. Messy. Alive.

And this? This was a pretender wearing its skin.

The thought gave Ashe comfort. If they could see through this lie, they could see through whatever trap waited inside.

They pushed the wolf down and stepped through the glass doors.

Inside, a woman in her forties greeted them from behind the front desk. She had a broad frame, a warm smile, and an accent as thick as the humidity outside.

"Hi there," she said, her voice twanging. "You must be Ashe. Mr. Damon's real excited you could make it on such short notice. Want a cookie or some coffee?"

Ashe raised a brow. *Throwing it on a little thick, aren't you?*

"No thank you, ma'am."

The woman frowned briefly, but then chuckled. "Well, alright, suga. Just take a seat, and the big man'll be down in a bit."

Ashe eased into one of the overstuffed chairs, trying to ignore the buttery scent of cookies drifting in from somewhere nearby. They scanned the lobby for design elements they could genuinely compliment during the interview. It would help establish their credibility as a graphic designer rather than an obvious intruder.

But the more they looked, the more unsettling everything became. Every detail in the lobby felt deliberate, almost obsessive. Carpet in labyrinthine swirls of grey and black, not a single thread out of place. Chairs lined the wall, each precisely spaced and untouched. The air was chilled against the summer heat and laced with synthetic citrus and linen.

Photos hung on every wall. Staged forests. Model homes. Corporate retreats. But none showed people. Even the art, geometric patterns in soft earth tones, seemed curated to calm without connection. Its beauty was engineered, polished to perfection and utterly devoid of life.

The sterile perfection was broken by movement as a heavyset man emerged from the back hallway, wearing a bright green shirt with Dum-Prot Land stitched across the chest. His dense black beard framed a wide grin, and he moved with purpose, each step brisk and assured.

"Hey-ya, Ashe," he said with an easy grin, voice upbeat and hand outstretched with practiced charm. "I'm Damon. Hope I didn't keep you waiting too long."

They knew better than to trust him, but southern politeness ran too deep. The shake was over before Ashe even registered the choice. His grip was firm. Polished. Practiced.

"You sure you don't want a cookie before we go up?" he asked. "Everyone takes one." He added, "Folks who say no usually regret it later."

"Uh, no thank you, sir."

He laughed. "Sir, huh? Gotta say I like someone who knows how to show the proper respect." He waved them on and headed toward a lone elevator at the back of the hall.

As they walked, every door shut before Ashe could peek inside. It was difficult to chalk it up to coincidence. A man stepped from a side hall, caught sight of Ashe and Damon, and froze. His face betrayed nothing, yet he pivoted and retreated, as though some warning had brushed across his memory.

This is what you wanted, Ashe reminded themself, keeping their expression neutral as they walked.

The elevator carried them to the third floor. Damon led them through a series of winding halls to a door marked **Branch Manager**. With a flourish, he opened it and gestured for Ashe to enter.

They were immediately put on edge by the space: a small room, ten by ten at most, but immaculately kept. Faux leather chairs, a pale wooden desk, and a corner window completed the upper middle management aesthetic. Ashe had learned to distrust people in rooms like this, administrators who used policies as weapons and hid cruelty behind procedure. What concerned them more was that the Wolf Spirit was quiet. Since they had been marked by Gaia, the wolf had been a constant presence. Eager to take control. Pressuring Ashe to hunt. Now, there was no growling or pacing. It was resting, distant, as if unconcerned.

Ashe tried to focus on the situation at hand. "Thanks again for inviting me on such short notice. I've been following your work and would love the chance to be part of it."

"We're so glad you could come in so quickly. We usually like to keep things movin'. Less time for people to change their minds." He chuckled at his odd joke and followed Ashe inside.

The door clicked shut behind him with a mechanical hum as it locked. From the corner window, Ashe caught sight of the RAV4 at the far end of the parking lot. Though sun glare on the windshield prevented them from seeing inside, knowing Renae was there steadied them.

"Please sit down," Damon offered. He continued forward behind the desk, resting his large frame in a rich brown leather office chair.

Ashe sat, opening their interview folder. "I've worked with several national brands on logo design and site layout. I'd be happy to show you some of my portfolio."

Damon waved away the folder, pulling out his own.

"I saw it on your résumé," he said, flipping through some pages. "Very impressive. I am curious about one thing, though." He never looked up but they could still feel something eyeing them from behind the folder.

"Ashe," he said, voice softening. "That's a chosen name, right? Folks like you usually pick theirs." The smile on his face didn't falter. But something underneath it shifted.

"People like me?" The words hit like a slap. Ashe's face flushed as they sat up straighter. "What do you mean, people like me?"

Damon gave a sympathetic wince. "Free spirits," he said. "Those who don't conform. Don't fall in line with the sheep. I like that. You think for yourself. I can see it."

Ashe didn't answer. They wanted to get off this topic as quickly as possible.

"I'd like to discuss the position," they said, forcing composure into their voice. "And maybe a tour, if that's possible."

It sounded clunky the moment it left their mouth. Too eager. Too rehearsed.

"Oh, I'm sure we'll get you that tour," Damon said, his tone dipping. "But for now, I'd rather talk about you." He set the folder on the table and casually leaned back.

"For instance, how long have you been a Lycan?"

The blood drained from Ashe's face. So much for playing it cool.

They reached for the Grayskin form, maybe they could beat some answers out of this smug bastard. Nothing. They tried to tap into the memory of that first transformation: the violation they'd felt when Ryan forced his kiss on them, how rage and helplessness had called forth something different from their usual Warhide. Rage surged through them now. But the Wolf Spirit didn't respond to the familiar trigger. It still felt sedated, far away.

Damon never flinched. His smile never wavered.

"You tried to call the wolf," he said. "I saw it on your face. But it's quiet in here. Funny, ain't it?"

Shock flickered across Ashe's face. They suppressed it quickly but he'd already seen it.

"Yeah, we know," Damon boasted, leaning forward. "And if you thought you could go big bad wolf and eat me in here, you must be new. This building's warded against things like you."

He reached beneath the desk and pulled out a long, narrow silver blade, the handle loose in his hand.

"I'm guessing you already know what this does."

Ashe stood, placing the chair between them and Damon.

"Why are you coming after me and my pack?" They tried to look intimidating, and even without the wolf, three years of CrossFit gave them enough of a presence that most people now left them alone.

Damon didn't move. His face stayed relaxed, easy.

"Pack?" He let out a low chuckle. "Lord of Order and Darkness, you're really that gullible? These people aren't your pack, kid. They're not your friends."

Ashe opened their mouth to argue, but nothing came. They'd only met Cole, Renae, Grace, and Ryan a short while. They didn't really know them, not deeply. A flicker of doubt pulsed in their chest.

Damon went on, voice patient, persuasive. "The Lycans use people like you. And when you're burned up by their enemies, they toss your ashes to the wind."

His gaze sharpened. A curl of something cruel twisted his lip. "Seems like you picked a fitting name."

"Can't you just let us be?" The plea felt sickening in their mouth. It didn't feel like their words.

For the first time, Damon's face looked more sympathetic. "We weren't targeting you and your little group."

The doubt was stronger now. Ashe tried to dig for something. Anything to contradict what he said.

"You came after us. Your people shot at us. Your monsters tried to kill us. Whatever lies you're spinning, you started this."

Damon shrugged, smile widening. "You sure? Our shooter was meant to take out Pines."

Standing suddenly, Damon moved to the side of the desk. His stance still showed no attack posture, no concern. Ashe took a small step back, adjusting their stance.

"He's been recruiting eco-terrorists and hurting people. That 'monster' that attacked you was a werewolf who realized what the Lycans really are. You all attacked *us* at the brewery. We were only defending ourselves from the Huntsville pack before you ever showed up."

The doubt thickened, shifting into something heavier. Surrender.

They ran through the events of the past week. Ryan had stepped in front of Pines just before the shot. Maybe it really *was* meant for Pines. Sebastian *had* been a Lycan. Pines claimed he'd been corrupted, but also said Gaia's guardians couldn't be corrupted. Maybe Sebastian had seen something, or known something, that got him hurt by his own kind. And Ashe had been late to the brewery. They hadn't seen how it had started.

It all lined up too easily.

The Wolf Spirit had slunk away as something else crept in, whispering confirmation. Damon set the silver blade down on the desk.

"I'll make you a deal," he said, voice soft. "You leave us alone, and I'll tell the higher-ups to leave you and your friends alone."

He raised both hands in mock peace.

"You seem to be aware we've got Pines. I'm sorry, but you're not getting him back. Still, if you walk away now, we'll let the four of you go."

Four?

The number snagged on Ashe's thoughts, but their mind was too clouded to parse it. A burst of static crackled from their blazer. A voice followed, metallic and rough.

Renae.

"Ashe," she said, small but fierce. "You better not be buying this bullshit. Don't make me come in there and yank your ass out."

The fog lifted. Not fully, but enough. Ashe steadied themself.

"We both know we can't trust anything you say," they said, shoulders square and chest out. "You came after us. You're poisoning the land. Whatever you're doing here, it's wrong."

Damon's mask cracked. "Fine," he said, walking back behind the desk. "Let's see how you feel after the Judge gets its hands on you."

Ashe caught the flick of his hand beneath the desk and the soft click of something mechanical. Outside the window, they spotted the RAV4 creeping forward. Whatever was about to happen, Ashe didn't plan to wait for it.

They grabbed the chair in front of them and hurled it across the desk. The heavy wood cracked against Damon's chest, knocking him backward into the window.

Without hesitation, Ashe snatched the second chair and rammed it into the wall of glass. A crack splintered across its surface, but it didn't give. Gritting their teeth, they swung again. This time, harder. Wood splintered in their hands. The window cracked further but still held.

Damon groaned and rose to one knee.

"It's reinforced glass, moron," he spat. "You're not breaking it."

He stood and grabbed the blade from the desk. Ashe braced themself. Damon stepped forward. Quick. Unnatural. Relaxed.

Fine. Plan B.

Ashe faked another swing at the window. Damon advanced. At the last second, Ashe pivoted and drove the broken chair straight into his chest. It shattered on impact, and Damon landed on the desk with a grunt.

Pain flared across Ashe's arm. The silver blade had caught them as Damon fell, carving a slender cut deep into their biceps. Through the haze of pain, Ashe saw the branch manager wasn't moving.

Ashe fumbled for the burner phone. "Catch me!" they shouted, panic tearing through their voice.

A horn answered from below.

Without pausing, Ashe tucked the phone behind a shelf. Hopefully, it might still pick something up. They sprinted to the office door, but it was already creaking open.

Ashe launched forward and kicked hard, slamming it shut on whoever stood beyond. A muffled grunt answered. No time to wait.

They spun, planted one foot against the doorframe, and launched across the room. Shoes tore at the carpet, threads ripping underfoot. Ashe leapt into the air, curling their body inward.

The third strike hit true.

The cracked window shattered outward, and they plunged through a rain of glittering glass. The rush of open air blasted away the last clinging threads of doubt and despair.

The Wolf Spirit surged awake. **Fight,** it howled. **Turn. Tear. Kill.**

Ashe gritted their teeth. *Too late.*

Bullets screamed past overhead. The sky pitched and spun. Wind roared in their ears.

The RAV4 rose to meet them.

The roof caved in upon impact. Bones popped. Pain screamed through their body. They rolled off the top, landing hard on the pavement. One ankle refused to hold weight. Broken.

Ashe dragged themself to the passenger door and clawed it open, collapsing onto the back seat.

"Get..." they gasped, the world whiting out at the edges. "Get us the hell... out of here."

The tires screamed, the RAV4 jolting over curbs before catching the road and racing into the distance. Ashe cried out, a sound sharpened by rage and the Wolf Spirit's demand to fight, then cracked into something weaker. Bitter. Human.

Hands wouldn't stop shaking. Breath came in sharp, shallow gasps. Everything felt distant: the car, their body, even the pain in their ankle. The scream had drained what little strength they had left.

Spent, they surrendered to the mercy of dreamless sleep. The last thing they felt was Renae's hand in their hair, her voice whispering that it was okay.

Chapter 21

Cole slowed as the tug from Gaia faded. They returned to the grove where Ryan had been shot. But the presence that had guided them earlier was gone.

Birds had resumed their lives. Forest creatures moved along the edges, neither hostile nor curious, only distant. The sun had risen fully now, painting the grove in sweltering light.

Beneath it, Cole spotted signs of their earlier fight. Disturbed earth, broken branches, and faint marks that might've been left by the Huntsville pack when they'd come to clean up.

Grace had taken to scouting the grove's perimeter. Amber eyes scanned the woods, alert and measured. She had asked if she could turn wolf, but Cole asked her not to. Their bond hadn't been tested since the brewery, and communication in that form was still foggy. If anything happened, he needed everyone clearheaded and speaking.

Crouching in the dirt, Ryan poked at a patch of grass with a stick. Blood and bits of fur clung to scattered roots. Cole realized Ryan was examining the spot where he'd been shot. Ryan didn't seem to notice the other Lycans watching him as he absentmindedly pushed leaves over the bloodstains, covering what little remained.

"Why are we out here again?" he asked, not looking up.

Cole exhaled. "We're trying to figure out why this spot was chosen for the ambush. Pines said we were supposed to meet Gaia here. I'm hoping he meant that literally."

Dropping the stick, Ryan glanced around the grove. "Maybe that forest-pressure thingy from earlier was her?" He turned to Cole. "You could try singing again."

"That felt like a onetime thing," Cole said, shaking his head. "It had just felt right at the time, ya know?"

"Won't know unless you try. I mean, it's that or we're literally turning over rocks."

Grace nodded silently from the edge of the grove when Cole looked her way. With a sigh, he climbed onto a flat stone and began the same song he'd sung before. His voice carried through the trees, strong and steady.

But nothing happened. No sudden hush. No presence stirring in the woods.

"Try *Twilight's Dusk*," Ryan offered.

Cole groaned. "Seriously? That one?"

"It sounds naturey. Might be what she wants."

Cole grumbled but gave in. The song was among his least favorites. The performance felt flat and clumsy as an acappella.

Grace turned away, disinterested, but Ryan still clapped enthusiastically.

"Do *First Thoughts* next," Ryan said, settling on the ground with his chin tilted up.

"This isn't your private concert," Cole snapped.

Ryan stood, wounded. "Yeah, man, I was just trying to help." He let the words hang in the air, shoulders sagging with exaggerated disappointment before turning away.

Cole sat back down and closed his eyes. He shouldn't have snapped. Ryan was trying to help, even if his suggestions felt off-mark. But the pressure of being looked to for answers, of somehow magically solving their problems with a song, was getting to him.

Rain began to fall. Light. Steady. Warm. Cole let the water kiss his face as he looked up. He sent out a prayer to the Earth. It had answered in his dreams, so hopefully it would now.

Lyrics flickered in his mind. Lines he'd started after his First Tearing. He'd never finished the song, afraid to rush what felt sacred. But now, the melody returned.

Standing, he opened his chest and sang. It wasn't polished. It wasn't even finished. But it was honest. A raw offering to Gaia. Grace returned to Ryan's side, her hand in his. They hummed beneath his voice, soft harmonies beneath Cole's melody.

My claws dig deep into the ground
And rip apart the verdant mound
The green spreads and the light shines
Like a cancerous growth expanding with time

When life expands and becomes overgrown
A creature is chosen to protect and maintain its home
When weak are threatened, the creature blooms
When the strong flourish, it consumes

When Cole opened his eyes, the world had changed.

The grove was gone.

A vast, open field replaced it. Surrounding colors shimmered too saturated to feel real. There was no sun, yet everything glowed from a source he couldn't see. Trees pulsed with veins of violet and blue. The stone beneath him was now a massive tree stump with a carved spiral staircase leading downward.

He knew this place. The same waterfall from his dream roared in the distance.

They had made it to the Wildlands. This wasn't a dream. Not a vision. It was real.

He stepped down the staircase carefully. Ryan and Grace met him at the bottom.

Ryan glowed. Literally. His skin radiated a faint bronze light. A small bird perched on his shoulder, nuzzling beneath his chin.

Grace had partially shifted. Her torso remained human, barely, dappled with fur and faded scars. Below the waist, she was a massive cinnamon-colored wolf, muscles tense but calm.

"You both see this, right?" Cole asked. They nodded, still absorbing the surreal landscape.

Far ahead, towering shapes emerged from the haze. Nearly human, but ever-shifting. Their movements stirred the air with a fluid grace, more dream than flesh.

Grace fixed her gaze on the figures. Her posture stiffened, and she began walking toward the shapes. Cole and Ryan looked at each other and followed in unspoken understanding.

Time unraveled as they walked. The colors of the world slowly dimmed. No true sunset, but a muted shift in hues. Cole's legs ached. He glanced at Ryan, who was also beginning to struggle.

"It's not fair; she's got four legs," Ryan whispered to Cole, rubbing a cramp out of his thigh.

"You should Veil."

"Nah. With my luck, I'd have human legs carrying a wolf's head. This place feels too weird. I'm staying pretty."

Cole laughed softly. "You do look good."

"Really?" Ryan grinned. His smile relit the darkening sky, and several wild animals gathered closer. He looked Cole up and down and hesitantly added, "You, ah... you look good too."

As Cole prepared to ask Grace for a break, the figures ahead condensed out of the haze. They were too vast to comprehend. Always shifting. Always disappearing to reform again.

At any moment, there were five, then eight, then three. One bore the Rocky Mountains across its shoulders, crags stretching down a thick, root-like leg. Another shimmered like the ocean, dark blue skin streaked with pulsing green currents.

"Our mother," Grace whispered, bowing low.

Green threads connected the beings, weaving them together. They were not one entity, but aspects of the same force. The land given shape.

Warmth swelled within Cole and the others. Not just comfort, but memory. Cole felt his grandfather's arms on Christmas morning. The roar of his first live performance. Rebecca's voice, laughing, as they shared a lazy day in bed.

Love wrapped around him in an invisible embrace.

Ryan collapsed to his knees, trembling. Cole rushed to help, but the other man waved him off.

"I'm good, man," he murmured. "Just... give me a second."

Cole turned back to Gaia.

"Thank you for bringing us here," he said, "and I'm sorry if this is too forward, but... our mentor's in trouble. Can you tell us if he's alive? Where he is?"

Silence.

He tried something else. "Our mentor told someone that we," he gestured toward the other two, "and two others were important to you. Can you tell us why?"

The figures dissolved into brown dust.

And Cole was lifted.

His body floated high above a version of the Southeast United States untouched by cities or roads. The land stretched wild and endless. Mountains swelled beneath him, proud and still. Forests tangled together, with no sign of human interference. A world unspoiled.

For a moment, Cole felt awe.

Is this what it was meant to be? No scars. No roads. No hunger. Just the world as it should have been.

And then the sky darkened.

Boils rose from the soil. Red. Black. Seething. They burst, spilling glowing fluid. Corruption spread, devouring color. What remained was ash and rot. Rain fell, thick and toxic. It burned Cole's skin, boring into his flesh.

Make it stop. Please.

He turned, desperate to see something real. Someone real. And found only horror.

Grace and Ryan were collapsing, their forms melting into heaps of bone and blood. They reached for him as they dissolved, eyes wide with terror and confusion. Fingers stretched toward Cole, grasping desperately at the toxic air.

Cole called for them, but their mouths had no voices. Only silent screams, lips moving frantically as if trying to warn him of something he couldn't see.

There was nothing left. And then he fell.

The corrupted landscape rose beneath him. Endless decay, vast and suffocating. A single warped tree remained. Dead. Twisted. Alone. Only a single flower clung to one of its broken limbs. Then it withered, carried away by the wind.

He plunged through the rot into darkness. Images struck his mind in flashes.

Pines, bound to a stone slab, laughed through blood-stained teeth as a human-shaped figure carved into him with trembling hands. Cole wanted to scream, to reach him, to stop it.

Then the angle shifted.

The slab now held Rebecca, torn and bruised, her arms pulled tight in restraints. She looked up at Cole, mouth trembling, pleading.

"Help me."

The figure turned. Its jaw unhinged, skin tearing as fangs ripped through. Its face collapsed inward, reshaping itself into something monstrous.

Cole gasped awake beneath a reddening sky. The sun had dipped low, its rays cutting sharp through the trees.

He sat up, heart racing.

"Grace! Ryan! *Rebecca...*" the last name escaped in a whisper. Only two voices called back. Grace and Ryan stirred and rose nearby, shaken but whole.

"We need to get back to Ashe and Renae," Cole said, breath still uneven.

He climbed behind the wheel of Renae's sedan. The others barely got inside before he sped into the trees, headlights tearing through the gathering dark.

Chapter 22

A she wasn't sure if they were being followed, but they weren't about to risk leading anyone back to Jericho. They convinced the others to meet at Lowe Mill, a once-abandoned textile mill now humming with music, murals, and misfits. It was an unlikely refuge for those the world had no use for.

The place felt safe. Not because it was hidden but because it was alive. A maze of old factory bones reworked into studios, indie galleries, coffee roasters, and experimental music venues.

Ashe had sold paintings there once. Danced down the halls without apology. The place was all mismatched couches and second chances, a beautiful chaos that made sense to them. People here accepted Ashe without hesitation. No questions, no masks. And now, what they needed more than anything was a place where no one would bat an eye at someone limping through the door looking like hell.

Renae drove, focused and silent. Ashe, almost recovered from the three-story swan dive, lay along the back seat, checking behind them every few blocks. Renae took the back roads and dead-end cut-throughs, watching for any sign they were being followed. Neither of them was trained in evasion, but they did their best.

The car rolled into the fenced lot behind Lowe Mill just as the last rays of light stretched across the asphalt. Outside, an artist led a collage workshop in the courtyard, her pink hair piled like whipped cream. Inside the SUV, Ashe and Renae sat, listening to Damon's voice crackle through the phone speaker.

"Find the bitch."

Renae cringed and turned the volume down. Ashe leaned back against the seat as their ankle bones shifted and clicked back into place, the break sealing itself with waves of sharp, burning pain.

"They already went to my place and my parents' house," Ashe said, grateful to no longer see white bits sticking out of their skin. "At least they didn't do anything to my family." The words blended relief and guilt. Despite everything, Ashe still loved their parents, and they weren't sure what they would do if something happened to Kyle.

Renae muttered, "Can't believe you used your real name on the application."

Ashe gave her a dry look. "Didn't think I'd need a burner résumé. Most places I've applied to won't let you in the door without ID, and I lost my fake one after I turned twenty-one."

Flipping to a blank page in her leather notebook, Renae scratched a quick reminder. "We're gonna need safe houses."

"Unless being a Lycan suddenly comes with a paycheck and a pension, I'm gonna need someone else's couch," Ashe grumbled, testing their ankle. It was still tender, but it would at least hold their weight if they took it easy.

Damon's rant faded. A door opened on the other end of the call, filled with a long silence. Ashe wasn't sure if Damon had left until they heard keys tapping.

Ashe and Renae were discussing what to do next when they heard the door open on the other end of the line. Then another voice. Cooler. Controlled.

"The surviving Lycan escaped the hospital, and no sign of Cole yet. We still don't have IDs on the other two. The chat app Pines used scrambled phone numbers, so we can't trace them."

Ashe froze at the names.

Cole.

Pines.

Hearing it from their hunters made it real in a way nothing else had. Dum-Prot had him.

Ashe went still, shoulders pulling tight. A low growl prickled at the back of their throat. They glanced at Renae, but her expression hadn't changed. Maybe she didn't care. Maybe showing it hurt too much.

Ashe pushed the dread aside and forced themselves to keep listening.

"Should I put more people on this?" Damon asked.

The other voice replied, slick and cold as oil. "We're already stretched thin. If I request more resources to chase new pups, they'll question our competence. We still have their mentor. The Judge can pull more from him. And other leverage."

The line went dead.

"Shouldn't that have lasted longer?" Ashe asked.

"New phone," Renae said, pocketing hers. "Didn't have time to charge it before you went in. We got what we could."

She glanced toward the lot and spotted headlights. Her posture eased slightly as the other three Lycans pulled in.

"Finally."

The pack slipped inside, nearly invisible amid the color and chaos. As they moved through the halls, bits of their stories surfaced. Snatches of breathless updates, half-joked trauma, and fragments of visions and fear. Renae spoke quietly to Cole. Ryan nudged Ashe, asking if they'd really jumped from the roof. Grace didn't say much, her attention focused on possible traps.

Then Ryan, almost offhand, mentioned the Wildlands.

Ashe stopped mid-step. They'd missed it. The other three had seen Gaia. Actually seen her! They had walked the Wildlands. Spoken with the spirit of nature, or maybe even more than one.

A flicker of envy rose sharp and hot. This was what they had fought and bled for. And they'd missed it. *Twice!*

They all but tackled Cole, words tumbling out.

"You saw her? You were there?"

Cole nodded, his attention pulled from whatever Renae had just told him. Ashe turned to the others, eyes fierce.

"This is it. This is why we're doing this. Not just to survive. We're supposed to embrace it. Claim it. Let it shape who we are."

Grace nodded, her eyes burning with purpose. The others stayed quiet, but Ashe didn't need their agreement. They'd already chosen.

Renae glanced around the still-busy hallway. "Let's continue this in the studio."

They climbed to the second floor together, the buzz of music and incense fading behind. When they reached the forgotten studio, Cole stepped aside, saying he needed to make a call.

The others slipped inside, with Ashe shutting the door behind them.

Renae didn't waste a second. She opened her laptop on the paint-stained table. Ryan dropped into a chair, feet up. Grace stood at the window, watching the street. Ashe hovered behind Renae, reading over her shoulder.

"These are the development plans," Renae said, swiping through images. "Four sites, all being fast-tracked. Dum-Prot's pushing clustered neighborhoods and oversized clubhouses, built on land that was supposed to be state-protected."

Her gaze stayed fixed on the screen. "We don't have time to check them all. Not with them tracking us. We need to narrow it down."

Ryan sighed and pushed his chair back. "Why not wait for Jericho to get back on his feet? The Birmingham pack's coming too, right? Let them handle it. We've got no experience in this."

Cole stepped back in. His face was unreadable, but Ashe felt a flicker through the pack link. Anger. Worry. And for a moment, an image of a young woman. They blinked, startled. They hadn't known the link could project like that while human.

Then the feeling vanished as Cole caught himself. He turned to Ryan instead.

"No one's getting here in time," Cole said, his voice cold and low. "You saw what Gaia showed us. We have to stop that. And we have to find Pines."

It was the first time Ashe had heard steel in Cole's voice. Knowing Dum-Prot had been to his house, had crossed that line, must have landed just as hard for him as it had for them.

Renae nodded. "We don't know how long we have. And we can't trust anyone else. This falls to us."

Ryan stood, arms wide, staring directly at Renae. "Why trust us and not the other Lycans?" he demanded. "We don't know what we're doing. We barely survived the last fight. And now you want us to handle this alone?"

Cole opened his mouth, but Ryan waved him off and turned back to Renae.

"No offense, Cole, but I want to hear it from her. You've been throwing shade at Pines since day one. You don't know Jericho or the others. So why us? Why now?"

All eyes turned to the older woman.

Cole's voice was low, deliberate. "Why did you bring a gun and a bulletproof vest to the Brewery?"

Ashe's breath caught. A bulletproof vest? No one ever mentioned it. A memory surfaced. Renae firing through the door. The creature's flesh bubbling where rounds hit.

They added quietly, "Does your gun have silver bullets in it?"

Grace turned at that, her body suddenly tense.

Renae didn't answer right away. Her eyes stayed distant, the mouse scrolling absently as images flashed by too fast to track. Then she froze, turned to Cole, and spoke.

"I told you my husband died." She paused. "I didn't tell you he was a Lycan."

Cole took a step back. Ashe's mouth opened reflexively, though they were unsure what to say.

"Jay was *chosen*," she said, her voice turned venomous on the word.. "About ten years into our marriage. He told me against his pack leader's advice. He trusted me."

Her voice trembled.

"He used to Veil into the wolf when we camped. Said it felt like breathing with his whole body. He'd tell me stories of spirits, the land... Gaia."

Turning back to the screen, she started flicking through the images again.

"He was a lawyer. Fought pollution in the courts by day. At night, he and his pack sabotaged equipment to stop illegal, and even sometimes legal, dumping."

Raising an eyebrow, Ryan challenged, "Are you saying your husband was Batman?" He immediately looked shocked at his own words. "Sorry, I—"

Renae let out a short, surprised laugh despite herself. "We definitely weren't billionaires, but..." Her smile faded quickly. "He was my super-hero."

Ashe leaned forward. "Did he ever tell you about... things like what we saw? Like the blob or the Banewolf?"

"No." She shook her head. "Nothing like that."

Grace broke in. Low. Lethal. "How'd he die?"

Her eyes lingered on the back of her hand, searching for a ring that hadn't been there in years.

"There was a plan to torch a facility poisoning a lake. Jay disagreed. Wanted more time to work through the courts. But when they went, he went. He wanted to make sure no innocents got hurt."

She bit her bottom lip.

"When he didn't come back, I looked into it. A pack leader had at-tacked him. Left him unconscious. Let the explosion finish the job."

"And those bastards got away with it." She was blinking back tears. "No one looked into it. The elders looked the other way. I had to track them myself. I had to..." Her voice faltered. Her shoulders trembled.

"You don't betray your pack," Grace said, gold flashing in her eyes.

Renae's head snapped up. "To them, it wasn't a betrayal. He challenged them, and that was enough justification." She spat out the next words. "No justice. No trial. Just a bruised ego and bullshit politics."

Then she slumped back in her chair. "So, no, I don't trust the Lycans."

Silence.

Scared at first of what her reaction would be, Ashe took a small step toward Renae, reached over and hugged her. A moment later, Grace followed. Cole wrapped his arms around them both.

Ryan hovered for a second, uncertain, until Renae reached out and pulled him in. The pack stayed like that for a long time. In that moment, the outside world didn't matter.

They were sweaty. Smushed together. Ashe couldn't breathe.

They loved it.

"Wait," Ryan mumbled, still pressed against Cole's side. He pointed at the screen. "I know that place."

The image showed a wooded lot with a dirt road snaking up a hill, and the ruins of what looked like a small cabin.

"We used to own that," Ryan said. "Well, my parents did. They'd go up to the cabin for the weekend, and I'd throw some killer parties while they were gone."

His grin faded as he caught the others' expressions.

He cleared his throat and continued. "They leased it to the state for a while. Conservation groups used it for educational hikes. There was this huge hole near the cabin," he said. "We used to throw stuff down it as kids, and it never hit bottom. I think it's some kind of natural well."

Renae clicked through to the next image.

The land had been bulldozed. The trees stripped bare. The cabin was gone.

Cole glanced at his phone, his mind half elsewhere. "How could a private company buy land that was under state lease?"

Ryan shifted awkwardly, realizing no one was interested in his childhood stories. "My... uh... my dad was able to break the lease and sold the land."

Ashe stared at the screen, a current buzzing beneath their skin. Their ribs pulsed. Something ancient, older than the wolf, was shifting inside them. They turned to Cole. His eyes were locked on the image, his face a mask of stillness.

"You feel that too?" Ashe asked.

"Yeah," Cole said. "Gaia. It's the same feeling I had on the mountain."

"This is it," Ashe whispered. "This has to be where they're keeping Pines."

Why only they and Cole could feel it, Ashe didn't know. Maybe they were closer to Pines. Or just more attuned. It didn't matter. This felt *right*.

Renae tapped the screen. "Then this is where we go."

Ryan frowned. "What if it's nothing?"

Cole crossed his arms. "Then we wait for Jericho. Or the Birmingham Pack. But we need to know."

Hesitation was building in Ryan again. He was on the verge of backing out. Ashe couldn't let that happen. Not now.

Facing him, they swallowed the bile that rose with the next words. "We need you. You know that land better than any of us. Maybe Gaia called you for this."

Ryan blinked. "That's... kind of a stretch."

Ashe didn't argue. Honestly, they agreed. But if Ryan didn't come with them, he might get caught. Or worse, he might get them killed. And by the look in his eyes, he was already halfway out the door.

Grace stepped in behind him and wrapped her arms around his chest, resting her head on his shoulder. "We will need you," she said softly. "You are the bravest warrior."

Ashe almost snorted but held it in as they turned away. When they looked back, Ryan's ego had already made the choice for him.

He exhaled. "Fine. One more night at my place. Then we go."

Chapter 23

They gathered walkie-talkies, tactical gear, and an assortment of knives and weapons from Renae's house. She had explained most of it was left over from when Jay was still alive. Ten or fifteen years ago, it might've been top-of-the-line. Now, it was bulky and outdated.

Ryan scoffed at the gear.

"It still works," Renae told him. "And it's all we have right now."

Cole noticed Ryan still looked a little green at the thought of what lay ahead. Cole couldn't blame him. He wasn't sure about any of this either. But if Pines was out there, he deserved to be found. And Gaia was pulling him toward something. The vision she'd given him, the land hollowed and ruined, still clung to his thoughts.

Even with that urgency, his thoughts kept drifting to Rebecca.

At Lowe Mill, Renae mentioned that Dum-Prot knew where he lived. He'd immediately started texting Rebecca but got no response. He just needed to know she was safe, that she didn't hate him. His last message had warned her to stay away from the house.

He'd been replaying that last night with her over and over. At the time, he had wanted her to stay. But now, after hearing Renae's story and seeing how loss had gutted her life, he was seeing things differently. Maybe Rebecca leaving had been the safest thing, for both of them.

Now they were loaded down with Renae's gear and driving toward the mountain. He'd asked Renae to drive by his place and her parents' home, but she refused. She patiently explained that it would only put everyone in more danger. Maybe she was right, but the need to know overwhelmed his own sense of safety.

They pulled into a neighborhood just outside Monte Sano Park. GPS had shown a narrow creek that cut toward a trail leading to the backside of the worksite. The sun was beginning to dip, but they had time to reach the natural well Renae had marked.

With their packs slung over shoulders, they left the road behind and descended into the woods, letting the edges of civilization fall away.

The hike began in peace. Sunlight filtered through the trees, scattering happy, dancing shadows across the ground. With every step deeper into the woods, Cole felt Gaia's pull grow stronger. He caught Ashe's eye and they gave a reassuring nod.

Inside, the Wolf Spirit stirred. It hadn't surfaced since the night Rebecca had left. But now, out here in the wild, it twisted and writhed, desperate to run.

And something darker stirred with it.

This was a part of the Wolf Spirit he had not experienced yet. This part didn't just want to roam. It wanted revenge. It wanted to strike back at those who hunted his friends. The spirit wanted to destroy.

They reached the stream, and Renae called for a break.

"Rest up, hydrate, take care of anything you need to," she said. "We've got about an hour hike left before the back end of the site. Stay fresh."

Grace immediately squatted downstream. Everyone respectfully turned away, hiding faint smirks.

"We haven't covered modesty yet," Renae noted dryly.

Ryan lay back in the moss, eyes on the limbs swaying above. "What do you think we're going to find?"

They had driven past the worksite earlier, doing their best to stay inconspicuous. Dum-Prot Land had thrown up a tall wall. Cole doubted it had anything to do with privacy for future residents. It was there to keep prying eyes out. And whatever was inside, in.

"The enemy," Grace eagerly provided, walking back toward the group.

"Sure," Ryan said, "but are we talking about another Banewolf? Something worse? That wall doesn't look like it's keeping out hikers."

He glanced toward Renae, who only shrugged.

Cole chimed in, "Pines said what they did to Lycans shouldn't even be possible. If that's true, they probably can't make too many more."

Ashe added, "And they'd be wasted guarding a site no one suspects is evil. If they've got more of those things, they're probably out hunting, killing or converting."

Ashe's words lingered in the silence. The forest had gone still. Cold. This wasn't just nerves. This wasn't a forest. It was a hunting ground. And all of them were prey.

Renae stood, checked her pistol, and holstered it. "And with that cheerful thought, let's move."

The sun had finally disappeared behind the treeline, and the full moon was already visible in the deepening twilight, silver light beginning to filter through the canopy.

"Huh," Ryan muttered.

"What?" Ashe followed his eyes up toward the night sky.

"I dunno," he said. "I figured I'd feel different. Like we'd get some kind of power boost. Or start turning into werewolves or something."

Renae laughed. "Jay said the same thing his first full moon. Some Lycans are affected by it, those with a stronger bond to the Wolf Spirit. But for most of us? It's just light in the sky."

Ryan looked over at Ashe. "Are you good? You don't feel like eating anyone?"

"Just you," Ashe replied, already moving ahead.

Grace shifted, subtle and instinctive. She stepped between them, her body taut with tension.

"I think they were joking," Cole offered.

Grace gave a small nod but didn't relax.

Her wariness made Cole turn his attention to Ashe, studying their back as they moved ahead. Steady. Unreadable. Distant. His own wolf was squirming harder now, eager to be let out. And if it was that strong in him... what was Ashe feeling?

Maybe they weren't joking.

They were about a hundred yards from the natural well when the terrain changed.

The air turned colder. Not a crisp mountain chill, but a damp, crawling cold that sank beneath Cole's skin and into his bones. The warmth of summer vanished all at once. No wind stirred. The trees stood still.

Birdsong was gone. No rustle of squirrels or insects. Just the crunch of their boots on brittle underbrush.

Up ahead, a young doe lay crumpled near the path. Its eyes were clouded white, its body sunken and half-rotted, as though death had come days ago. But the wound on its flank was fresh, still wet.

The smell hit Cole. Sweet rot, cloying and thick. He held his breath, trying not to let the putrid air coat his throat. Grace crouched near the carcass, taking a careful sniff before pulling back sharply. Ryan turned away, nearly losing his last meal at the sight.

"Grace, you sniffing it made me smell it," Ryan said between quick gags.

"Different from the Banewolf," Grace said, standing. "But not natural death." Grace's assessment caused Cole to give the surrounding a closer inspection.

The leaves around them had begun to fall, still green, curling at the edges. Even the trees looked sick. Bark peeled in strips, and a dark fuzz coated the undersides of branches. Sap oozed thick and black from old wounds, trailing like tar.

Beneath their feet, the ground had softened. Moss squelched underfoot, slick with moisture. Cole spotted patches where the soil had turned gray, ashen, stripped of life. Whatever was happening, it was spreading out from their destination. A wound in the forest, radiating death.

"Not good," Grace murmured. "Nature flees. She says to run."

Ashe's voice was low, disturbed. "Why hasn't anyone reported this?"

Cole was caught between the urge to run and the wolf's desire to punish. The question lingered as he glanced at Renae and Ryan. They were wrestling with the same conflict.

Grace and Ashe were different, though. They showed no conflict. The desecration wanted them gone, but those two pressed forward, regardless.

He forced himself to speak. "There's no real trail back here anymore. If anyone did come this way, they probably turned around before they got too close. They'd feel something was off and just leave. I think that's how this corruption protects itself."

Renae squared her shoulders, like someone forcing off a heavy coat. "Let's find the well," she muttered, drawing her gun. "We'll figure out the rest when we get there."

The well was unremarkable. A rough ring of limestone, cracked and worn smooth by centuries of weather. Moss filled the crevices. Dead ferns hung limp around the edges, bowing toward the darkness below.

Cole stepped closer and aimed his flashlight into the opening. The beam vanished into blackness. No bottom. Just depth.

Then he heard it.

Faint at first. Just echoes, he thought. Water dripping on stone.

But then the echo shaped itself into words.

Come to me. Save me.

Rebecca's voice.

He dropped to his knees, straining to listen, when Grace yanked him back with surprising force. He started to ask why, but the look on her face silenced him. She shook her head, gave the well one last glance, and walked away. Rejoining the group, Cole forced himself not to look back at the well.

Through a break in the trees, he saw artificial light ahead.

Renae crouched near the edge of the woods, setting her pack down. "This is close enough," she said, pulling out binoculars. The others dropped their bags and joined her.

Construction floodlights bathed the site in harsh yellow. Skeletal house frames jutted from the earth at various stages of construction. Near the center stood a larger, completed building, its dark windows catching the floodlights. Workers in reflective vests moved around, hammers tapping, machines humming. A bulldozer groaned in the distance.

"Why are they still working?" Ashe asked. "I can't even get a plumber after three."

"Maybe they're trying to finish before anyone sees too much," Renae said.

Grace tensed. She sniffed the air as the wind shifted.

"Something dead moves."

"Does it smell like the rot from the brewery?" Cole asked.

She shook her head. "Different. But rot is here too."

"That's not all," Renae said. "Three patrols, same gear as before. Assault rifles. Circling the perimeter."

"So what, more skin-bags?" Ryan stepped back. "I think we should come back later. Or, I don't know—*wait for the other Lycans.*"

"Jericho said the Fäulung thing can't make those things unless the host's already completely corrupted," Cole replied, trying to calm him. "Either way, I'm not leaving."

"Neither am I," Ashe said, voice low, eyes never leaving the site.

Renae and Grace nodded.

"Fine," Ryan muttered. "My luck, I'd get lost and wander these woods alone for three days."

"Then let's get started," Renae said, stashing the binoculars.

The plan was simple, but risky.

Grace and Ryan would Veil into their wolf forms and circle the perimeter, searching for anything unusual outside the worksite. They would watch for signs of the land's corruption or for anything the company might be hiding. If the cause of the rot lay beyond the fence, they would find it.

Meanwhile, Cole, Ashe, and Renae would slip into the site itself. Renae's path would lead her to the large clubhouse at its center, while Cole and Ashe moved through the skeletal rows of half-built houses. They would search for traces of corruption, hints of experimentation, or any evidence that might reveal what Dum-Prot was truly doing here.

If things went sideways, the wolves would be their backup. Grace and Ryan could reach them faster on four legs than any human could run, distract or disable whatever threat emerged, and buy enough time for the others to escape on foot.

She handed Ashe a pair of silver daggers, rough walnut handles gleaming.

At Renae's house, she had offered Cole several different weapons, but he refused. The one time he had goofed around with some nunchucks a friend had, he'd ended up giving himself a black eye.

Besides, Jericho had made it clear that not everyone here would be a monster. That was how the enemy worked: hiding among the innocent, forcing hesitation.

If he was seen, Cole would Veil and run. He'd fight if he had to, but wasn't going to hurt any innocent bystander.

Waiting for Grace and Ryan to Veil, Cole's panic briefly spiked. Gaia's pull hadn't vanished, but it felt weaker now. Muted. The corrupted land was muffling her voice, thinning the bond between them.

He was afraid they might not be able to shift, like what had happened to Ashe at the Dum-Prot building. But thankfully, Grace and Ryan stripped down and Veiled without issue.

Two wolves emerged from the brush, strong and solid.

Ryan sneezed and shook his head, clearly overwhelmed by the tangled web of scents. Grace waited, watching as he regained his footing. Then she vanished northeast in a blur of fur and shadow. Ryan lingered, then finally turned southeast, his pace more tentative. In seconds, both wolves were gone. Silent shapes melting into the forest gloom.

Ashe was rigid, barely breathing, their stare fixed like a sniper's scope on the construction site.

Cole studied them with growing concern. They'd been through so much physically and emotionally. Not all of their wounds had healed.

Last night, Ashe had opened up about their doubts regarding the Lycans, about whether any pack would ever see them as more than a weapon or an outsider. They were still searching for a connection, a place to belong.

He couldn't promise what the others would do. But he could promise this: he wouldn't leave them behind.

Stepping closer, he asked, "You okay?" He placed a reassuring hand on their shoulder.

Ashe flinched, their head snapping toward him, eyes flashing with something primal. Cole jerked back, startled by the intensity. Renae glanced over at the commotion. Ashe's expression softened, blinking as if pulling him into focus.

"Sorry," Ashe said, a faint blush rising. "I just got distracted."

Cole wanted to say something. To tell them to hang back. Take a safer role. But Ashe didn't want to be protected. And the last thing they'd accept was being pulled from danger just to spare Cole worry.

He wanted to keep them safe. But trying to save Ashe by sidelining them would only feel like betrayal.

So instead, he met their eyes. "I've got your back. I know you've got mine."

Ashe met his eyes and gave a small smile. Tired but sincere.

A sharp click brought his attention to Renae racking the slide on her pistol.

"Let's do this," she said.

Chapter 24

The forest gave way to raw earth and rigid artificial order. Dirt was packed in straight lines where trees had once stood. Gone was the damp green scent of the woods. In its place: diesel and something chemical beneath it all. Churned soil stretched between half-laid driveways and gravel piles. Main roads were little more than veiny tracks of loose rock and jutting rebar. Orange fencing flapped weakly in the breeze, marking the land like a wound stitched with synthetic gauze.

Keeping low and out of the floodlights, they scurried across the open ground, exposed and unwelcome in a place that wasn't meant for them. Once they reached the shadows near the first house, they split up.

Renae peeled off toward the clubhouse. Something in the building plans had bothered her, and she needed to see it with her own eyes. She paused, perhaps catching the strain Ashe tried to hide, but when they managed a passable smile, the older woman gave one last glance and disappeared into the dark.

Cole continued ahead toward the next unit, stepping around loose piping and unfinished framing. From behind, Ashe watched him move like someone holding something back. They weren't sure if it was fear, concern, or whatever had been eating at him since Lowe Mill.

Ashe stayed behind to investigate the house in front of them. They crouched beneath a window where the plastic wrap hung partially torn, like half-shed skin.

The house was nearly finished. Artificial turf stretched across the front and back yards. Neat. Organized. Sterile. It didn't sway or yield underfoot. It was a lie. Bright green polyethylene concealing dark, poisoned earth.

Ashe peered through the open window. There was a drifting scent of sawdust and drying paint, but beneath that was something worse. A sour, chemical bite clung to their sinuses. The smell reminded them too much of the Dum-Prot Land complex. That same manufactured calm stretched thin over something festering. A pleasant facade hid rotted teeth.

The wolf thrashed inside them, wild and relentless. It didn't care about the mission. It didn't care about stealth or strategy. It wanted to hunt. It craved blood.

Ashe clenched their jaw and focused on breathing. In through the nose. Out through the mouth. Each breath felt like a fraying thread. Every nerve, every thought, locked on keeping the beast contained.

Was this the full moon's doing, like Ryan had teased? Or had they wandered too close to the enemy for the spirit to sense blood in the air?

Maybe they should've stayed behind? Sweat slicked their spine. Their hands had gone numb, skin clammy. When Cole startled them earlier, it had nearly broken loose.

Before, they'd always pulled back from the edge. Now, the edge felt too thin. Too brittle.

Kill them all. Find the mentor.

The voice came low and coaxing. Not a command, but a suggestion. Soft as a caress against the back of their neck.

Ashe shivered. The words curled around their spine, warm and heavy, like sinking into dark water. For a heartbeat, they could see it. Claws unsheathed. Teeth snapping. The mission erased beneath a flood of violence. It would be easy. It would feel so good.

"No," they hissed, teeth gritting so tight they ached.

Ashe ducked low, scanning the site. But the sounds of construction masked their voice. No one seemed close. The workers were still focused on the unfinished homes farther out.

With a grunt of effort, Ashe shoved the wolf back into its cage and stepped inside.

The interior was still a work in progress. Drywall was missing in patches. Appliances sat wrapped in plastic and stacked to one side. Copper pipes snaked through the open rafters above.

With each step, the silence pressed in closer. It was as if the house was keeping something hidden, a secret tucked just out of sight. The deeper Ashe went, the more the light disappeared, choked off by bare studs and exposed framing.

Pressure swelled beneath their skin. A weight that hadn't been there before, as if the house itself was seeping into them. They moved faster through the rooms, unsure of what they were even looking for.

Their entire body seized, muscles cramping as they reached the center of the house. Through the pain, an invisible force dragged at their body, pulling downward through the subfloor.

A wave of dizziness hit. They dropped to their knees as a malevolent force clawed through the floor and seized them. Sound vibrated somewhere in the walls. Low and almost wet.

Apathy seeped in. A voice in their blood told them to lie down. Rest. Never rise again. Maybe they just needed to close their eyes for a moment. Just to gather strength. The dark wrapped around them, warm and quietly suffocating.

***

Cole ducked behind a propane tank near the next house, heart pounding. He hadn't seen the security guard, but the static pop of a radio check had tipped him off. The man was just around the corner.

Pressed flat against the cool metal, he held his breath. The guard was only fifteen feet away, boots scuffing dry dirt.

"Guard Four checking in," came a bored voice as the guard walked a lazy path. Then the steps stopped. Right on the other side of the tank.

Cole's heart hammered against his ribs. His lungs ached. He didn't dare exhale. Not even a whisper. One breath too loud could get him killed.

His eyes stung. A faint ribbon of vape smoke drifted past. Sweet. Synthetic. Bubblegum flavor.

Seconds stretched. His chest spasmed, a reflex he couldn't suppress. He was moments away from gasping. Desperate for even a shallow sip of air...

Then the footsteps turned.

The guard circled back around the house, boots crunching away toward the front entrance.

Only then did Cole let himself inhale. Slowly. Controlled. The smoke still clung to the air, stinging his throat. He fought down a cough as the pounding in his skull began to ease.

Blinking away tears, he peered over the tank. The man was gone.

Great. Ten minutes in, and you almost get caught by a guy on a smoke break.

Cole shook the thought away. He crept toward the house, hugging the wall of unfinished plywood, then slid through a window frame where the glass hadn't been installed yet.

The room was empty, surrounded by bare concrete and open studs. Probably meant to be a bedroom. Maybe an office.

Then the pull hit him.

He staggered, cold shivering up his spine. A vision burst into his mind: a Hispanic man drowning in a river of sludge. Brown. Thick. Choking. The man clawed for air but only swallowed more, jerking as the muck filled his lungs.

Cole hacked out a cough, nausea rolling through him. The taste clung to his mouth, sour and toxic. An invisible burn slid down his throat.

Still shaking, he sat back down before his legs could give out. This wasn't like Gaia's gentle guidance or images he had gotten through the pack link. He hadn't just witnessed it. He hadn't just felt the man's fear. He had lived it. Every breath. Every desperate second.

The pull toward the center of the house deepened. Fear churned in his gut, but the need to know outweighed it. Cole dropped to his hands and knees and crept forward, careful to stay below the windows.

The subfloor hadn't been installed yet. Sheets of it leaned against a wall, stacked and ready. In the dining room, something caught his eye.

A latch was embedded in the concrete, nearly invisible.

When Cole pressed the center, a handle popped up. He twisted it, and a three-by-five hatch unlocked with a soft hiss. As he eased it open, he was met by a dim green glow pulsing from below.

As he slid down through the opening, he thought he felt his radio vibrate. Only a flicker of motion at his hip. Landing with a soft thud, he turned up the volume. No static. Not even the faintest crack of an open channel.

He paused, debating whether to climb back up or press on. Deciding to risk a quick investigation and radio out once he was clear, Cole clicked on his flashlight and moved forward.

The room was a fifteen-by-fifteen concrete box, lit by faint green runes etched into the walls. They pulsed in a slow rhythm. The symbols looked Celtic, or close enough to remind him of a friend's band logo.

The soft earth squished beneath his boots. Cole had expected the entire space to be concrete, but the floor here was soil. Wet and strangely warm.

Aiming the light down revealed a blackish-brown substance oozing across the surface. It shifted thick and slow, almost as if it were a living thing.

At the center of the room stood a dark orange fifty-five-gallon metal drum. Chains wrapped around it in a crude cross-pattern, bolted into the earth by heavy hooks. Small holes had been drilled around the base, and something foul was leaking from them, soaking into the ground.

Renae had given Cole and Ashe a small pouch of thief's tools, including a miniature bolt cutter. Cole pulled it out, snipped the simple padlock, and popped the latch.

The lid creaked open.

The smell hit him first. Raw sewage laced with rotten eggs and a sharp chemical bite. The odor was so pervasive he had to turn away and gather himself. It was as if the stench itself were physically assaulting him.

A splash from the barrel turned him back. Then he saw what was inside.

A man. Hispanic. Face partially dissolved, features warped beyond recognition. One skeletal hand reached upward through the thick brown sludge. The same sludge from the vision.

"Cole, help us," the voice rasped. Cole stared back. He still had no idea who this man was.

So how did he know Cole's name?

***

Their hip buzzed with a soft chirp. Ashe cracked their eyes open. Heavy lids threatened to drag them under again.

Working past the fog, they reached down and turned up the volume on the radio.

"Here," they croaked. Even that one word nearly pulled them back into unconsciousness.

"You need to get to the clubhouse," Renae whispered. Her voice was tight, urgent. "I need your help."

Ashe clung to the sound. They pushed upright, limbs trembling. The lullaby tried to draw them back, but they focused instead on each breath, each flexing joint, each movement that proved they were still in control.

One step. Another. Then another.

Each movement was a small rebellion against apathy, their body breaking free inch by inch.

The pull never left completely, but the haze began to lift.

"Ashe? Cole? I need someone to respond." Panic now laced Renae's voice.

Ashe reached the front door and clicked on the radio.

"I'm... I'm here," they said, voice hoarse, barely recognizable. "I'm on my way."

A relieved voice answered. "Good. Come in through the east-side door. It's unlocked, and the lights don't hit that section."

"Gotcha." Ashe shook off the last of the lingering haze and eased the front door open.

The clubhouse sat about two hundred yards away, its exterior mostly untouched by the floodlights. A couple of guards passed nearby, casually glancing through the windows. Construction workers walked across the front of the building, chatting as they moved.

How the hell did Renae get there without being seen?

Scanning for a way across, Ashe caught movement near the front entrance. A lone figure drifted away from the clubhouse. Not walking. Gliding.

Everything about him felt off. His clothing was completely wrong for a construction site. Period garments hung just below the knee in stiff, heavy fabric. Dark brown and green cut broadly across the shoulders and narrowed at the waist. A high collar rose sharply behind his neck. A leather scabbard was strapped at his side, with the black hilt of a sword jutting from it.

His physical form made it worse. Ashe couldn't get a good look at his face, but the skin on the back of his head sagged and was covered by only a few random strands of grey hair. The torso wasn't symmetrical; one arm looked withered or entirely missing, making the elaborate costume hang awkwardly on his frame.

"Never seen this guy at the Ren Fair," Ashe whispered, but the joke rang hollow even to themselves.

Then came the smell. Rot, as if flesh had been left out too long in the sun. His aura crawled across their skin. It wasn't just tainted. It was alien. Sick. Viscous.

The Wolf Spirit recoiled. If it could have clawed its way out and run, it would have.

That terrified Ashe more than anything. The predator didn't run from danger. It ran *to* it. Whatever this thing was, it didn't just threaten the body. It violated the soul.

As if sensing the Wolf Spirit's panic, the figure halted mid-stride. It slowly scanned the area.

Then turned toward Ashe.

Panic shot through them like ice water. They jerked backward, slamming their elbow hard against the doorknob. Pain flared, but they barely felt it. The front door was still cracked open. Had it seen them? No time to find out.

Ashe ducked back into the house, staying low as they cut through the rooms, avoiding the windows. They slipped out the back patio door, hands shaking as they eased it closed behind them.

Reaching the clubhouse turned out easier than they expected. No one seemed to be seriously looking for intruders, not this deep in the site. They reached the east door and carefully pushed it open.

Inside was a large open space meant for a restaurant. A bar stretched along one wall. Dining tables and stacked chairs filled the floor. Dim lights hummed along the walls. The building already had power.

Quickly shutting the door behind them, Ashe saw Renae with her arm raised, elbow bent, gun pointed in the air.

"Good. Follow me."

She was already in motion, weaving her way through the restaurant and toward the kitchen. Ashe stayed low, careful not to let their silhouette reflect against the walls or catch stray light from outside.

The moment they stepped into the kitchen, Gaia's pull struck them like a harpoon to the chest, dragging them forward. Her influence, barely a whisper since the well, now pressed in like a scream behind lay-ered fabric. Muffled, but urgent. Impossible to ignore.

It led straight toward a tall stainless-steel door. Ashe took a step for-ward, hand reaching toward the handle.

"Stop," Renae hissed.

They turned, frowning. "We don't have time to..."

Renae held up her hand. A blistered red burn marked the inside of her palm, the shape unmistakably matching the freezer's handle.

Ashe's expression tightened. "I'll risk it," they muttered, reaching again.

"It's not just the silver handle. It has a coded lock," Renae said. She pointed to a small electric keypad beside the door, its digits laid out in a standard grid. "I didn't want to risk putting in the wrong code and set-ting off an alarm. When I tested the handle, I got this." She nodded at the burn.

"We could probably bust it open, but I can't do it alone. Have you heard from Cole?"

Ashe shook their head. "No, but it doesn't look like he's been caught. No one's raising an alarm."

"Then it's on us."

Renae's voice wavered, just for a second, a flicker of doubt. Through the pack link, Ashe caught something else: a brief surge of frustration, protective instinct warring with necessity. Renae didn't want to risk people like Ashe and Cole, but she couldn't let that stop her. Not now.

Ashe had sensed it before at Dum-Prot. Both times, Renae pushed past it. The mission always came first.

Pulling out a roll of duct tape, Renae carefully wrapped it around the handle.

They both gripped the door and pulled. Nothing. No creak. No give. No flex.

Both of them stepped back, breathing a little harder.

Renae looked to Ashe. "Do you think you could take the Grayskin form? We need more muscle, and I don't want to waste time looking for Cole."

Dread raced down Ashe's spine.

"Maybe. Why don't you do it?"

Renae shook her head. "I've only ever Veiled. I don't want to go past the wolf, and even if I did, I'm not sure how."

The Wolf Spirit stirred eagerly. It felt Ashe thinking and whispered back, full of approval.

Yeah, I bet you're all for this, Ashe thought. They took a few steps away from Renae to get a head start.

"Okay... be ready to run if this goes bad."

The memory of the night Ryan had kissed them flooded their mind. All that embarrassment, anger, and frustration. Unlike in front of Damon, when the change hadn't come at all, this time the wolf spirit surged forward, quick and greedy.

Ashe bent the cage inside themselves, cracked it just enough to reach the beast without letting it loose.

Muscles swelled. Bones stretched with a slow, grating ache. Skin tightened across expanding limbs, threatening to tear. The wolf wanted more, demanded it, but Ashe held the line. Strength, without surrender.

Renae's eyes widened.

"Yeah," Ashe said, their voice a low, rumbling bass. "Caught Ryan off guard when he saw it too."

They stepped up to the door together. Gripped it. Pulled.

Metal groaned. Bolts popped. Ashe's arm trembled under the strain, thick cords of muscle flexing tight.

CRACK.

The doorknob snapped free, and the door ripped open. Both Lycans stumbled backward from the sudden give, landing hard and skidding across the tile.

Ashe scrambled up first and bolted into the freezer.

"Pines!"

A figure huddled in the corner. Back to Ashe. Naked. Shivering.

Deep cuts slashed across their body. Some were still bleeding. Hot-iron brand marks seared cruel shapes into the skin.

Ashe slowed, heart sinking. It wasn't Pines. The person was too small. Too slender.

Gingerly, they reached down. The figure flinched, her muscles seizing tight, but didn't pull away.

They turned her from the wall.

Her face was a wreck. One cheek swollen, raw from multiple hits. Frozen tears clung to her skin in jagged streaks. Her lips were cracked, breath barely stirred. Her whole body carried the color of death. A soft mottled blue beneath the bruises.

Ashe's stomach clenched. Even through the damage, they knew her.

A flash from the pack link at Lowe Mill. Images along with emotions. Cole's fear. His devotion. The desperate ache in him for someone out of reach.

That woman had been warm. Laughing. Whole. Not this. Not broken and carved and left to freeze.

And yet...

"Radio Cole," Ashe said. Their voice came out flat, hard-edged. "Tell him to get here. Now."

They slipped their arms beneath her and lifted. She weighed almost nothing. Bones and ice and torn skin.

Ashe held her close and carried her out of the cold.

***

"You will help me," the man croaked.

Without thinking, Cole stepped forward and gripped the exposed bone and tendon of the outstretched hand. He pulled.

The figure slid out of the barrel and collapsed onto the earth. Brown sludge followed, oozing from his ruined body, seeping into the dirt beneath him.

Where they touched, the sludge clung to Cole's skin. A creeping numbness spread across his palm and wrist, cold and wrong.

Then Cole's mind caught up. He stumbled back, breath quickening. "Who... who are you?"

The man's body was full of holes. Literal gaps where flesh had burned away entirely. Parts of him were translucent with decay. One lung was fully exposed, pink-grey and sickly, spattered with black. It inflated and deflated with wet, rasping breaths.

"I am The Seer," the man rasped. "I am a spirit of time."

His eyes locked with Cole's. Then the pupils blackened, and it was no longer eye contact.

It was *Sight* boring through him, past him.

"You will ask me, 'How did you get here.'"

"How did you get here?" Cole repeated, only realizing after that the words hadn't felt like his own.

He stumbled backward, seeking space in the cramped room.

"I was taken," the Seer said, "by Fäulung. The Rotting Essence."

He turned to reveal a burn on his lower back. A glyph glowed faintly red beneath a web of fluorescent green runes. Twisting shapes that danced on the edge of recognition. Too many lines curved where they should've intersected. Angles bent in the wrong direction. It wasn't a symbol meant to be read. It was meant to bind. To burn.

"I was branded. Bound. I cannot leave this body."

Staring at the twisted symbol, Cole wasn't sure whether to recoil or reach for the spirit again.

"There are others," the Seer said. "Spirits like me. Trapped. Poisoned. Our essence spills into the land. Into your world."

Cole swallowed hard, mind racing. "Let's get you out of here."

He reached down. The Seer lifted his mangled arm. Intact in form, but hollow in substance. Somehow, it moved smoothly, as if the body didn't need to obey natural law anymore.

The memory of ichor crawling across his skin made Cole pause. He tore a strip from his pant leg, wrapped his hands, and crouched beside the spirit.

Bracing himself, he grasped the cold, wet hand and pulled. Skin sloughed away. Tendons unspooled. The body rose in pieces and came together again.

The spirit was light, too light. Sixty pounds at most. Cole lifted him easily and boosted him through the hole above. Then he jumped, caught the edge, and pulled himself up after. He landed steady, heart still pounding.

Even now, the strength startled him. In high school, he'd never once touched the basketball rim.

Closing the door behind them, he turned to the figure, now crumpled more than seated.

"The Seer huh," Cole said, brushing his hands off. "You're the one who told Pines to gather us, right?"

No response.

"Okay," Cole paused, letting his mind unscramble. "Why did you tell Pines to gather our pack? Why us?"

The Seer's voice came slow and brittle, like it was dragging each word from the wreckage of memory. "You are meant to slow what is happening," the decayed man said. "The deterioration of this land beneath the reach of Tzelut's tentacles."

Before Cole could respond, the Seer pressed on.

"They trap spirits. They poison us. Spirits of the Wildlands. Spirits of Renewal. The corruption twists the connections. Tainted essence spills and tears through all realms. Where it seeps, nothing grows."

Cole tried to keep up. "How do we stop it?"

"It will not be stopped," the Seer said quietly. "It will be slowed."

His radio crackled to life. Renae's voice burst through, panicked and breathless. "Cole, you need to get to the clubhouse."

He looked between the Seer, the clubhouse in the distance, and the nearest patch of woods.

"What can I do to help you?" Cole asked.

The Seer didn't look at him. His gaze drifted away, unfocused.

"You have done it," he said. "There are other spirits who will need help."

Cole stepped forward. "Let me at least get you to the woods..."

"YOU HAVE DONE WHAT WAS SEEN. YOU WILL DO NO MORE TO AID ME."

The Seer's voice detonated through the house. The walls cracked. Cole was hurled backward, hitting the floor hard as a wave of force rolled through the room.

Now floating in the air, The Seer's eyes went wide and wild, burning with something beyond pain. Something ancient.

"DO NOT PRESUME TO CHANGE WHAT I HAVE SEEN."

The sound wasn't just heard. It settled into Cole's bones. His skin went clammy. Cold raced down his spine. Goosebumps bloomed across his arms and neck.

Then, just as suddenly, The Seer collapsed. He crumpled back to the earth like a puppet with its strings cut.

"They come," the Seer murmured. "You will go to the others."

Cole didn't remember turning to run. His feet were already moving, mind blank. He slipped out the way he'd come in, boots hitting the dirt, breath ragged.

By the time he raised the walkie-talkie, he was halfway to the clubhouse. He clicked the button hard, voice spilling out faster than he could think.

"I found The Seer! Said he was trapped. Burned. Corrupted. There are others here like him."

His words came out in gasps. "We need to find them. We can't leave them down here to rot."

Static crackled in the speaker. Cole didn't care. He kept moving, breath thinning, hands shaking.

Renae appeared from a side door leading into the kitchen, her expression hard.

"You need to come with me," she said. No hesitation. No explanation. Just command.

Cole opened his mouth to speak, but she didn't give him the chance. She grabbed his wrist and pulled him inside. The air in the kitchen was stifling. Every stove had been turned on, heat radiating through the space.

Ashe stood near the center of the room, noticeably larger and more muscular than usual. Heat shimmered around their bulked-up frame. They moved carefully, methodically rubbing warmth back into something small and still on the countertop.

Cole stepped closer.

A form lay beneath a pile of tablecloths. Crumpled. Unmoving.

Rebecca.

Time seemed to stall.

Somehow, someone from Dum-Prot had followed Cole home. Either the night of the brewery or after he'd dropped off Jericho at the hospital.

They'd waited. And when she'd left, when she'd walked out on him after their fight, they'd taken her.

Renae stepped forward, arms open as if to steady him. Ashe was still working Rebecca's limbs, trying to push life back into her frozen skin.

"She's alive," Renae said gently. "We're getting her out of here."

Cole dropped to his knees beside her. Her hand was ice against his burning palm. He held it as if it might vanish.

"Let's see if we can find more blankets," Renae said, glancing to Ashe. They moved off toward the storage rooms, giving him space.

Rebecca's eyelids fluttered.

Blue lips parted.

"C-Cole..."

Then her body went limp again.

He pulled his hand back, staring at her broken form. His mind struggled to process that she had spoken his name. That she was here. That this was real.

They took her. Beat her. Tortured her.

Because of him.

The rage started as a tremor. A pressure behind the eyes. A crack in the dam.

Then it hit.

His body convulsed as bones cracked beneath the surface like gunfire, his spine arching sharply. Vertebrae ground into new alignment while muscle tore and re-knit across his frame. Flesh rippled as new mass swelled beneath it.

Skin split along his back and thighs. His legs twisted, ankles snapping and reforming as his heels lifted off the ground. Feet lengthened into a forward arch. He dropped low, center of gravity shifting to the balls of his feet.

Hands curled. Nails blackened into claws.

This wasn't brute strength. This wasn't Warhide.

He grew taller, but not wider. Lean. Efficient. Built for speed.

Every part of him sharpened.

Not a brawler.

A hunter.

Cole's breath steamed through clenched teeth. His gaze locked on Rebecca.

His thoughts were no longer racing. They were clear. He was going to find them.

And he was going to kill every... single... one.

Chapter 25

A she returned to the sound of splintering wood. The silver daggers glinted beneath the stovetop glow, looking almost delicate in their massive hands. Tension carved deep grooves into the wooden handles.

No threat. Just the empty kitchen.

Rebecca still lay curled on the counter, shivering uncontrollably, but with no new wounds. The same cold, broken girl they'd left.

Where was Cole?

Ashe stared at the hole in the wall, their mind refusing to catch up. Refusing to admit what they already knew.

No. Not Cole.

He wasn't supposed to break. He was the steady one. If *he* couldn't fight it, then what was the point? Why were they still clinging to control?

The Wolf Spirit stirred, emboldened. Its breath was warm in Ashe's throat. Its teeth, Ashe's teeth. The boundaries between them were thinning.

"Renae! We've got a problem!" Ashe shouted, their voice edged with more than one meaning.

Renae sprinted in, a bundle of blankets in one arm, a gun in the other.

"What?" she snapped, lowering her weapon when she saw only dust, drywall, and panic.

Ashe pointed wordlessly to the yawning hole in the dining room wall. Jagged wood and exposed studs jutted out where something massive had torn its way into the night.

"Oh. Shit."

Renae knelt beside Rebecca, draping the blankets over her trembling form, tucking them tight.

"You've gotta find him," she said. "Before he gets hurt. Or before he hurts someone he doesn't mean to."

"Renae..." Ashe panted. Sweat soaked their collar. Their skin flushed hot, the predator pacing beneath it like a caged blaze. "I can't hold it back much longer. If I go out there, I might make it worse."

Renae stepped in and rested her hand on Ashe's hip. The contact was soft, softer than Ashe expected. Not domination. Not Pines' forceful stillness. Just trust.

It was the touch a mother gave a frightened child, promising they weren't alone.

Something inside Ashe stilled. Not caged, not beaten. Just... held.

Renae wasn't afraid of them. And somehow, that made Ashe feel more human than anything had in days.

"I'll try to stop him," Renae said, then corrected herself. "To help him."

But Ashe could hear the blade beneath the mercy. *If he's gone too far... I'll do what I have to.*

She looked to Rebecca, whose color was slowly returning. "But she needs someone too. Can you be that person? Are you safe enough to stay with her?"

Ashe hesitated. The comment felt manipulative, a dig to get Ashe to go.

They couldn't imagine hurting someone like Rebecca. Couldn't picture lifting a hand to someone so clearly shattered.

But the memory came anyway.

The Wolf Spirit back at Ryan's house. The way it had looked at Grace, its tongue slipping out, its eyes gleaming with hunger. It hadn't seen her as a friend. Or a packmate.

Just a rival.

Or a meal.

"I'll go help Cole," Ashe said, the words scraping from their throat like splinters.

If they were going to lose control, better it happened out there. Not here. Not near her.

Renae nodded. Then stepped forward and wrapped her arms around them, resting her head briefly against the larger Grayskin.

"You've got this," she whispered.

Ashe gave a final nod and turned toward the hole in the wall. Their heart rattled in their massive chest, uncertainty clawing at every step. But Renae's faith stayed with them, just enough to move forward.

Behind them, Renae raised a dog whistle to her lips and blew, calling for reinforcements.

Then, gunfire ripped through the distance.

Followed by screaming.

***

Claws shredded a rifle in half, tearing through steel and Kevlar like wet cardboard. He swept across the gunman's chest, raking through ribs and spine in one smooth motion.

The man gasped. Then dropped, lifeless.

YES! MORE! The Wolf Spirit howled. Cole didn't need the push.

He wanted to hurt. To punish.

He craved the crunch of bone, the collapse of bodies. The agony. Someone else's pain to drown out his own.

He bared his teeth and scanned the gravel road for movement, for breath, for prey.

A gunman had climbed into the rafters of an unfinished house, hoping to catch the Lycan from above. But Cole heard him. The creak of lumber under nervous boots. The shift of weight above.

Cole dropped to all fours, claws scraping furrows into the loose stone. Then leapt into a graceful soaring arc. Panic shots barked but didn't land in time.

He collided with the man mid-fall; the impact broke the beam beneath them.

The two bodies tumbled downward.

The gunman hit the concrete with a sickening crunch. Cole landed atop him, the man's ribs folding under the Lycan's weight.

He will never hurt anyone again.

The Lycan burst from the skeletal frame of the house, a blur under the artificial light. Renae had said there were three patrols. Just three.

He had just ended the third.

But it wasn't enough.

A group of construction workers ran from one of the houses, scattering into the open.

They were human. Unarmed. Terrified.

Cole tasted it in the air. The fear was sharp and cloying, sweet on the tongue like bloodied sugar. The animal inside surged with hunger.

More.

He paused. They weren't shooting. They weren't even looking back. Just running.

But they worked here. They had to know what was buried beneath this place. Maybe they hadn't pulled the trigger, but they built the walls that trapped the spirits. They poured concrete over the bones of the land.

That made them part of it.

Even as the thought twisted in his chest, the Lycan moved. Its need was simple.

Cole dropped low and charged.

***

Ashe arrived too late.

The first body was little more than a smear. Black sludge mixed with torn muscle, bones shattered and scattered across the dirt. The next two weren't much better.

But the last ones...

No rot. No taint. No signs of spirit corruption. Just blood. Red. Human. Real.

And fear.

These hadn't been monsters. They had just been people.

Ashe wanted to believe Cole had been driven to this. That his Wolf Spirit had twisted his hand. But even their wolf recoiled at the carnage.

These weren't prey. They were victims.

"Cole!" Ashe shouted, their low bass cracking as it echoed into the dark.

They sensed the movement a half-second too late.

A worker swung a two-by-four at their head. Ashe caught the blow with a raised arm. Wood splintered against it. Pain flared sharp and hot. Something cracked deep inside. Their dagger clanged against the gravel.

"Wrong move, asshole."

With their good arm, Ashe grabbed the man by the throat and hoisted him off the ground, feet kicking in the air.

The monster inside urged them forward. Squeeze. End him. But it wouldn't help Cole, and Ashe had to stay in control.

They hurled the man backward. He hit the gravel and rolled, scraping across stone until he came to a stop. Blood dripped from his face.

Ashe stepped close and crouched beside him.

"Take this as an opportunity. Run."

The man scrambled to his feet, gave one last look, then disappeared into the trees.

A scream tore through the air, yanking Ashe's attention.

They sprinted toward it, boots pounding across uneven ground. The Wolf spirit tugged at them and they weren't sure if they were running to stop Cole or join him.

Bursting into the main roadway, they spotted a group of men hurtling toward them. Ashe tensed, ready to fight.

The faces stopped them.

One man, barely older than Kyle, stumbled at the front. His hardhat was gone. His eyes were wide, wet, pleading. Not a soldier. Not a monster. Just a kid who'd taken a construction job.

Then Ashe saw what was behind them.

Cole.

The werewolf barreled forward, his frame massive and unmistakable. Brown and red fur rippled with motion, and over one eye, that patch of white. The only part still undeniably him.

The men faltered, caught between two terrors. The Grayskin ahead. The beast behind.

"Get behind me!" Ashe shouted, waving them past.

Cole didn't slow.

The workers swerved around Ashe in a frantic rush, desperate to avoid getting too close. The werewolf skidded to a halt just feet away, claws carving deep trenches in the gravel.

A low, guttural warning growl rumbled from his chest.

"You got the guards. Now we need to get the others and get out of here. We need to get Rebecca to a hospital."

The growl shifted. It was no longer a warning. Anger now. Vibration. Rage. It rattled Ashe's bones.

Oh, well, shit. I guess that was the wrong thing to say.

Cole lunged.

Ashe sidestepped, but claws ripped across their arm, nerves igniting like live wires. A backhand landed a heartbeat later, smashing into their face and hurling them through the air. Blood streamed behind them, painting red ribbons in the dark.

They crashed to the ground. Something snapped deep inside.

The cage shattered.

Cole's blow had broken more than bone. It had tipped the balance. Ashe had held on through blood and breath and sheer will. Now they were going to fail. Fail Renae. Fail themself. Fail everyone.

A howl ripped from Ashe's throat as their body convulsed. Muscle swelled. Flesh tore. Bone cracked and rebuilt itself.

Hunt. Chase. Kill.

The drumbeat rose in their blood.

And Ashe howled the answer.

***

Both Lycans collided. Freight trains of rage and muscle crashed together, the impact cracking the air. Fur tangled, teeth snapped, claws tore through skin. Ashe's weight slammed into him, the heat of their Warhide bulk pressing against him, the impact of their bodies hitting hard ground.

Ashe went for his shoulder, teeth digging in deep. Only for Cole to twist, spin, and rake across Ashe's ribs with three brutal claws that peeled back strips of skin.

The Warhide snarled and surged forward, using their size to drive him back. Cole's feet skidded over gravel, then wood. The half-built house loomed behind him, then shattered. A window frame disintegrated as they barreled through it in a storm of splinters and nails.

Cole tumbled and rolled away, fast as lightning.

Ashe was already swinging.

He ducked beneath the Warhide's swipe. Too slow. Too heavy.

Cole's jaws found flesh and clamped down on their thigh. Ashe roared, pain and fury ripping from their throat. He felt the femur grind, tasted blood, and part of him reveled in the suffering he caused.

A knee smashed into his face, snapping his head back. Then came the shoulder, solid and brutal. It slammed into his chest and sent him flying.

He hit the far wall hard. Wood blew around him. The frame gave way, and part of the house collapsed under the force.

Debris fell like rain, but neither werewolf cared.

He clawed his way out.

So did Ashe.

They met again without a word, without hesitation, and without mercy.

They circled, blood matting their fur, eyes locked. Their growls filled the empty space between unfinished homes. The scent of copper and sawdust hung heavy in the air. Somewhere behind them, humans screamed.

Cole ignored them as Ashe lunged.

He dropped low, muscles snapping tight, and slashed upward. His claws tore under their jaw, nearly severing their throat. Blood sprayed across his muzzle, hot and fresh.

Ashe reeled. That was his opening.

He didn't understand why they had stopped him, why they got in the way. Maybe they thought they were saving him. Maybe they thought there was still something worth saving.

But Ashe had made their choice.

They'd stood between Cole and justice. That made them just as guilty. For Rebecca. For the spirits. For every wasted second.

The wolf agreed.

Find. Tear. Punish.

He pounced, slamming Ashe through another wall. Wood snapped, plaster shattered, and they hit the concrete slab with a thunderous crack.

He landed on top and struck.

Once. Then again.

His claws carved deep into their side, ripping open their shoulder. Blood poured between them.

And still, it wasn't enough.

Ashe's body arched under the assault. But they were still the stronger.

In a wild surge, a knee smashed into Cole's ribs, and a massive arm hurled him aside. Ashe rolled clear and pushed up to their feet.

They faced each other, chests heaving.

Blood dripped from Cole's mouth. Ashe's eyes burned. Not just with pain, but recognition. Grief. Resolve.

A flicker of movement behind him caught his attention. Two wolves running to a nearby house.

Ryan and Grace.

He tracked them without turning his head, instincts razor-sharp. If they interfered, he'd be ready.

Behind them, more movement. A few of the construction workers bolted for the trucks parked down the road. One engine revved, tires squealing as it shot backward, then peeled out into the dark.

But not everyone was running.

Just before the gated exit, a man stood. Unmoving. A statue amidst the chaos. His frame was small, almost pathetic, with one shriveled arm barely visible beneath the sleeve of his coat.

Not afraid. Uninterested in the fight.

He was just waiting.

Hands relaxed at his sides. Posture calm. Like he knew exactly when his moment would come.

Cole's Wolf Spirit recoiled, instincts curling away from the figure.

And for one fleeting second, Cole blinked. It was the thing from Gaia's vision.

The haze split, and his mind surfaced. He could feel it all. The pain. The weight. The wrongness.

Then Ashe hit him.

They barreled into his ribs, knocking him flat. Cole hit the concrete hard; the breath ripped from his chest.

Ashe's fist came down like a hammer, but Cole rolled, slashing claws across their leg. Blood followed his slash in an arc. He twisted, using their momentum to flip them both.

The Warhide struck the ground shoulder-first, a sharp crack echoing off the slab.

Cole landed on top.

Seizing their arm, he drove it into the concrete. Bone snapped.

Ashe roared in pain, but Cole pinned the shattered limb beneath one clawed hand. The other hand rose, claws slick and red, poised to strike deep.

Ashe didn't flinch.

They bared their teeth and growled through the pain, eyes locked with his.

The beast howled inside him, screaming for blood. Demanding the kill. But through the fog of rage, he saw them. Not just the Warhide. Not an enemy.

Ashe.

Even in pain, even with fire behind their eyes, they were still trying to stop him. Cole wanted to hurt those responsible. To burn the rot out. But not this. Not them.

The Warhide's legs shifted, tensed. They were about to kick.

The kill would have been simple. Claws could have come down and finished the gash along their throat. But he wasn't going to murder a friend. Not now. He was finally back in control.

Reaching for the pack link, he tried to project something. Peace. A warning. Anything. A signal that the fight could end. But his mind remained too fogged, too tangled with the beast's fire to form clear thoughts.

Whatever he sent, it didn't land.

Ashe kicked with both legs, hard.

The blow launched him off. Cole flew back, skidded through the gravel, and landed in a pile of cinderblocks. Dust and stone exploded around him.

He lay still for a moment, ribs screaming, the world spinning.

Ashe was already on their feet. Staggering. Bloodied. One arm limp at their side. Chest heaving with effort. But they were ready for the next round.

Then, the headlights blinded them both.

Two tan work vans tore through the main gate, engines roaring. They skidded into the gravel lot, tires chewing up the earth. Doors burst open, and a dozen men spilled out of each vehicle. They drew their rifles, armor gleaming in the overhead lights.

Voices barked as muzzle flashes lit the night.

Chapter 26

Bullets tore through the construction site, kicking up sprays of dirt and shattering concrete. Cole howled as rounds punched through his shoulder, then his thigh. Ashe dove behind the splintered frame of a half-finished house as the wall collapsed under a relentless hail of gunfire.

The real battle had just started.

Ashe sucked in a breath, blood-sharp and laced with the metallic sting of ozone. The crack of gunfire echoed off rebar and skeletal walls, a deafening rhythm of chaos. Somewhere behind it all, someone screamed.

The sudden shock of a new threat shoved the Wolf Spirit down. Instincts pulled inward, driven by the need to survive something the wolf was not familiar with. Ashe's focus snapped back into place just as the pain surged.

Every bite, every claw mark Cole had torn into their skin flared with heat. Those wounds refused to close, slower than the rest. But everything else was already knitting back together. They could feel their broken arm, the cracked ribs, pulling into place; each shift scraping bone on bone in a raw, grinding ache.

The fight had hollowed them out. But that pain belonged to another world. This one, filled with bullets and blood and ruin, was all that mattered now.

The gunfire had settled into a rhythm, providing cover for movement. Ashe used the lull to assess their position, scanning the chaos beyond their shelter.

Gunmen swarmed the site, moving with cold precision. Their gear seemed to drink the light, faces hidden behind glowing sights that swept the dark. The vans still idled, engines purring, headlights spilling across the gravel in sterile white. Warped shadows stretched and stalked between the shattered frames.

Cole was already moving, a blur of motion and blood. He darted through muzzle flashes, claws slicing clean arcs before the soldiers could react. One dropped, his stomach opened like a zippered pouch. Another slammed into a truck with enough force to bend the fender.

Ashe broke from cover, their arm finally snapping back into place as they ran. They collided with a soldier mid-sprint, their Warhide mass cracking his spine beneath the impact. The man's rifle skittered across the gravel. Ashe didn't stop to watch him die.

Gunfire barked behind them. Ashe twisted, catching the rounds in the shoulder. Something popped deep and wrong. The flare of agony locked them in place, sharp enough to keep them grounded. Ashe grabbed a slab of broken concrete and hurled it. The chunk caught the shooter in the chest. He dropped hard, breathless and crumpled.

Grace and Ryan flowed in like ghosts. Brown eyes gleamed with amber in the dark, claws slick. Grace lunged at a soldier reloading behind a van, dragging him down in silence. Ryan toppled another, jaws clamped deep into a thigh.

Even two additional Lycans weren't going to turn the tide.

Gunfire erupted from all sides, a storm of noise and motion. No safe angles. No rhythm to follow.

Ashe stumbled behind a propane tank, lungs raw. The stench of gas clung to their throat.

I guess it's not empty.

Sparks shrieked against the metal, sharp enough to drown everything else. No time to think. Legs launched them into the open, body twisting as they hit the ground in a tumble.

The world detonated.

Heat slammed into them, flattening the breath in their chest. A jet of fire ripped into the sky, and the 2x6 frames of a nearby house went up in a single violent breath. Wood curled and blackened in seconds.

Through the smoke and fire, the world seemed to pause. The chaos faded, replaced by a stillness too complete to feel natural.

Then, Ashe saw him. The figure. The same one from the clubhouse.

Perfectly still beneath the unfinished archway, meant to welcome some future community. A monument to a future that would never come. Watching. Unblinking. Unbothered.

Renae saw him too. She stepped from behind a trailer, weapon steady, and fired three times. Each round aimed dead center.

The figure was already gone. Or rather, never truly where he appeared to be. One moment he stood in place. The next, two feet to the left, as if he had always been standing there instead. The bullets passed cleanly through where he wasn't.

He hadn't flinched. Hadn't moved. He had simply not existed in the space she fired.

Renae's mouth curled, a flicker of awe and revulsion, before she ducked back down.

Cole roared and charged the line of gunmen fifty yards ahead. Their rifles were steady, bodies locked in firing stance. He was fast, but Ashe saw it.

He wouldn't make it in time.

The space around Cole blurred like boiling oil. Ashe felt a pulse ripple across the earth, like the heartbeat of something buried. Then Cole vanished. Pulled into the Wildland between seconds.

He reappeared in the middle of the squad. One moment the soldiers stood together, clean and ordered. The next, bodies came apart. Blood sprayed wide. Limbs flew in every direction.

Across the battlefield, the figure spoke just loud enough for Ashe to hear. *"Faoil na haislinge."*

The Wildlands had cracked open for a breath, just enough to let something through. Ashe felt it in their soul.

The pack link didn't just ignite. It flooded them. For Ashe, it was sunlight behind their ribs, too bright to contain. Gaia's breath, suddenly close.

Fierce. Undeniable.

Ryan and Renae pulsed at the far reaches of the bond, like pressure behind glass. But Grace, Cole, and Ashe moved as one. The pack link pulsed stronger than it ever had. Images flashed with perfect clarity. Emotions passed between them like breath. Words didn't need to be spoken; they surfaced and slipped through without friction.

The Lycans flowed through the remaining gunmen like a single body. Ashe saw a soldier creeping up behind Cole and pushed the vision through. Cole turned and tore the man open without hesitation. Grace herded a panicked soldier into Ashe's path, and he never saw it coming. Cole's thoughts came steady and calm, pressing upward through the link, lifting them all.

They were synced. They were pack. Ashe's Warhide eyes shimmered, filled with the terrible certainty of it. They had never known anyone like this. Never felt anyone like this.

The gunfire had faded. Bodies lay broken across the lot, limbs twisted, blood steaming in the dirt. The vans were riddled with holes, sagging and smoking.

Grace limped toward a crumbling wall, her fur streaked with blood. Ryan hovered near her, his growl low and constant. Renae knelt beside a pile of shattered fencing, one hand clamped over a wound, still breathing, still watching.

And at the far edge of it all stood the man.

But Ashe knew he wasn't a man. They felt it in their bones, a slow, instinctive revulsion. The bond confirmed it, humming with unease.

The scent of old death clung to him, thick and rotting. His presence was heavy, full of hunger and age.

A vampire.

Yet he didn't attack. Didn't lift a hand. He simply watched, calm as if the slaughter were nothing more than a prelude.

His eyes were milky, clouded with cataracts, but not blind. They shimmered faintly, tuned to something beyond the visible world. Strips of flesh clung to his face, slack and rotted, bone dark beneath. His left arm curled into a shriveled claw. The right gripped a short sword edged in silver, held by four remaining fingers. Two long, hooked fangs jutted past his lip, ancient and blackened but still razor-sharp.

His strength radiated from every still inch of him. Ashe's Wolf Spirit didn't want to fight. It wanted to run. Even at full health, the pack couldn't win this. Its instincts had narrowed to two options. And flee was winning.

***

That pale, rotted face tilted toward them as its voice spilled from dead lips.

"You are scattered and broken," the vampire said, voice dry and low, like wind passing through hollow bones. "You reek of Gaia's touch. I will release that burden from you."

Cole's lip curled. A snarl tried to rise in his throat, but it came out strained. They were too weak to posture.

His muscles quivered with exhaustion. Blood ran in slow, sticky rivulets down his chest and soaked into the gravel at his feet. One silver bullet was still inside, trying to burn its way out of him.

Every part of him screamed to rest. To drop. But the figure standing at the far edge of the ruined construction site made rest impossible.

It took a step forward; the earth tensing beneath its feet. The runes on the hilt of its short silver sword pulsed a dull red.

"I am Lugh the Judge. And while Gaia demands your death to feed her forest, my judgment is kinder."

The blade turned toward Grace and Ryan, still bracing together near the wreckage.

"You will be chosen for domestication. We must replenish the stock animals your kind has slain."

The sword arched lazily toward Ashe and Cole, its glow deepening.

"You two will nourish what's to come. Rooted, not wasted. Eternally alive, spreading Tzelut's reach."

Then the blade swung toward Renae's hiding place.

"And you... you will be my personal payment for delivering this verdict."

The pack link surged. Renae sent not a word but an urgent flash of intent. *Light. Blind. Eyes closed. Now.*
Cole shut his eyes a breath before the world detonated in white.

The flashbang hit Lugh full force. The creature could dodge bullets, but not the speed of light.

The Judge screamed. The sound tore through the air, raw and skin-peeling, as he staggered backward, sword dropping low.

Renae emerged from behind a concrete mixer, already shifting. Her body ripped itself apart as fur blanketed her skin. She fell to all fours, bones snapping and realigning, claws grinding into the concrete.

Now!

Cole charged. Ashe was beside him. Grace and Ryan flanked the Judge.

For a single heartbeat, they had him.

Ashe struck first. Their claws tore across Lugh's torso. The flesh split. No blood. Only smoke and a chemical burn from contact with its skin.

The vampire reeled but recovered quickly.

Claws caught the vampire's throat. Skin burst. A chunk of jawbone spun through the air.

Runes on the sword flared blood-red, and Lugh lashed out blindly. The blade struck Cole's shoulder, and cold fire bit into his flesh. Blood sprayed, drawn into the blade. The silver drank it in, the red in the runes deepening, glowing brighter.

Cole stumbled back, roaring in agony.

Ashe lunged to help, but the Judge turned, sudden and sharp, and carved across Ashe's leg. The wound burned. Ashe fell hard, teeth clenched.

The vampire's movements became fluid again. Sight returning.

He vanished and reappeared behind Grace. His sword cut her down in one motion. She hit the ground, bleeding and gasping.

Ryan charged to protect her. The flat of the blade caught him clean in the ribs. He flew into the wall and stayed down.

Fear flooded the pack link. But Renae pressed forward anyway, leaping at the Judge from behind. The vampire twisted and slammed his shriveled arm into her side mid-air. Something cracked. She hit the dirt, groaning, eyes flickering.

Cole tried to rise. His legs folded beneath him.

Blood poured from his side, hot and unending. The air turned to sludge in his lungs. Too thick. Too slow.

Through his failing vision, he glimpsed movement. Probably just smoke and shadows playing tricks on his dying eyes. He could only hope it wasn't more reinforcements.

But hope felt pointless now. One by one, they were falling. Grace. Ryan. Renae. Because of him. He was the one who'd lost control. The one who tore off into the dark. The one who let the monster speak for him.

Rebecca.

The thought hurt more than the sword. She had been right to try to run. She'd only done it too late.

Lugh The Judge stepped forward, blade low and glowing, its edge eager to feed again. Cole could only watch, body failing, as the vampire advanced on Ashe.

A rifle cracked from the shadows.

Silver rounds slammed into Lugh's back. He snarled, turning, but more followed. One hit his shoulder. Another struck the sword.

It flew from his hand, clattering into the dirt with a splash of blood. Lugh staggered, smoke rising from each impact.

Ashe made a desperate lunge. The vampire tried to blink away but was a hair too slow. The Warhide tackled him full force, driving him to the ground in a tangle of claws and rotting flesh.

Claws tore at his throat; teeth ripped through chest and face. Flesh gave. Bone cracked. Black ichor splashed over Ashe, and they ignored the burning. One more pain among a thousand. The bloodied, misshapen thing reached out and dug four fingers into Ashe's sternum. The Warhide stuttered as pain pulsed through the pack link, causing Cole to double over in shared agony, unable to move. The last ebbs of life slid out of Ashe as they struggled to pull free from its good arm.

Lugh's fingers tightened in Ashe's chest. His voice bubbled through ruin.

"You little nothing!" Lugh's black-red blood spat from his mouth onto Ashe's muzzle. "I am going to take your brother and make him like me. Make him like the other's belov—"

Two more bullets found the vampire: one struck its mouth, teeth flying in yellow-and-white bits; the other sank into its skull, mushrooming inside the brain. Lugh screeched, gurgled, then stopped.

Cole saw something snap inside Ashe. Not bone. Not will.

For the first time, the Wolf Spirit recoiled at Ashe's intensity.

Ashe dragged it back. Their claws yanked free from Lugh's grip and plunged back into his chest. Again. Again. Tearing through ribs, shredding what remained of dead organs. Black ichor sprayed across their muzzle, burning, and they didn't care.

"Not Kyle! Never Kyle!"

They found something that might once have been a heart and ripped it free. Held it up. Crushed it in their fist until it burst.

Then they slumped forward. The Warhide peeled away like wet bark, leaving Ashe naked, crumpled, and unconscious.

Cole collapsed onto his elbows. His own form wavered, then gave in. Flesh rippled. Claws receded. Bones cracked as they reset. He shifted back with a final, shuddering breath.

His body screamed. His soul felt hollowed out. Through his ringing ears, he heard footsteps. Light. Bare.

Rebecca.

She ran across the broken earth, nearly slipping in the pools of human remains. Her blanket fluttered behind her like a banner, stained and scorched.

Her voice reached him, soft and steady, rough at the edges.

"I've got you," she whispered. "It's over."

Cole tried to speak. His throat was raw, his voice barely a rasp. "I killed... I couldn't stop..."

Her hand found his face. Steady despite everything.

"I know." No judgment. No flinching. Just her, holding him in the wreckage. "We'll figure it out. Together."

He didn't deserve that word. Not after what he'd done. But she said it anyway. And in that moment, it wasn't a warrior or a wolf who held the pack together.

It was Rebecca.

Cole leaned into her, not because he was weak, but because she was strong.

Without teeth. Without claws.

She had saved them.

Chapter 27

The Uber stopped at the edge of the long driveway, refusing to take the dirt road down to the house. He had tried to convince the driver. Just a little farther. Just through the trees. Just to the door. But she shut him down fast. Liability concerns. After a little more prying, she admitted the place creeped her out and told him to get out.

Fine.

His physical therapist had told him to keep moving. Let the muscles settle, and they would seize. Let the pain get comfortable, and it would never leave. He just hadn't pictured a one-mile trek in the middle of August as ideal exercise for his injuries.

He stepped out into the stillness, the sound of tires on gravel already fading behind him. A soft breeze carried the scent of pine and moss. Somewhere up ahead, buried in the hush of the woods, was the house. And beyond that, whatever came next.

Dozens of birds filtered through the canopy, their voices layered and constant. He had never heard so many calls at once.

Chipmunks darted across the path in pairs, fat with acorns and too bold to care about the human passing through their domain. Squirrels skittered overhead in the branches, tails twitching. A fox paused just beyond the trees, watching him for a moment before vanishing into the underbrush.

Even the air felt different here. Humid with loam, dense with motion and sound. The forest wasn't just alive. It was brimming. Every inch of it seemed to press inward.

It sounded like every animal in Madison County had gathered here, huddled on this patch of land like this was the last safe harbor.

On the plus side, Jericho had reassured them the pack had made a serious dent in Dum-Prot's local manpower. The company was still busy managing the fallout from the construction site fire and trying to spin the near-destruction of Monte Sano as an accident.

For now, the pack was in the clear. As long as no one dug deeper into the company's business, it would focus its attention elsewhere.

That had never been this group's strong suit.

The others had thrown themselves into their next missions. Chasing ghosts. Digging up half-buried leads. Renae was already investigating other Dum-Prot Land sites. Ashe was pushing hard to find Pines. Grace wanted to track down the corrupted spirits they had unleashed.

He couldn't blame them. He just didn't know what his next move was. That was why he was here now.

The dirt road curved ahead, the trees thickening with every step. Pale light filtered through the leaves in shifting streaks. Somewhere in the distance, a power tool shrieked to life.

The hair on the back of his neck prickled.

It came from behind the house. Pines' old workshop. The one Ashe had unofficially claimed. They said it was temporary, just keeping watch in case the old man came back. That had been weeks ago.

He slowed as the sound cut out, replaced by the clank of metal on metal, then a sharp burst of swearing.

The air smelled of oil and burnt rubber. Something about it made his chest tighten. He told himself he could leave. Turn around. Head back before they noticed.

But his feet kept moving.

He stood just outside the open door, watching. The memory of starlight flickered behind his eyes. The last time they had been alone.

The fury in Ashe's voice. The threat they had made. Clear. Sharp. Unmistakable.

He didn't know if they had forgiven him.

He didn't know if he had forgiven himself.

Inside, Ashe's RAV4 sat jacked up on ramps. The Enby lay underneath it, grease-slicked and frowning, a laptop open beside them streaming a repair tutorial. He knocked on the rolling door, and the clatter made them jolt.

They slid out from beneath the SUV, wiping their hands on their jeans. Scabs still marked their arms and neck, wounds that refused to heal cleanly. One jagged gash ran from collarbone to jaw. That one would scar.

They looked at him with sharp unease. No effort to hide the tension.

"Why..." they paused, catching their breath. "Why are you here, Ryan?"

So much for just stopping by to say hi.

He stepped closer. "We've got air to clear if we're going to work together."

That got their attention. He still didn't know why Ashe wanted him in the pack at all. He had guesses, but they had sent too many mixed messages to be sure.

Ashe paused the DIY tutorial and stood with their arms crossed.

"Fine. I think you're a dick."

He took a step back, angling his hip out of reach. He didn't think they would actually follow through on the threat from the night they met. But some risks weren't worth taking.

"I sold the property to Dum-Prot Land," he said. "And it wasn't the only one. There were others under my name. Looks like they ended up with some of those too."

"What?" The word landed hard. Blue fire lit Ashe's eyes. He could have sworn they stood an inch taller.

They really were beautiful when they were mad. But now wasn't the time.

"I wanted to tell you at Lowe Mill," he said, lowering his voice. "But I didn't think I'd make it out of that studio alive. You still deserved to know."

He took a breath.

"My parents died six months after I graduated high school. They left a trust, but my Dad had poured everything into some corporate project. I was left with nothing. I tried to hold on to what I could, but lately, I've had to sell what I could just to get by."

Ashe's expression softened. "Why didn't you just sell your house? You didn't need that big, ugly thing."

He laughed, then looked down, face warming. "Couldn't. Dad mortgaged it a dozen times over. Even if I sold it, I'd still be in debt. I kept hoping that the project he was working on would pull through. But when he died, it fell apart."

Ashe uncrossed their arms, head tilted.

"Look," they said. "I get you didn't *mean* to sell land to an evil corporation bent on corrupting the world with rot and darkness. But... not a great look, you know?"

He snorted. "Yeah. Hard to argue with that."

His voice dropped. "The worst part is that it didn't matter, anyway. I'm probably going to have to declare bankruptcy. The only thing I still owned outright was my car..."

"Oh, Ryan." Their voice softened, just for a moment. Then they turned back to the SUV. "Actually. Just a second."

They opened the back door and pulled something out. It was an 8x10 sheet, matte-backed and heavier than standard paper. They handed it to him.

"I promised anyone who helped me Veil I'd give them pizza and a drawing."

He took it carefully. His breath caught.

It was him, standing on the roof of his yellow Charger, with leather reins in one hand and a whip in the other. The car soared through the sky, aimed at the burned-skin monster from the brewery. It was wild. Gory. Beautiful.

But what hit him hardest wasn't the scene. It was the expression on his face. Captured in ink with impossible precision. Brave. Fierce. Grinning like a man who *knew* he mattered.

Goddamn, he looked like a hero.

"Thank you," he whispered. He moved forward, arms half-raised, but stopped when he saw their shoulders tense. Not yet. He'd earn that.

There was more he wanted to say. Maybe even needed to. But not after this. He didn't want to ruin the moment.

Instead, he nodded toward the RAV4. "You need a hand?"

Ashe raised an eyebrow. "You know how to work on cars?"

"Not really."

"Yeah, me neither." They smirked and handed him a tool he didn't recognize. "But it's got to get fixed. And I'm not giving up on it."

They worked in silence after that, communicating only when it involved grease, bolts, or busted parts. The sun dipped low. Crickets began to chirp. He wiped his hands on his jeans and glanced at the Enby beside him.

They were stubborn. They were brilliant. They were a warrior.

Maybe he wasn't ready to walk away just yet.

***

The wind blew through her whiskers as she stood atop her territory. The overlook showed Grace the vast land surrounding her den. No other hunter laid claim to this section of Monte Sano. It was hers and hers alone.

Which had been the problem for her for so long.

After she had escaped that prison the humans called a zoo, she'd lived up here alone for several years. It was better than the cage, but she had always known something was missing. Now, as Cole trotted up behind her, his wolf form larger and more striking than hers, she knew what it was.

She had needed a pack.

And Mother had given it to her. Surely, there is a reward for what she had endured. They were still too fragile, still finding their shape. But one day, they would be more than survivors. They would be strong. Untouchable.

Cole still hadn't healed completely from the fight with the vampire. According to Ashe and Renae, he had also been "sulking." They had suggested Grace take him for a few days, to work on pack tactics and give his mind something else to focus on. A distraction from his previous mate.

He had protested at first, but Grace had not relented. They had spent a full week up here now. Almost the entire time had been spent running, hunting, and sleeping in wolf form.

It had been a homecoming.

After so much time trapped in wood and brick houses, she was no longer walled off from nature. Out here, she felt Mother more than ever.

A mix of emotions filled Grace as Cole sent thoughts through the pack link. Her confusion must have been obvious, because he Veiled back to human while still sitting on the rock, looking out over the forest. His fur shimmered, then dissolved. Sweat formed quickly on his skin as it returned, damp and flushed.

Grace Veiled as well. Her deep brown skin showed none of the strain Cole's did. He was going to have to learn better control of his body temperature while Veiled, but that could wait.

"We are staying wolves so we can develop our bond." She tried to sound stern, with just a hint of the softness Renae was so skilled at.

"I'm too tired to focus," Cole said between breaths. "You went too fast through the last stretch of woods."

His naked body heaved with exertion, muscles twitching as they cooled. She didn't like this feeling. This always-burning heat that came with her human form. It had been difficult not to simply take one of the men. Renae had been patient when explaining that now was not the best time to seduce Cole.

"Human relationships tend to get messy," Renae had warned.

That was fine. Grace really had her eye on the other one, anyway. He was pleasing to look at, and she enjoyed being the dominant partner. He would submit soon enough.

She shook her head, clearing away the scent of lust. There was work to do.

"We were tired when we fought the vampire. The bond was strong."

"Yeah. I'm not sure why it was so strong then. Maybe we need to get Jericho out here to work with us on it."

"He will not be able to Veil or Tear again."

The conversation with the burned Lycan, after the battle, had been brief. He had been surprised the pack had survived such a fight. When the others arrived from the south, they helped clean up any trace of Lycan involvement and tended to Jericho's wounds.

But they had been too late, or the wounds had been too deep.

Jericho could walk without a cane most days, but his days as a hunter were over. Instead, he had agreed to help train Grace's pack until they found their true mentor.

Renae had been suspicious of the offer. Grace was too.

Cole spoke again, still looking out over the land. "I know. But there's still probably stuff he could teach us. We know so little about what we're capable of."

He was more trusting of outsiders. It was something Grace would need to help him fix.

"You want to understand what the vampire called you. What it means."

Faoil na haislinge.

The Dream Wolf.

"I don't like not knowing what I can do," he said as he threw a small stone over the ledge. "If we had known more, maybe we could have done better. Maybe I wouldn't have killed so many innocent people."

His eyes began to leak again.

Human sorrow always surprised her. But Grace was growing used to strange human feelings. Guilt. Morality. She didn't enjoy them, but she understood humans needed to process such things in order to grow stronger.

"You have rested," she said gently. "We will continue."

She placed a hand on Cole's leg to comfort him. Desire stirred again, unwanted and inconvenient. She withdrew quickly and Veiled back into her wolf form.

Cole remained human a moment longer. He stared out over the land, his gaze distant, looking for something she couldn't see.

Then, silently, he shifted again.

The wind rustled the canopy above them. Nature sang in the healthy woods around their ledge. But farther down the mountain, in the direction of the old construction site, the forest was silent. No birds. No small creatures. Even the wind felt reluctant to cross that scarred land.

They would hunt soon, then rest.

The corrupt roots would still be there in the morning.

***

It had been another dead end.

Renae sat at her kitchen table, half a pot of cold coffee at her elbow and an old file folder spread open beside her. The apartment smelled faintly of sandalwood and dust. One chair still held a pile of unopened mail. She had lived alone for years, but lately, the part that she had quashed was coming back. She was starting to care again.

She leaned back and rubbed her eyes. Her efforts to dig up more of Dum-Prot Land Inc.'s supernatural dealings had hit a wall. Her old contacts were either unresponsive or gone. It had taken time to build trust in the supernatural community back west. But she used every ounce of goodwill to chase down what had happened to Jay, who had killed him, and why.

Then she left. Moved to Alabama and buried the trail, along with the part of herself that chased it.

Now, in some cosmic joke, she had been chosen too. Just like Jay.

The bitterness never really left. Jay had loved being a Lycan. She had loved that *for* him. His stories used to fill her with awe. She used to imagine what it would be like, the two of them as wolves together. She never imagined being left behind.

Her gaze drifted to Jay's old law books, still lined up on the shelf. She could never bring herself to throw them out.

But he was gone. And she had been *chosen* too late to save him.

All she could do now was look out for the four kids Jay would've taken in like strays without a second thought. They were young, untested, and would be eaten alive by the politics of Lycan society. Ashe and Cole could protect them from external threats. Renae would protect them from Gaia.

Her phone rang, cutting through her thoughts.

"Probably Ashe," Renae muttered. "Looking to see if I found a lead on Pines."

A number flashed across the screen, familiar but unlisted. Not in her contacts. She answered without speaking, letting the silence stretch while she listened.

"Hello..." The voice was quiet. Vaguely familiar, but off just enough to raise her hackles. "I take it this is Mrs. Renae Whitlock."

Venom coiled beneath the calm.

Damon.

The bastard from Dum-Prot. The one Ashe had escaped from.

Renae shot to her feet, phone still pressed to her ear, and scanned the window for movement. She stayed low, checking rooftops, cross-streets, and parked cars.

She didn't answer. Not yet. Her mind raced. They must have found the phone Ashe hid. Renae didn't expect Ashe to leave it there when they used Renae's phone.

She cursed under her breath. It was stupid not to have bought a second burner. She was too old for this. She needed to be sharper, better prepared.

She moved fast, circling the living room, pulling the curtains closed and checking every corner for signs of an incoming strike team. Nothing. A couple walked hand-in-hand past her front yard. Children's laughter echoed from somewhere down the street. Everything looked normal.

Her stomach told her otherwise.

"Mrs. Whitlock," Damon said again, still calm. "I'm calling as a courtesy. I would appreciate a response."

His tone never wavered. But Renae remembered the way his voice cracked when Ashe and she had listened in on him. How fast that calm turned to rage.

She drew a long breath. "Fine. I'm here. You want to tell me why I'm not being swarmed by evil werewolves or deformed vampires right now?"

A low, humorless chuckle grated over the line. "Because those resources yielded no result. A waste. All of it."

He paused, and she heard the wet sound of his breathing. The way it filled the silence made her skin crawl.

"I offered your young companion a ceasefire," he continued. "They declined. I'd like to offer the same to you."

Renae grabbed her go-bag and unzipped it one-handed, checking her knife and sidearm. "Why?" she asked. "We tore up your operation on the mountain. You don't strike me as the forgive-and-forget type."

Another chuckle, even colder than the first. "You've seen the plans. The ones on our other sites. At least someone matching your and young Ashe's descriptions has. And those are just the ones in Madison County."

Her grip tightened.

"You and your little pack can't stop it. Even the Lycans won't stop all of it. You will be caught. Killed. Or canned like the rest."

Renae flinched at the word. *Canned.*

Her mind flashed to the broken things Ryan and Grace had pulled from the bunkers. Sickly spirits barely clinging to form, unable to be released from whatever they'd possessed before Dum-Prot captured them. Twisted, wrong.

The last one she saw had been a decomposing doe, floating inches above the ground. It had only one leg left, and where it drifted, wild grass and flowers sprouted, then withered to ash.

The Birmingham Lycans suspected it was once a spirit of renewal, left stuck in "on" mode, its purpose corrupted. Other spirits from the site had refused healing. Some fled into the forest. Others simply vanished.

The thought of being *canned*, of becoming that, sent a fresh shiver down her spine.

"Gaia showed us the devastation you are planning," Renae snapped. "You think we're dumb enough to sit back and let the apocalypse slide by?"

This time, the laughter was real. Deep. Unsettling.

"Mrs. Whitlock," Damon said, amused. "The apocalypse started decades ago. You aren't stopping it. You're plugging a hole in the broken dam with your finger. If you don't believe me, ask one of the pups from Birmingham."

She didn't respond. He didn't wait for her to.

"I'll hold on to this phone for now. If you choose to accept our terms, I promise you and your pack will be safe. From Dum-Prot's interests, and from the Lycans."

Renae didn't trust promises. Especially not the kind that came with a smile and the scent of blood. But the thought of Ashe, Cole, Grace, or Ryan ending up like that doe. That stuck with her.

"I'll keep in touch," Renae heard herself saying.

A soft click followed.

The line went dead. Somewhere across town, Ashe was fixing a car. Cole was running the mountain. Grace was hunting. And Renae was already planning how to keep them alive. She slowly added the number to her contacts.

Epilogue

Rebecca had stayed in the hospital for several days. She'd slept through most of it, waking only in brief, foggy stretches. Cole had been there every time, still in the stolen outfit from one of the gunmen, never leaving her side.

When he brought her in, he'd refused care until she was seen first. They'd both made a startling sight, covered in gore and cuts. Cole with multiple gunshot wounds. Both nearly dead.

Cole had told the staff they'd been mugged. The police came with questions, especially curious about someone walking in with a near-dead woman in his arms. But with no clear evidence, they handed Cole a card and left it at that.

In her sleep, she dreamed only of what had been done to her. The cutting. The burning. The cold that froze her down to the bone. One dream returned again and again: something slick and monstrous sliding down her throat. She remembered gagging. Choking. But never waking up.

The thing that had done it stayed with her. Even after lighting the bastard up in gunfire. Even knowing it was dead. It lingered in the corners of her vision, behind her eyes, just waiting. Ready to show itself whenever she closed them. Whenever her mind wandered.

Waking was a blessing. A rare moment of escape.

When she finally returned to full consciousness, Cole had hugged her like it might undo what had happened. Dried blood still crusted the folds of his clothes. Pain flared across his face when he moved. Hugging her clearly hurt. But if she had asked him to hold on, he would have, no matter the cost.

It felt warm. Human.

But something inside her, something new, twisted at his touch. Her body tensed, rigid in his embrace. Cole let go without protest and sat back in the chair beside her.

He didn't ask. Didn't complain. He waited. He waited for her.

When she was discharged, Cole offered to take her wherever she wanted. Her parents' place. A hotel, anywhere safe.

Breathing room, she had told him. She needed to walk alone for a while.

But the truth was harder. Harder to say. Harder even to think.

Because when she looked at Cole now, she didn't see the boy who once curled beside her on lazy Sunday mornings. She saw what he had become. What he had let happen. The blood on his hands wasn't theoretical. It was in the creases of his skin, clinging no matter how hard he scrubbed.

And worse than that was the voice.

He's dangerous, it whispered. *He's the reason you hurt. He's the reason you woke up wrong.*

When had it started? Maybe during the dreams. Maybe in the icebox where her body forgot how to warm itself. It didn't matter. The voice was here now. Threaded through her thoughts like mold in bread.

At first, it only whispered. Then it began to suggest.

On her last night in the hospital, she woke to find her hands hovering inches from Cole's throat. He was asleep, lips parted, chest rising and falling. The voice was speaking then, low and smooth. Like a friend. Like a lover. Only a knock at the door snapped her out of it.

That moment haunted her more than the blood. More than the burns.

Because in that moment, she had wanted to follow through.

A few days after she was released, she met Cole under a gray sky at a soccer field where they used to play. She knew he was hoping the memory of them laughing and running would spur something in her. It nearly did.

A light drizzle settled on the grass. He looked like he hadn't slept in days. His shoulders were slumped, his eyes rimmed with exhaustion, and he carried the weight of everything like he still thought he could fix it.

"Where will you go?" he asked softly.

Somewhere. Anywhere. She'd figure it out as she went.

"I can come with you," he offered. "Not to crowd you. Just to make sure you're okay."

For a second, she was lost in the eyes she fell in love with. For a heartbeat, she almost said yes.

But the voice stirred. Coiled behind her eyes. *Yes, go. And when he sleeps, we will end him. Then, find the others.*

"I don't feel safe," she said. "Not with you." She didn't say the rest.

I don't feel safe with anyone. Not even with myself.

Cole's mouth opened slightly, then closed. He looked down at his hands, flexed his fingers like they didn't belong to him.

Nothing more passed between them, but just before she turned the corner, she thought she heard him whisper, "Be safe."

Her steps were slow but certain, carrying her past police tape still fluttering on a broken bench, past ambulance lights reflected in puddles. The destination didn't matter. Only the moving.

Trembling hands. Aching body. She wanted to turn back. Fall into his arms and pretend none of it had happened.

But pretending was a luxury she couldn't afford. There was something living inside her now, and it had teeth.

The city stretched out ahead of her. Traffic swept by in gusts of hot wind. Neon signs flickered over dim storefronts. Strangers laughed nearby, their voices drifting past as if from another world.

Life had moved on.

But Rebecca hadn't.

The voice inside her quieted, sulking. But she felt its shape. Like a second spine. Like a shadow that didn't follow the light.

She needed to find a way to fix this. And she had to believe there was still time. Time to tear it out. Time to find her way back.

To be whole.

To be human.

She just had to hope there would be something left of her when she did.

The End

THE FIRST TEARING

ACKNOWLEDGEMENTS

This book wouldn't exist without the generous support of many people.

To my beta readers—Noah Palma, Samantha Recker, Seanna Estes, Catherine Sotomayor, Rachael Damiani, Carynn Ireland, and Gavin Steely —thank you for your honest feedback, your encouragement, and for catching the things I was too close to see. You made this story stronger, and I'm grateful for every note, every question, and every "wait... this doesn't make sense" you sent my way.

To my editor, Melissa Stone, your insight and expertise were invaluable.

To Ashe Steely... again, thank you for bringing The Marked Pack to life visually. The cover is everything I hoped for and more.

To anyone that picks this up new or in a bargain bin—thank you for taking a chance on a debut author and a new series.

And finally, to every person who has ever felt unseen, misunderstood, or marked as different: you belong. Your pack is out there. Keep howling until
you find them.

ABOUT THE AUTHOR

Christopher J. Steely is fashionably late to the professional writing party, having spent years crafting science fiction and urban fantasy worlds exclusively for tabletop roleplaying sessions. What began as compulsive worldbuilding has evolved into an unstoppable urge to share these stories with actual readers. This is his first novel, with the second nearly complete and several short stories that poke at what makes us human, just with more monsters. When not writing, he's killing houseplants despite his best intentions and absolutely demolishing his wife at board games—though she may dispute this claim.

Find out what he's working on next at www.witherbound.com